LARRY GENT

ALSO BY LARRY GENT

The Benedict Forecasts
Be All That You Envy
Never Been To Mars
To Money And A TV
Bedroom Walls That Save Us
The Future Sold Out (2019)

The TOP SECRET Mac Files
She Who Trains Under Death

Avalon Lost
Lightyears To Go Before I Sleep

Vörissa's Catalyst Online
Patch 1.01:   New Game+
Patch 1.02:   Escort Mission
Patch 1.03:   Corpse Run
Patch 1.04:   In Another Castle
Patch 1.05:   Silent Protagonist

BEDROOM WALLS THAT SAVE US

LARRY GENT

MIDNIGHT READING PUBLISHING

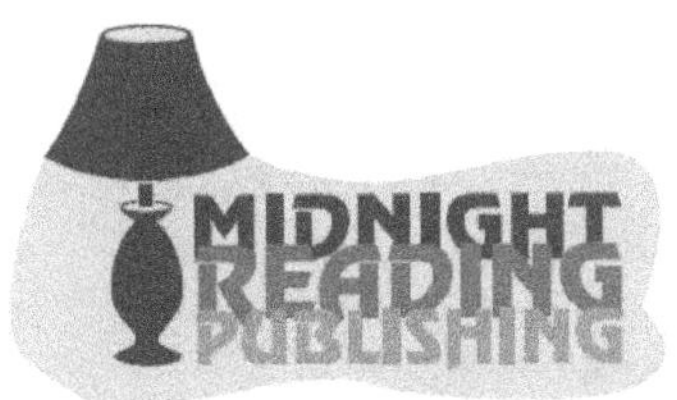

Published in Canada by **Midnight Reading Publishing**, Ottawa

Gent, Larry, 1983-, Author.
       Bedroom Walls That Save Us / Larry Gent
ISBN: 978-1-989152-03-4
Ebook ISBN: 978-1-989152-04-1

Cover Design: Valérie Gent

Midnight Reading Publishing
511 Brittany Drive
Ottawa, Ontario
K1K 0S1

To my Mom!

You have always encouraged my love of reading. You fed me new book, helped expand my horizons and always showed me the power of slowing down and go back over what I had written. I am an author now and that is in no small part because of your doing.

Thank you, Mom, for everything.

I love you!

Five Years Later

Five Years ago I published *Never Been to Mars*. I never thought I'd be a published author. Two years later I followed up with *To Money and a TV*. Shortly after, things changed when my contract with my old publishing house came to an end.

I am grateful for the start that my old publisher gave me. He saw potential in me and took a chance. I like to think we both benefited from it. I hold no ill will towards my former publisher, I owe him for my start, but it did leave the future of Ben in limbo.

Until Now!

Ben is back! He's packed up his stuff and moved into a new house, one where he and the rest of the Ben-Verse can grow. Ben's returned with a new sequel and a brand-new spin-off series starting with *She Who Trains Under Death*.

For those long time fans, you'll notice there have been some changes. There are new names, like Croxallé medical and the Visegar Company. There are also familiar ones like WhiteStar and Lepton Enterprises. But worry not. Our story still remains the same and Ben and company are just as we left them.

Thanks to all who return and to those who are new.

Welcome back to the Cowboy's world.

- Larry Gent (November 2018)

The Benedict Playlist

Music has always been a big part of my life. I use it for everything. I use music to sleep, I use music to play video games, I use it to read, to exercise (as if), to play Magic and above all else I use music to write.

When I want to write a certain character I need to get into his mindset, I need to feel what he's feeling. I do that by music. A happy song has the power to energise me, a sad one to turn my mood foul and a raunchy song will.....well you see where I am going with this.

Sex. I was talking about sex.

So below is what I am calling The Benedict Playlist (because I can't call this I Stole This from Carrie Vaughn PS I love your work Carrie). These are the songs that I listened to over and over in the writing process of the Ben Books. They are the songs that, while not always being lyrically appropriate, had verses in them that related to what Ben is doing now.

I don't own any of these songs, sadly paying $0.99 on iTunes doesn't count as owning them; they belong to the talented people who wrote them. So to them I give as many thanks as I would anybody else who helped me out. For without your lyrical skills I wouldn't be where I am today.

Here's to the Cowboy and his music.

Songs

- Is Anybody Home? – Our Lady Peace
- Heart Of Novocaine – Halestorm
- Frank's 2000" TV – Weird Al Yankovic
- Lay Down Sally - Eric Clapton
- Is This The World We Created - Queen
- Don't Leave Me Now - Supertramp
- Sympathy For the Devil - The Rolling Stones
- Here's to Us – Halestorm
- Lean On Me - Bill Withers
- Leaving on a Jetplane - Peter, Paul and Mary
- Bodies - Drowning Pool
- My Father's Eyes - Eric Clapton
- Jealous (I Ain't With It) - Chromeo
- All You Did Was Save My Life - Our Lady Peace
- Take Me Home, Country Roads - John Denver
- Layla - Eric Clapton

Chapter 01
Minnesota Isn't Fictional

I love my bed. It's warm, comfy and it never judges me for the things I look at on my phone when I cannot sleep. After a hard evening I love to just fall back into my bed, wrap my arms around the warm body next to me and drift off into never-never land. What I hate is when my phone decides to wake me up at 5:30 am. My phone isn't warm at all and it's always judging me with questions like d*o you want push notifications* and *Are you still watching? It's been 9 straight hours of Top Gear. Is there someone I can call?* I grab my phone and thumb it on. Lifting it to my ear, I mumble some half-coherent greeting.

"Wake up, Benny-Boy, we have work to do." I scowled. Nobody called me Benny except Annie and I wasn't thrilled when she did it either. The voice on the line definitely was not my sister, it belonged to Iris Scott, a lawyer I tried to sleep with. She turned me down but offered me a job. I still wasn't sure if that was a better deal or not.

"Don't call me Benny," I grumbled. "What the hell are you doing calling me at 5:30 am? I thought 5:30 am was a myth. I thought it was fictional like Hogwarts, Gotham and Minnesota."

"Weren't you military?" Iris asked. "You should be familiar with 5 am."

"I also was familiar with a uniform and I ain't seen

that in many years either."

"Just get your ass out of bed and get down here. I'm texting you the address."

"And if I say no?"

"Then I say *double pay*." My eyes shot open. "You've been itching for work and this will be a nice one." Money versus sleep; I hated that debate because sleep rarely won, especially not lately. I had just made a big purchase and I needed to get out of debt.

"I'm on my way," I sighed. I sat up and ran my hands through my scraggly black hair. Lately I had been pushing myself hard. I had been taking any job that came my way. I needed money and the only way I was going to get it was by working. Damn, I needed a job that paid me to watch Netflix and sleep.

"Minnesota isn't fictional." This voice came from the naked body in my bed. Her name was Rachael Puzo. She was a good ol' girl with long blond hair, smooth skin - minus a tear or two - and a thin scar that ran the length of her neck. Some called her boss and others called her Senior Special Agent of the FBI. I simply called her my girlfriend. "Minnesota is a real place."

"Have you been there?" I asked. She shook her head. "I've never been there and neither has anybody I know. The only people who have ever seen Minnesota are friends of friends of friends. That makes it an urban legend."

"Get out of here," she mumbled. "I don't have to be at work until eight so I'm going back to sleep."

"Lazy FBI," I muttered. A pillow flew from the bed and slammed into the back of my head.

I sped across town in my Chevelle. It was a 1971 Chevy Chevelle SS. It was a cherry red car with black strips down the hood. It had a black and red leather interior. While the car was in my possession, it *technically* belonged to my nephew Robby. I was holding onto it until he was of age to appreciate it. It was weird driving again, it had only been eighteen-months since I was bequeathed this car and I was still getting used to having vehicle freedom. I had spent so many years afraid to live my life that I was missing it. I didn't drive; I didn't even leave my house. I just plopped myself down on my Lay-Z-Boy and watched TV and movies. Now, I was forced out in the world and I was adapting. I still missed my TV - to be honest I still spent a lot of time in front of it - but it was no longer the only thing I did.

I pulled up to an empty Porche dealership. It was easy to see that I was in the right place. There were cop cars everywhere. I parked a block away and, with my cane in hand, I climbed out of the car. I instantly regretted stepping out in the open. Even at this early hour it was ungodly hot. This summer had brought the worst heat wave in decades. I glanced at the situation as I hobbled down the street. The dealership was downtown, off of a major city road, and had a large building that acted as their display room and offices. Uniformed officers were everywhere. They were cornering of the street while the CSI brain patrol was out in full force, searching every inch for evidence.

Iris Scott met me at the police tape. She lifted the tape and escorted me in. Iris was a sexy woman with long brown hair. She was a Latino woman with a set of shimmering eyes that always got my attention. Despite it being ungodly early, she looked prim, proper and well rested in her suit. "Morning, Benny. Thanks for coming."

"Ben," I corrected. "What's up? What do you need?"

Iris was a high-priced lawyer. When I first met her she was new to the game, now she was climbing fast and making a name for herself. She worked for Kemp, Slott and Bendis. It wasn't as big as Pearson, Specter, and Litt from *Suits* but it was miles higher than any business Jimmy McGill ever ran.

"My client is Rutin Haley," Iris began. "He owns nine dealerships across the city. Most of them are more middle-class but this is his high-end store. Last night someone broke in and robbed the place blind. They hit several locations and his warehouse. Sixty-seven high ends cars and two dozen more common cars were stolen."

They stole ninety-one cars in one night? I would take at least three Nik Cages and Angelina Jolie's to pull that off. In my experience, though, when pulling off a car heist you shouldn't use actors. Use car thieves, they actually know what they're doing and none of them need Donny to play *Low Rider.*

"This is a major heist that has the attentions of police, reporters and insurance companies. A lot of eyes are on Mr. Haley and I have to make sure he stays clean."

"Is he?" I asked. Iris glanced at me. Her sparkling eyes were suddenly stern. It was like I had just crossed a line with that question. I've crossed that line before and experience had shown me there was only one right thing to do. "Is. He. Clean?"

"Clean enough," she snapped.

"Who do the cops like?"

"It's too early for the official stuff but the way the detectives are whispering, they're looking at Pepito Navarro, the security guard," Iris explained. "Obviously, Navarro swears up and down that he didn't do it. Haley believes him and wants to go all in behind his employee but he needs to be one hundred percent sure that his guy didn't do it. A heist this big screams mob and he has to make sure that he isn't seen as supporting the mob." I nodded. It wasn't often that a boss went all in for their employees like this.

"What is this guys doing, running for office?" I joked. Iris raised an eyebrow and smirked. Holy shit, he was running for office. "Okay, I'll see what I can do."

The dealership building was a three story stone building with large glass walls. From the outside you could see several spinning platforms where several super expensive cars should have been. Iris guided me in and introduced me to

Rutin Haley.

Rutin Haley was a man of obvious mixed descent. I'm not an expert, on literally anything, but if I had to guess by the names I would put money down on Indian and Irish. He was wearing jeans, t-shirt and a jacket. His hair was a mess and he looked tired as all hell. He looked like the type of guy who normally wore a suit - the expensive shoes were a give-away - and was uncomfortable in casual wear. He eyed me with a hesitant look before looking back to his lawyer.

"Mr. Haley," Iris said in a soothing but professional manner. "This is the man I was telling you about. This is my investigator."

"Him?" Haley asked in disbelief. Iris nodded.

I get that a lot. I don't look like the gumshoe type. I'm not dressed in a yellow trench coat with a matching fedora and I'm not wearing a suit. I don't look tough and I've never been accused of looking smart. I was the polar opposite. I wore jeans and a blue hoodie. A cowboy hat was on my head, gloves on my hands and I was using a horse-head cane to keep me up.

"Is your name really Benedict?" I nodded.

Benedict Butler Thompson; I was named after a famous Cowboy who walked with a cane. To my family, westerns were a religion. We had all been named after one famous cowboy or another. My sister was named after Annie Oakley, my niece after Poker Alice and my nephew was named after Robert E. Cunningham.

It's a family thing.

Then there was Clint.

I watched the police work. I've seen the police investigate missing children cases and I've seen them investigate murder charges. Watching the police investigate grand theft auto is a whole other beast. The police don't need to move with the same urgency. Stolen cars almost never get returned in a regular theft. In a coordinated strike like this one, there was no getting them back. They were either chopped up or shipped out. Either way, there was no rush. There were several uniforms walking around and a couple detectives acting as bosses. One was a bigger guy who looked like a bald Robert Baratheon. He walked around with his hands in his jacket pockets, loudly complaining about everything he saw. He was the type that wore a jacket no matter the heat. The second was a dark-skinned woman. She had a notebook out and was silently writing down everything she saw and heard. CSI were studying the locks and the alarms.

Baratheon spotted me and started an angry swagger over. He was loud, boisterous and pointing as he shuffled. "Who the hell is Cowboy Jim and what is he doing on my crime scene? You're bringing a construction worker, an Indian and a sailor with you as backup?"

"It's Cowboy Ben," I replied. The thing with cops is you have to play it cool. They were fragile creatures who wanted to be shown the respect they so greatly desired. If I wanted to make things easy on me for the rest of the investigation I'd have to play it diplomatically and smoothly. "Cowboy Jim was my inbred second cousin. He's busy banging your mom."

Smooth as ice!

"Funny guy. I love a funny guy," Baratheon snapped. "I love arresting the funny guy who thinks it's okay to walk onto an active crime scene."

"I'm with Mr. Haley's legal team," I said quickly. "I'm from SRG Security. My name is Ben Thompson."

"I'm Detective Hale Boseman," he grumbled. He pointed to his partner. "That's Detective Letitia Bassett. She's the one that will bust your balls if you mess up my crime scene."

"I'll behave. I quite enjoy my balls in their un-busted form." He smirked. "Can you tell me where you two are at?"

"I can tell you to go fuck yourself and you'll have to like it," Boseman said. He had me there.

"Dude, I get it. I'm sorry," I began. "It's an ungodly early hour and I don't want to be here but someone woke me up for a job and now look where I'm at. So how about you tell me to fuck off one more time and I'll go home to my bed and my naked girlfriend and I'll just go back to sleep."

Boseman stared at me with a stern look but eventually a grin formed, like I had just earned a sliver of his respect. "If I can't sleep then neither can you. Let's go."

"This was a professional job," Bassett said as we walked. She gave me the lowdown and spoke at a speed that was normally used for an auctioneer. "This job was professional to the core. They slipped in, knocked out the cams and alarms, took out the guard and were gone. They left no evidence and no witnesses."

"No witnesses? What about the guard?" Bassett stopped by a laptop. She tapped a couple keys and brought up the security footage. I leaned in and watched.

Pepito Navarro sat at a standard security desk with several screens around him. Each showed a glimpse of the lot and surrounding area. I expected to see him with his feet up watching some game on the TV like the guard from *Die Hard* but he wasn't. He was studying a law book and writing an essay on the work computer. The guy was going to school during the day and being a security guard at night. He was ambitious and smart. I liked him. I also hated him for being the two things I wasn't but that was jealousy talking.

As Pepito worked, the security screens suddenly went blank. He turned to a second keyboard and quickly tapped on the keys but the screens never changed. Pepito opened up a drawer and withdrew a pistol. He checked the weapon, loaded it, turned on the safety and attached the holster to his belt. Then he cautiously moved to where the downed camera was. The video I was watching had no sound so I don't know what it was that he heard but suddenly Pepito spun and drew his firearm. He kept his arm straight but his hand still shook.

It was clear that whatever security training Pepito took taught him how to properly use his gun but the man didn't have much in the way of experience with it. A person could have all the book learning in the world but when it came down to *actual* experience there was no replacement for muscle memory that came from hundreds upon hundreds of hours of practise.

Pepito stared at a door and yelled something loudly. I could see the intensity in his face. But as he looked at one door, another one opened behind him and a man dressed in black clothes while wearing a Donald Trump mask entered. He tasered Pepito and the guard went down. Eight more people entered, each wearing a different mask of various presidents. Regan moved to the security system while Obama moved to the video cameras. Then the video ended.

"Cameras go down and that's all we have."

"Yeah, it looks like ObamaCare'd enough to cut the feed." Both cops stared at me with disgusted looked.

"Really? Are you proud of that one?"

"It's five in the morning," I protested. "I'm not using my A-Material at five in the freaking AM."

"The masks can be bought anywhere which is no help," Bassett said, moving past my Dad joke. "CSI is looking for car treads but all they are finding are the treads of the stolen cars."

"Do you mind if I look around?" Bassett gave me a warp speed lecture about not contaminating the crime scene but eventually gave me permission. I walked towards the security desk and removed my gloves. It was time for this superhero to go to work. Yeah, you heard me, superhero.

I am Benedict Thompson and this is the life of a superhero.

I'm not a great superhero. I'm not super strong, I can't fly or climb walls – hell, because of my bum leg I'm forced to hobble everywhere with the assistance of a cane, so I'm not likely to be fighting crime anytime soon but what I can do is read items.

The technical term is psychometry. According to Wikipedia, it's the ability to relate details about the past or future condition of an object or location, usually by being in close contact with it. It was on Wikipedia so it must be true. In the normal tongue of everyday people, if I touch an object

I see a moment from its past. It doesn't work on anything that lives or breathes and it is always a moment from the past, well *almost* always.

I pressed my hand on the faux-wood table and felt a shiver up my back, a twitch in my eyes and I fell into the past. I saw Pepito on the ground and several presidents standing around him. Richard Nixon pulled out a gun and leveled at Pepito's skull.

"What the fuck are you doing?" Bill Clinton asked.

"He saw us; I'm ending him," Nixon snarled.

"If he dies then so do you." Clinton snarled.

"I ain't risking it."

"Let me do my job and you do yours. Get rid of those lowjacks, now." Clinton pointed to George W. Bush. "Get the keys."

"Cams are down," Obama said. He reached to pull off his mask but Clinton stopped him.

"Masks stay on," he ordered. "There may be some idiot out there has with a cell phone pointed at us."

Reality returned and I swore. I hated when bad guys were smart. It made my job so much harder. I walked towards the key locks. The cabinet had been pried open with a crowbar. I gave it a touch and felt the shiver and the twitch and fell into my vision.

George W. Bush came into view. He slammed his crowbar into the large steel cabinet and started to pry. From behind the grunting I heard music. Bush II was whistling. The cabinet opened with a snap. George H. W. Bush walked over and grabbed several keys. It was at the moment that whistling became singing and I suddenly recognized the song.

"Why do you build me up?" Bush II sang.

"Build me up," Bush I added in a higher pitch.

"Buttercup Baby, just to let me down," Bush II continued.

"Let me down."

"And mess me around." Both Bush men walked towards the cars, keys in hard. They kept singing. "And then worst of all."

"Worst of all."

"You never call, Baby, when you say you."

"Say you will."

"But I love you still."

Reality returned and I cursed. They were singing car thieves. Who the hell hired singing car thieves? But that wasn't the worst part. The absolute worst part was now that that ear worm had taken hold. I was going to have that stupid song in my head for the next couple days.

I walked to the empty spinning platform. It normally held some super flashy car for all to see but now it just endlessly spun, showing the world nothing but circular motion. I gave the sad piece of hardware a touch and fell back into the past.

Bill Clinton stood at the platform, watching a Porche 911 GT2 RS slowly spin in circles. He turned his head at the sound of approaching music.

"I'll be over at ten I told you time and again but you're late," Bush II sang as he walked past. "I waited around the bend."

"Bah-dah-dah," Bush I sang as he tossed Clinton a set of keys. Both Bush men then each walked to a separate car, climbed in and within seconds were speeding off the lot. Clinton just nodded.

"Alarms are clear, lowjacks are disabled and we're ready to burn rubber, Boss." Trump said as he approached from behind.

"Get to the docks and regroup. We're going straight into the third hit," Clinton ordered. He held out his fist to Trump. "Drive safe, Wonka."

"Good luck, Erwin." The two men bumped fists and my vision ended.

I started walking towards the detectives when I spotted Iris. I waved her over. The two cops eyed me suspiciously but I didn't speak until Iris was beside me. I pulled my gloves back on as I waited.

"Does the name Erwin mean anything?" I asked. Boseman and Bassett eyed each other.

"He's in jail," Bassett said.

"He got out a month ago."

"He's doing a job already?"

"He must be desperate." Boseman turned towards me. "Why you askin'?"

"He was the ring leader or at least for this job," I offered. "Who is he?"

"Johnny Baker: car thief. They call him Erwin because he got arrested as a kid trying to do the Cannonball Run in a stolen car. Since juvie he did a nickel for grand theft auto. He just got out."

"Does he know a Wonka?" I asked.

"Yeah, that's his brother William Baker."

"Both of them were here. The cars are down at the docks but I don't know which one."

"How do you know all this?" Bassett asked. "Words like that make me think you're involved."

"My client is a private investigator with a current license," Iris began. I paused. Was my license up to date? "He's here at the request of my firm. Any information he offered up *freely* is not an admission of guilt or involvement. It is an example of his co-operative nature and his willingness to work with the police."

Having psychic powers doesn't mesh well with cops. Nobody takes me seriously and it tends to get me into more trouble. So when I was going to reveal facts that I had stolen from the past, having Iris nearby to wield her legal hammer makes my life easier. I may not be a smart man but I am a guy who learns from *some* of his mistakes. If I learned from *all* of my mistakes I'd be a freaking genius. I am clearly not.

"If you hear anything else, keep me in the know," Boseman said as he handed me his business card. I nodded and said I would. Iris and I walked away and towards my Chevelle.

"What do you got?" she asked.

"So far nothing I saw says the guard was involved. Did you know he's a law student?" Iris gave me a *keep it on target* look. "I'll keep investigating before I give it the ol' Ben Stamp of Approval."

"This is why I'm glad I didn't sleep with you," Iris joked with a smiled. "This is much better for me."

"Agree to disagree," I grumbled as I climbed in.

Chapter 02
Sex on a Stick

It was 7:30 by the time I got back home. I stepped through the door and immediately sighed in relief at the feel of a running air conditioner. We were well into summer and this year's heat wave was killing me. First it was hot, then the humidity kicked in and made things unbearable. I had been in heat overseas but this was still disgusting. It was the type of heat that made your body feel like it was endlessly covered in one layer of sticky sweat after another. I dropped my cane in the basket and limped to the kitchen. I saw Rachael finishing up her morning coffee while getting ready for work. She was dressed in a pants suit and had her Glock 22 holstered at the hip. I limped over and planted a kiss on her cheek.

"How long before you're gone?" I asked.

"I have to leave in a couple minutes," she said. Rachael didn't live with me, not officially. She had a key, had several drawers and had somehow conquered my closet. She was here four or more days a week but she still kept her own place. She placed her mug on the counter as she walked into the bedroom. I took a sip and nearly spat it out. It was sweet. It was more than sweet. It was like Juan Valdez had relation with not just Willy Wonka but with his brothers, Wallace Wonka and Winston Wonka, and the coffee was the result.

For those that are wondering, Wallace Wonka is a diabetic accountant that wasn't invited to the baby making event but showed up anyways.

"What the hell is that?" I called out.

"Coffee," she called out with a confused tone.

"Are you sure? It doesn't taste like it," I coughed.

"I added more sugar," she said. "I needed a boost."

"Have you tried cocaine? It might be healthier than your thirteen sugars." I shook my head. "By the way, did I tell you that you were super beautiful and pretty and sexy and awesome?"

"What do you want?" Puzo asked as she walked back into the kitchen.

"If I gave you a name could you run it and give me known associates?"

"You need to make friends with *other* cops so they can do this instead of me," Puzo said with a smile. "Good detectives have their own police informants."

"I'm trying, I swear," I pleaded. "Cops don't seem to like me."

"Did you make a *banging his mom* joke?" I nervously looked away. Damn she was good. "Text me the names and I'll see what I can do."

"You're the best." I glanced at the thick brown envelope. "Is this police stuff?"

"No." Puzo's reply was cold and icy. I cursed. I knew exactly what this was and I was in shit. "A man came by today to drop this off."

"Blonde hair, well built?" I asked.

"Hot as all hell and built like sex on a stick," Puzo finished. She was speaking about Ian Kenser. "I wouldn't kick him out of bed for eating crackers."

That said a lot. Puzo *loathed* crackers in the bed. She didn't crumbs of any sort in her bed. I found that one out the hard way. Needless to say, I got kicked out.

"He's super gay," I said, breaking her heart. It was a common response. Twenty-One months ago Ian Kenser was an overweight student studying for his PhD in theoretical physics. Then he underwent an experiment that Chris Evans'd his body. Now he was Steve Rogers-ing all over the place looking like a Greek god with abs for days.

"What makes him *super gay*?" Puzo asked, ready to lecture me on my word choice.

"He has super strength and he likes guys." I shrugged. Puzo rolled her eyes. I opened the envelope and took a look at the various papers that poured out. They were various written reports and files. They were from Hotwire.

"They are about *her*, aren't they?"

There it was.

It had been eighteen months since Nouri Allawi and since Puzo and I had been in a relationship. Things were good but there was one large elephant that hung around like an uninvited guest: Zoey Harris.

My ex-girlfriend, who I thought was dead, came to me in a vision and told me she was alive. Then she told me she was being held captive and I was the only one who could save her.

What's a guy suppose to do when that happens?

I began to investigate. I was going to find her and save her. The problem was I had no clue where to start and worst yet, I'm a shitty detective.

"How much did this intel cost?" she sternly asked. I opened my mouth to answer but she shook me off. "I'm not doing this again. I have to go to work." She grabbed her coffee finished it in a single gulp. Grabbing her suit jacket, she slipped it on. She gave me a tender kiss. "I'll see you tonight." With that she left for work.

I poured a glass of orange juice and carried it and the file into my office. My ground level apartment had four bedrooms. One was the main bedroom - the sexnasium -, the other was Robby's bedroom for when he came over, the guest bedroom and the room I converted into my office.

When my investigation into Zoey began I decided I needed an office to work in. I bought an old couch, an Ikea desk, a chair and several of those swivelling murder boards I always saw on TV. I wanted nothing more to stand by the murder board with Nathan Fillion and Stana Katic and quip about our case and the suspects.

"We think Mr. Thorton is the killer," Stana would say.

"In my book that would be the deception," Nathan would counter. "The real killer would be Mr. Notroht."

"That sounds like a *novel* idea," I would add. Then Nathan and I would high-five while Stana would debate shooting us both.

My murder board had a picture of Zoey in the center and lines chaotically shooting out of it like literally anybody's hair during this heat wave. Each line pointed to a different possible avenue. I had one shooting out to Croxallé, another shooting out to Visegar Company and a third shooting out to WhiteStar and Polaris Industries. From there dozens more lines shot out. Each touched a different location, company or rumour. Some were shrouded in mystery and government oversight like Port Alexander, others had so many lights on them, like Eureka, Nevada, that nothing new could be gained.

I slid into my chair and winced. I hated my office chair. It was stiff and uncomfortable but that was the point. If I wanted a comfortable chair, I'd go sit in my Lay-z-Boy. I was at my desk to work and I needed a firm chair to do so. I sipped my OJ and started to read through the files. They were hardcopies from a batch of files that Hotwire had scored for me. Each was pulled from the servers of a company that was owned by a company that was owned by a company that was *allegedly* owned by Croxallé. For several hours I flopped through the papers, examining each one by one. If something was relevant to a lead or a theory, I put it in that respective pile. I had a thick Croxallé pile, I had thin Visegar pile, I had an eerily large WhiteStar pile and I had several piles for potential secret projects and codenames.

Then there was the Malpaso pile.

I had come across a small mention of something called Project: Malpaso. I locked onto this immediately. Malpaso Creek was located south of Carmel-by-the-Sea in California. It was also the name of a film production company known for making such films as *Dirty Harry, Hang 'Em High* and the Oscar winning films *American Sniper* and *Million Dollar Baby*. The Malpaso Company also produced the two greatest films in the orangutan and his trucker bff film genre: *Every Which Way but Loose* and *Any Which Way You Can*.

The Malpaso Company was the production company owned by the one, the only, the legend, the man's man, the better than John Wayne: Mr. Clint Eastwood.

This meant nothing to most but to me, it couldn't be a coincidence. To me, this was related to *my* Clint. I looked at the file in my hand. It had mention of Project: Malpaso. I studied the spread sheet. It was numbers upon numbers and I am no good with numbers. I read it as carefully as I could and eventually sighed in boredom. This was simply a spreadsheet that showed Project: Malpaso requesting money and it being transferred from one account to another until it arrived. I'd have a money guy follow the numbers but chances were it would lead to the same result as last time: an empty account, no names and a dead end. I put the sheet atop the miniscule-sized Malpaso file and went to the next.

Two hours later and my door shot open with a loud bang. I leapt from my chair and came down on my leg, hard. Bad move: that was my bad leg. I winced loudly and limped for the door. I was ready to grab the first thing I could use as a weapon when I heard a familiar voice cry out.

"Ben--ny, we need a fa--vour." Aw crap, it was my sister. I exited my office, closing the door behind me, and saw Annie standing at the doorway with Alice in her hands. Annie and I look alike, dark black hair, strong piercing eyes, and sturdy shoulders. The only difference is she has long curls that reside in her dark mop and I'm a foot taller than her. Also our gender. Annie pointed outside. "Go help Robby and Dave."

I glanced outside. My nephew Robby and my BFF

David were grabbing a bunch of suitcases from the back of the minivan. I looked back at Annie.

"What the hell are you doing?"

"We need a place to stay for a couple days."

"Normally people stay in their own houses," I suggested.

"Ours caught fire. We're staying here."

"Oh well that makes sense. I mean if it caught fire then ------whhhhhaaaaaaaa?" I asked in an exaggerated Chris Griffin. "Okay, start over. What the hell happened and what do you mean fire?" Annie rolled her eyes like her explanation hadn't been super obvious.

"There was a small fire at our house. Nobody is hurt but until the insurance people and the safety inspectors finish checking the house, we have to stay here with my little brother."

"Do I get a say in this?"

"Nope." She leaned in a kissed my cheek. "Now go help David."

I limped outside, shaking my head as I moved. There was no fighting against an older sister. They were evil placed in human form. They had no other purpose on this Earth but to make the lives of the younger brother a living hell.

"Yo, douchebag," I called out.

"What up, jerk face?" David yelled back.

Staff Sergeant David Belledin was my best-friend/ brother-in-law. He was the soldier's soldier: six foot one, two hundred and ten pounds, dark hair maintained in a crew cut and a look of strength about him. David and I were infantry buddies that became real life buddies.

Robby was almost fourteen. He stood in that lanky teenager age with a blonde mop of hair atop his skull and an infectious smile that was three miles wide. I walked over and held up my fist. Robby bumped and we both blew it up.

"Sup, Spiderman?"

"Just swingin' and a slingin', Uncle Ben."

I grabbed a few bags and carried it indoors. Robby

took his bag and went directly to his room to drop off his stuff. I started putting the extra bags into the guest room. I entered the living room and saw Robby plopped down in my Lay-z-Boy. The TV remote was in his hand and his eyes were glued to the screen. I tapped the kid on the top of his skull. "You're in my chair."

Robby sighed, rolled his eyes and climbed out. He plopped down on the closer of the two couches.

"Un-kill! Un-kill!" I turned around and saw a familiar two year-old running towards me. I smiled at the black haired beauty and scooped her up with a grunt. She was getting heavy. "I go phwoosh!" She eagerly clapped her hands and giggled.

Holding Alice was like holding a blanket just pulled from the dryer. The girl was normally very warm to the touch. It was originally a concern with the doctors but when it didn't go away and she was remaining healthy, everybody just assumed she ran hot. Although, at the moment I was holding her, she didn't seem warm at all. She felt normal.

"So anybody want to tell me what happened?" I said loudly.

"A small fire started in one of the rooms," David said as he raided my fridge for a coke. He popped the tab and re-entered the living room. "I don't know what caused it yet but we're having the house checked for damage and wiring just to be safe."

I let out a low whistle. It was going to suck to have them all over here but I was glad everybody was safe. I adored my sister's family. She gave me two awesome kids to spoil and she married my best friend but going from living on my own to living with her entire family for a week was going to be an adjustment. But that was the type of sacrifice you did for family.

David plopped down in my Lay-Z-Boy. I smacked him. "You're in my chair"

Family or not, nobody sits in my Lay-Z-Boy but me!

Chapter 03
Keep the Clock in Double-Digits

I sat in the Chevelle looking across the street. It was an apartment building in a crappy part of town. It was the type of area that if a building had a security door, it was there for a reason. I climbed out of the car, locked it, and hobbled across the street. Stepping into the lobby, I glanced at the paging system. It was the type of speaker system that had a list of names, a speaker and a twelve-key dial pad. You were supposed to find the name of the desired person on the list, dial the corresponding number into the keypad and then they would buzz you in. I went for another route.

It is a little known fact that these keypads actually have a number you can dial that would auto-open the door. It's meant for supers and handymen. I didn't know the number but I was going to find out. I pulled off my glove and ran my fingers over the keypad. A shiver and a twitch and I fell into the past.

I saw a fat slob of a man waddle his way up to the building. He was your stereotypical New Jersey handyman. He wore jeans a size too small, had a tool belt that hung so low his tools bounced off his knees, had a wife beater that started out as white but was now some disgusting brown colour and a moustache that could get him a job as a guard in Netflix prison. He used his stubby fingers, stained with Cheetos dust, and punched in a number.

3765

The vision ended and not a moment too soon. I tried not to hurl as I punched in the number: 3765. The door buzzed and Detective Ben is in the building. One elevator ride later and I'm standing in front of the door of Johnny 'Erwin' Baker. I tested the door and find it locked. Running my gloved fingers across the top of the door frame I hit pay dirt. He kept a spare key there.

For a moment I couldn't decide what's worse, the fact that he decided to hide his key on the door ledge because he watched too much TV or the fact that it was the first place I looked because I also watch too much TV.

Erwin's place was nicer than I expected. I was assuming it'd have a run-down bachelor decorating motif going. It didn't; his place had nice stuff. It wasn't super expensive stuff but it was still nice. He even had a rug in the center of the living room that, to be honest, really tied the room together. There was only one problem with the rug: there was a dead guy on it. It was a black man with a shaved head. He also had a shiny new bullet hole in his skull.

Fuck. I hate walking in on a body. It's like walking in on your parents having sex, just with more movement. Both have the same symptoms upon discovery. First is a sense of shock, followed by an urge to vomit and then you're just confused as to why your dad is bent over in a sling while you mother is tightening the straps around her waist. The end result is you get traumatized and never forget what you saw.

My mind raced. I had to investigate quickly. I did not want to get caught with a body but I had to call the cops. I hobbled over to the coffee table. If I didn't do my psychic bit now, I wasn't going to get a chance before 5-0 showed up. I gave it a touch and fell into another vision.

Erwin stood in the room chatting to six other men and one woman. I recognized none of them but I assume that they were the presidents from earlier. Erwin stood in the middle. This was my first time seeing Erwin without his mask. He was tall and had good looking features. He had a Hugh Jackman chin and Ryan Gosling eyes. To be honest, he was good look-ing and I was close to swooning.

"Okay, every one shut up," Erwin snapped. "It's time to work. Y'all ready to shut up?"

"I'm ready, yes, I'm ready for you," One guy said. He was a black man with a bald head. He was also my dead guy. "Hell, I'm standing on my own two feet."

"Out the doorway the bullets rip," a second man add-ed. He looked identical. They were twin car thieves. "Repeat-ing to the sound of the beat."

The two twins looked at each other and started bounc-ing their hands in unison to a beat that only they heard. They started to sing.

"Bah, Bah, Bah, Bah," They sang. Suddenly I knew who the twins were. They were the Bush men. "Another one bites the dust."

They were singing twin car thieves.

I returned to reality. I placed my hand on a chair and fell into another vision. The room remained the same but ev-erybody had shifted. Everyone was a couple drinks in and were busy going over the plan.

"We've cut the feed and disabled the alarms," one of the twins said, "but what about the guard?"

"I'll shoot him." A thin guy, with a mullet and who was missing several teeth stood up. I had an odd feeling that this Mr. Mullet was Nixon.

"Whoa! Nobody said anything about killin'. I didn't sign up for killin'," the lone woman in the room said. She was a punk chick with a studded leather jacket, an arctic blue Mo-hawk and more piercings then I could count. She was swig-ging rum like it was pop and chain smoking to such excess that I swore she was trying to kick start lung cancer. "Jackin' is fine. Killin' ain't. I don't want that type of heat."

"You'll do as you're fucking told, bitch." Mullet was on his feet with a gun in his hand. The room all leapt back and Erwin stepped in. Mullet didn't flinch. "Back off, man! I ain't going down 'cause some bitch stepped out of the kitchen."

The room stayed silent until an unexpected noise filled the room.

"Why do you build me up, build me up, Buttercup Baby, just to let me down?" Everybody looked at the punk girl. The song was coming from her phone. A small chuckle rippled through the room. Erwin grabbed the gun and yanked it form Mullet's hands. He glanced at the girl.

"Seriously, Harm, *that's* your ringtone?" Erwin asked.

"Says the guy who uses the *Cannonball Run Theme* as his," Harm smirked.

"It's not what you do; it's how you do it." Erwin smirked. "Be anything you want to be."

"But seriously, you're not even using the original," one of the twins added.

"Is that the punk version from the *Mallrats* movie?" the other asked.

"That is going to be stuck in our head all day," the first concluded.

"Look Erwin, I love you and I'd do anything for you," Harm began. "But I ain't working with that guy. He's a loose cannon. I have to look out for me."

"I get it, girl. I need him though. He's the only low-jack I could get on short notice."

"Walk away from this job, Erwin. This is bad news."

"I can't. Ma got in trouble and I have to bail her out. This is the way to do it," Erwin said. "When Fenderbaum leans, I have to give."

"Family," Harm said with a grin. "I wanna help but not with him."

"I get it. No hard feelings, girl." My vision ended and I called the cops.

Twenty minutes later, Iris was by my side as I faced down the police stares of Detective Hale Boseman and Detective Letitia Bassett. I flashed a stupid grin on my face. I was nervous and I had no idea what else to do. Iris elbowed me until the grin went away.

"Do you believe in déjà vu?" Bassett asked.

"I'm beginning to," Boseman replied. He glanced at me. "We came from another crime scene with an identical victim."

"The other twin," I said suddenly. Boseman eyed me for a second before nodding. "They were both part of Erwin's crew."

"We picked up Erwin and Wonka this morning; caught them both in a surprise scoop. They aren't speaking so we're holding them until they crack." I gave Iris a quizzical look. She gave me a nod of approval.

"My client," Iris began, "would like to offer a suggestion. During the course of his investigation, he discovered that a man named Victor Fenderbaum is threatening Mr. Baker's mother. He forced the man to commit these crimes."

The two detectives hungrily eyed each other. Victor Fenderbaum was a big name in the crime world and both of these cops knew that a take-down would be big business. The cops did their police thing before letting me go. Iris and I exited the build and made our way to my car.

"Pepito Navarro had nothing to do with this," I said. "I watched them plan for hours. He was always an obstacle, not an ally."

"Thanks, Benny," Iris said. I tried to correct her but she didn't listen. God, I hated being called Benny. "I'll wire you the money."

"Anytime you need me," I offered, "but let's keep the clock in double-digits next time."

Iris laughed and walked to her car. I climbed into the Chevelle and started it with a roar but paused before taking off. A thought bit at the back of my mind. The cops surprised Erwin and Wonka and grabbed them both. Then both twins end up dead. Somebody killed them both and my money was on Mr. Mullet, but why? According to Stephen Cannell - on that episode of *Castle* - there are only three reasons to commit a murder: love, money and to cover up a crime. So which one was it? The obvious choice was money. They're fighting over the money. I ran that over and over in my head but something didn't feel right.

If this were a TV show - and I really hope my life isn't - then this would be a weak episode. This would suck. It's too straight forward. Even with banter, you'd only filled up about forty-five minutes. I still had fifteen to go. So what happened in the last fifteen minutes of literally every cop show?

The twist.

What was my twist? If it wasn't about the money then it had to be about the cover-up. When Erwin got pinched, Mr. Mullet got scared and killed whoever he thinks ratted them out. First he killed the twins and now.... My eyes went wide. He was going after the girl. I slammed my foot on the gas and sped off.

I had Harm's address from Puzo's text. She was listed as one of Erwin's known associates. Puzo's texts included her real name, her address and her phone number. I steered the Chevelle down the street, clumsily taking the turn. Since getting the car, I had become reacquainted with the art of driving. I was not, however, any good at it. This car was honestly a waste on me.

I pulled up to an ugly green apartment attached to the side of an uglier green house. I climbed out of the Chevelle and hobbled to the front door only to find it kicked in. I crouched down and crept inside. The apartment didn't have many rooms. It was a one bedroom bachelor pad or, in this case, a bachelorette pad. I peered around a corner and spotted Mr. Mullet holding a gun to Harm. I reached for my belt and silently cursed. Why didn't I bring my gun? Three months salary my ass; this wasn't worth it. I glanced around and spotted a side table with Harm's phone on it. I had an idea.

"I didn't say nothing." Harm protested.

"You lying bitch!" Mullet screamed. "You bail and then we all get pinched. It had to fucking be you." Rage built up inside the man. With each second that passed, his face became redder and his hand began to twitch. "I'm gonna end you before you say anything about me. You got any last words?"

"Why do you build me up, build me up, Buttercup Baby, just to let me down?" Harm's phone sang as it signaled an incoming call.

"That fucking song is everywhere; I can't get it out of my head!" he screamed. Mullet pivoted towards the phone and readied a shot. That's when I hobbled into action.

The phone call was from me. It was meant to be a distraction. I knew I could probably disarm Mullet but I didn't want to while he was pointing the gun directly at her. When he aimed at the phone, I dashed forward. I swung my cane down upon his wrist and heard a small cracking sound. He screamed and the gun fell from his grip. I went to swing back and strike at his neck but I never needed to. Harm dashed forward and slammed her fist across his chin. Mullet went down faster than the appeal of the actual mullet. Business up front and party in the back; too bad the party's over, bitch!

Damn, I should have said that out loud. Wait, maybe there was a chance. I glanced at Mr. Mullet and watched as Harm kicked her steel toes into his chest.

"You don't harm me," she yelled. "I harm you. It's in my goddamn name."

"Yeah and the party's over, bitch." Her eyes snapped up at me, a fire burning within them,

"What did you just say?"

"Nothing," I quickly added. Damn, I totally ruined it. Harm quickly scooped up the gun and pointed it me. I raised my hands quickly. "You don't need that. I'm not here to hurt you. I promise. I'm here to do the opposite. I'm here to unhurt you. No wait, that's not a word."

"Who are you?" I slowly pointed to my back pocket and slowly reached into it. I pulled out a business card. I slowly handed it to her.

"I'm Ben Thompson," I said. "I work for SRG Security. I was hired to investigate a massive car theft. Now the cops have already pinched Erwin and Wonka."

"I didn't do anything," she quickly replied.

"I know. You bailed when this guy started waving a gun around." Harm's eyes went wide. It was the standard *how did you know that* look. I get it frequently. "Normally I'd say you were in the clear but then Mr. Mullet started killing people. He off'd the twins and was trying to kill you."

"The twins are dead?" she asked. I nodded. She fired another kick into his side. Mr. Mullet coughed and spat up blood. I shrugged it off. I really didn't care about him.

"The cops are looking for a murderer now. The way I see it you have three options," I began. "1) Kill him. 2) Let him live and run, forever. 3) Call the cops and turn yourself in. You are looking at conspiracy charges but the cops are building a case against Victor Fenderbaum. They know he was involved and will be getting Wonka and Erwin to turn against him. You can add to the case."

"What do you get out of this?" she asked. I shrugged.

"I already got paid. I'm just here because of poor life decisions combined with a decent upbringing. It's a weird combo." She smirked at that. I started to slowly back away, retreating to the door. She didn't stop me. "I'm out of here but if you do go to the cops, ask for Iris Scott at Kemp, Slott and Bendis. Tell her the Cowboy sent you."

With a tip of my hat, I backed out through the door and left. The rest was up to her. I climbed back into the Chevelle and glanced at the time. I sighed. It was time to go get my ass kicked.

Chapter 04
Uncle Ben is Calling Me Sherriff Justice

Everybody in this world has a different set of thoughts that run through their mind when a good looking man puts his hands on their body. Some find themselves getting tingly and weak in the knees while thinking *this is going to be good.* Others find themselves getting tense and ponder *who does he think he is*? I often find myself swept off my legs and think *well crap, here we go again.*

I gripped my bat tight and swung it at the man who stood before me. I aimed for his chest. It was a solid swing that would have knocked a baseball clear out of the park if I had connected but I didn't hit a damn thing. My opponent stepped into my swing, blocked my hands with his left arm, grabbed my shoulder with his right and next thing I knew, my legs were in the air and I was floating. The thing about floating is that it's very misleading. Although it feels like you're floating what you're actually doing is enjoying that fraction of a second before you hit the mat, hard.

I landed with a thud and let out a loud groan. My opponent, Mr. Jack Walker, stood over my body. He looked down at my pained expression and did what all decent human being did when they saw another in pain, he laughed.

"You really suck at this," Jack laughed. "Your stance is too rigid, you're too squared off and you're an idiot gimp." Jack was a brick of a man with blonde hair in a military buzz.

He was an ex-Ranger who now made a living by cashing in on the fitness racket. He was also a complete asshole.

He was the kind of guy you assumed had a rough exterior and had a heart of gold beneath it but he didn't. He was an ass through and through but he was a brother. Truth be told, he was the type of asshole I enjoy playing with.

That sounded bad.

I grabbed my stick and swung for his legs. He casually lifted his leg and watched the stick swing by. I pushed myself to one knee and swung again, this time aiming for his knee. Jack was fast, one of the fastest men I'd ever known. With his speed he could have just slid backwards and dodge the entire attack. Instead, in a move I *still* don't understand, he pivoted on the balls of his feet, swung his far leg around and somehow judo kicked the weapon from my hand. The staff bounced across the room, skipping off the mat. I saw my opening and took it. I pushed myself forward and charged. I was Bill Goldberg and I was going to spear Jack for the win and continue my epic win streak. Sadly, my streak never even got started. Jack pivoted to the side, grabbed my arm and next thing I knew, I was back on my back whining about the pain.

"Do you treat the housewives like this?" Jack's fitness center taught many things. He taught how to *properly* lift weights and build strength. He taught martial arts and he taught women self-defence classes.

"Nope," he shrugged. "That is a different type of class, Ben."

"Oh. Can I sign up for that class?" Jack offered me his hand. I took it.

"Women self-defence classes are not about the actual self-defence," he explained as he hoisted me up to my feet. "While I do teach them how to properly defend themselves, they come to me to regain their confidence and to gain some control in their lives. Something happened that rattled them. They come to me and I give them back the confidence they desire."

I got to my feet and struck, hoping to catch him by

surprise. I fired with a solid crossover punch, my old military muscle memory *finally* kicking in, but I forgot that when I first trained in fighting I had two good legs. Now, I barely had one. By instinct, I shifted my weight to my bad leg and instantly regretted it. The leg buckled, my punch came up short and I started to topple. Jack blinked at me in disbelief before simply pushing me towards my bad leg. I crumpled down and returned to the mat. Hello, darkness, my old friend.

"You, on the other hand, didn't come to me for confidence. You came for actual skill." He crossed his arms and rubbed his nose. "You really are pathetic though, you know that right?"

"I've gathered that."

He hoisted me up again and I took my stance. For the next twenty minutes we worked on shuffling. The idea was to re-learn how to move my legs in a fight. I couldn't avoid my bad leg forever; I had to adjust to it. I had to learn just how much weight I could put on it before things went sour. We trained with a mock cane that Jack built for me. It was Jack's logic that if I was always going to have the cane on me, then I should learn how to use it during a fight. He didn't want me to train without it only to then trip over it when shit turned bad. He wanted it to be as much a part of me as my dick was (his words).

When the twenty minutes came, Jack walked back into his office. He emerged a couple minutes later with a pair of beers. This was his signal that our session was over. He cracked both opened and handed me one.

"Rangers lead the way," Jack said. I replied in kind as we tapped bottles. Each of us took a big swig. I knew Jack from back in the day. He was part of the same Ranger battalion that David and I were in. That was years ago, before I switched to Odin Squad.

"I was asked about you the other day." I raised my eyebrow. Jack continued. "Anderson was asking if we ever saw one another."

"Leo Anderson?" Jack nodded. Anderson was also a

member of Odin Squad. "Shit, what's he up to? You got his number?"

"He's out; he went private," Jack explained. "I'll text you his number. He's in the city now. He was saying your name has popped up in the circuit a couple times now. He's wondering if you're back in."

"Are you pulling a *John Wick*?" Jack just smirked. I shook my head and tapped my bad leg. "Trust me, the game don't want me. I'm out and I'm staying out. I'm just making ends meet."

"Good. The game just gets people killed." Jack took a long swig. "I've attended way too many funerals."

"We both have."

I got home, ready for some peace and quiet and the ability to take a nap. But as I pulled up into my driveway, I was reminded of the chaos that surely waited inside. I love my family, there was no question about that, but I also loved my alone time. Inside there was going to be a nosey older sister who was now taking time to go through my stuff and question every decision I have ever made. God help her if she looks at my internet search history. I'm not saying I'm a pervert. I'm just saying Puzo and I have some shared interests that we enjoy watching. With a sigh, I climbed out of the Chevelle and hobbled towards the front door. I stepped inside and was greeted with a wave of sound and noise. It was a combination of nagging, laughter and the TV. I dropped my cane at the door and carefully placed my hat atop the rack. I limped inside.

"Un-Kill! Un-Kill!" I looked and saw Alice waddling towards me. I scooped her up and hoisted her into the air. She giggled and laughed. I noticed that her natural warmth had returned. "I saw a birdie. It flew away. I wanna fly."

"Me too," I admitted as I carried her to the door. We

opened the door and stepped outside onto my porch. I pointed to the birds in the sky. "I want to fly too. I want to fly up in the sky, in the clouds."

For several minutes, Alice and I stood outside. We stared at the clouds and pointed to each bird we saw. Then she saw a squirrel and we talked about them. Then we saw a neighbour walking a dog and we talked about dogs. Perhaps I could get used to having them around.

"Cowboy." Alice pointed across the street. I spotted a man dressed in cowboy boots, blue jeans, black blazer and had a white cattleman style cowboy hat. He was walking past my house on the opposite side of the street. He kept stealing glances towards me. I nodded at him. I decided to take Alice indoors. You didn't see many folk wearing cowboy hats in this city. It used to be just me and then I saw Van Cleef.

Eighteen months ago, I had a vision that changed my entire life. I looked into the past and saw Zoey. She was with another cowboy. This cowboy could look into the future and somehow we met in the middle. On that day I learned that Zoey was still alive and she was being held captive. On that day she asked me to do three things:

1. No matter what happens, stay who I am.
2. When the diamond in the rough shows up, protect her.
3. Find and save Zoey.

No pressure.

The worst part of all of this - the visions, the missions, the Van Cleef - was the one undeniable fact that ripped me apart: Zoey was hanging with another cowboy. I was -- no. I am her cowboy. What the hell was she doing with another one? Was I jealous? In the words of some wise Canadian men: I get jealous, I'm just too cool to admit it. When the fellas talk to my girl, I ain't with it.

I hated Van Cleef and his stupid Stetson hat. I know what you're thinking, I'm psychic, remember. You're thinking that I wear a Stetson as well so we must be wearing identical hats. No. Our hats are not identical and damn anybody who says that. Damn them all!

My Stetson was brown and was formed in a Gus Style fashion. The Gus Style, or Gus to his friends, has three steep slopes towards the front of the hat and has three creases. Van Cleef had a black Stetson formed in the Diamond Style. This method of hat forming put a pinch in the front of the hat and a pinch in the back, making a diamond on the top. This was the style favoured by John Wayne and I hate that guy. Eastwood or death!

I might be a little sensitive when it comes to hats. Just don't get me started on the trilby.

The tires let out a squeal as the car peeled out of the parking lot. Bullets bounced off of the car. Red and blue lights flashed in the rear view mirror as cops cars closed in. This was not good.

"Robby?" I called out from the passenger seat. "They're behind us."

"Yeah, yeah," the kid grumbled. He steered the car and took a hard left. The car drifted like a Vin Diesel wet dream. Robby smashed through a gate and drove into an indoor parking garage. He drove up the ramps, masterfully drifted around the garage, climbing floor after floor until he reached the top. We were on the roof. Robby pointed the car at a haphazard ramp.

"Are you doing what I think you're doing?" I shook my head. Robby was going to jump the roof. "You can't do this!"

"Eastbound and down, loaded up and truckin'," Robby sang as he applied more pressure to the accelerator. "A'we gonna do what they say can't be done."

I love that kid!

Robby hit the ramp and flew off the edge. Time slowed down as the car flew through the air. A look of panic crossed my face. "We're not going to make it."

"Yes we are," Robby protested. Then we crashed into a building in a fiery explosion. Giant red letters that said WASTED came across my screen. Robby put down the controler with a grumble. "Okay, maybe you were right and maybe you were wrong, Uncle Ben, but we'll never know."

"You just blew us up," I joked. "I think that pretty much confirms that I was right."

"Agree to disagree."

"Whatever you say, Sheriff Justice."

"Wow, that was just mean," Robby protested. He called out at the top of his lungs. "Dad! Uncle Ben is calling me Sheriff Justice. Make him stop."

"Is that bad?" David said as he walked into the living room. Robby's jaw and mine both fell open.

"Buford T. Justice, Sheriff of Montague County?" Robby hinted. David just shrugged. Robby cried out again. "Mom! Dad doesn't know who Sheriff Buford T. Justice is."

"Who did I marry?" Annie said as she walked into the living room. "He's the cop from *Smokey and the Bandit*. He was literally *the* Smokey."

"You and your car films," David laughed. "I always preferred the counter-culture films like *Easy Rider* and *Billy Jack*."

Robby was over at my place the day Burt Reynolds died. I was bummed out and tried to explain to the kid why. I showed Robby *Smokey and the Bandit* and since then he hadn't stopped quoting it. Now it was my job to show the kid all the good out there in the movie world. If it was geek he would find it on his own. I wanted to make sure the boy was well rounded in the movie world. We had been doing the car movie genre. After the *Smokeys* we moved to *Cannonball Run*. Since then we'd been trying to tackle them all. We'd watched *Every Which Way but Loose, White Lightning, Vanishing Point, Dirty Mary, Crazy Larry, Bullit* and both *Gone in 60 Seconds.*

He liked *Bullit* and *Every Which Way*. He adored *Smokey* and *Cannonball*. He was meh on *Vanishing Point* but that film was a very artsy fartsy car film and Robby was never an artsy type of kid. He was pure fartsy. Either way, it was less about the movies and more about the time the kid and I spent together. It was time like this that he would remember for the rest of his life but then again, Robby would remember everything for the rest of his life.

A couple years back, I learned that the Thompson bloodline was special. Our blood was filled with superpowers. The technical term, or so it was explained to me using small words, was our blood was rich in Lycotta genes. These genes existed in all people in varying amounts. The more you had, the more likely you were to develop superpowers. I had superpowers, Robby had superpowers and it was very likely that Alice would develop superpowers. Annie had no powers but she did produce offspring with massive counts of Lycotta gene. She was like the combination of a Pez Dispenser and a T-Shirt cannon when it came to producing meta-humans.

Robby's power was a perfect memory. When his powers were fully developed, he would remember every moment of his life, ever. He could not forget anything, ever. Each person underwent a considerable amount of pain, suffering and trauma in our respective lives. We get through it by dealing with some of those and forgetting the details of the rest. It was a defense mechanism. Robby wouldn't have that. Every bad - and the kid had seen a lot already - would be engrained in his mind for the rest of his life.

Nobody knew what Alice's superpowers would be. It was difficult to tell before they developed. Meta abilities developed in two categories. The first was natural powers. Those emerged when the body reached puberty. The second were called trauma powers. They developed when your body was put in a desperate life or death situation. It was like the extreme adrenaline awakened the Lycotta gene, like a set of booster cables used to jumpstart a dead car battery. Luckily

Alice hadn't been in any life or death situation since she first left the hospital. She was touch and go when she was born early. It turns out that a stressful gun fight is not recommended for pregnant women. Alice was put in a John Travolta-esq baby tube. It was actually called a Neonatal Intensive Care Unit but that's a lot of big words for a simple farm boy turned army grunt turned detective like me. The kid fought for life in the beginning and she won. Now she was kicking alongside the rest of us.

A knock at the door pulled everybody's attention but none more so than mine. At first I didn't recognize the sound. What the hell was that? Nobody knocked on my door. Literally anybody I knew didn't bother knocking. They just opened the door and walked in. So who was knocking? I limped to the door and carefully opened it.

There as a teenage girl standing in my doorway. She had violet hair and a large green leather bag slung over her shoulder. The girl looked like a homeless rocker. She looked up at me with a look of desperation and exhaustion.

"Ben?" I hesitantly nodded. "Help me, Ben Thompson. You're the only one who can."

Chapter 05
I'm the Italian Stallion

I escorted the girl into my house. I knew I shouldn't have let some strange teenage girl into my home but she asked for my help and I'm a sucker for a person in need. Man or woman, adult or child, if someone needs help I tend to be the first to volunteer. I led her down the long hallway only to find my family staring at her with curious eyes. The girl recoiled in surprise. I shook my head, rookie mistake. Don't mix family with business, especially not my family.

"You look hungry," I began. "Do you want something to eat?" She nodded. I asked her a few question to avoid allergies before limping off to make her a PB & J. I glanced up as Robby walked over to her. His eyes were wide and the kid was smitten.

"Hi, I'm Robby," he introduced himself. The kid was trying to put on a cool stance as he leaned against the chair. "I'm kinda a big deal around here."

From across the room David and I did our best not to laugh. The kid had no game. He was pulling from the Ron Burgundy school of thought. I could teach him better but that was more of a father's job. David was a life-taker and a heart-breaker before he got lassoed by Annie. Robby would do well to learn from him.

I handed the sandwich and a coke to the girl. She hesitantly took it from me while cyeing my staring family. She wasn't going to talk with everybody looking so I escorted her to my office. She glanced at the swivel board.

"Nice murder board," she said with her southern twang as she plopped down on the couch. The upholstery was an ugly plaid but the couch was surprisingly comfortable. The girl started to wolf down the food. She was very hungry.

I did the detective thing and looked the girl up and down. She was a head and a half shorter then I was. She wore tattered jeans, a screen-printed tee and had a black choker with a metal heart around her neck. She wore a man's black leather jacket. It was too big for her and she was basically swimming in it. Her eyes were like a pair of vibrant emeralds. Her chest-length hair was tangled and poorly maintained. The violet dye had begun to fade and her roots had begun to show her natural brunette colour. A pair of broken handcuffs was on her wrist. The chain that held each cuff together was busted, leaving her hands free but the cuffs still firmly attached. Her face and hands were stained with dirt. Wherever she had been staying, she didn't have access to a shower.

I grabbed my chair and wheeled it closer to her. She recoiled slightly as her right hand dropped to her jacket's pocket. I held up my hands to show no threat.

"My name is Ben Thompson." Great start, moron. She already knew that. "What can I do to help you?" She eased up with her right hand but she didn't say anything. She just continued eating. "Let's start with simple questions. What is your name?"

"Lucy," she said in a low tone.

"Pleasure to meet you, Lucy," I said. "Where are your parents?" She stiffened.

"My mom died a few years ago. She was sick," she said slowly. She gently ran the fingers of her right hand across the leather choker. A look of sorrow filled her emerald eyes.

"And your Dad?"

"He's dead," she snapped suddenly. "But I'm not allowed to talk about that."

"Then I won't ask," I said. "How old are you?"

"I'm eighteen."

"And I'm the Italian Stallion," I said, calling out her bullshit. "Seriously, how old are you?"

"I'm fifteen," she said sheepishly. I smiled at her.

"I was sixteen when I got a fake ID," I began. "I wanted to get into a bar and have a drink with some buddies and maybe meet a lady or two. The only problem was in a small town everybody knew everybody. The bartender knew my Dad. He took one look at me and my ID and laughed. He kicked me out so fast that my head spun. It was a stupid idea but I wasn't the sharpest tool when I was a young'n." Truth be told, nothing much had changed but I wasn't going to tell her that.

Lucy smiled and chuckled. I returned with a smile of my own. "So where are you living?"

"I don't live anywhere," she explained. "I'm just a toerag on the run. How did I get here? What have I done?"

I blinked. Her words were weird. "Everybody lives somewhere, kiddo. Where have you been staying?"

"Here and there," she said. "Who needs some loving care inside a happy home?"

Her words were confusing. Did I no longer understand how teenager talked? Was I ---- getting old? No. I swore that would it never happen to me. I swore I'd stay young forever.

"What can I do to help?" I asked.

"I'm in trouble but I don't know if I can trust you," she snapped.

"Then why did you come here?" I snapped back, my voice jumping in tone more then I wanted. Lucy's back became rigid and strength emerged. Her bottom lip stiffened.

"I came because you have powers," she snapped. "You have powers and you help people!"

Wait, what?

"H...h...how did you know that?" I asked.

"Benedict Thompson. Occupation: Retiree/private investigator. Classification: Delver." She flashed a cocky look my way. "It's a smart way of saying that you're psychic."

"I knew that, thanks." I actually didn't but I wasn't going to tell her that. "How do you know this?"

"Does it matter?" She asked. "The truth is I saw something bad and now bad people are after me. I need your help or I'll be dead by the end of the week."

"Then I'm in," I said without hesitation. After a statement like that, what choice did I have? "I don't know what I'm in but I'm in."

"Thank you," she said.

"I have to make a call," I began.

"No cops!" she desperately pleaded.

I paused in shock. I looked at her and rolled forward. "It's okay. The person I'm calling is a special agent in the FBI. She's a cop but she is different. I trust this one. She's my girlfriend. Is it okay if I call her?" Lucy didn't look convinced. I flashed a humorous grin. "I have pictures of her on her day off. She was in ugly sweats and covered in cheeto dust. Trust me; she doesn't want those to get out. She'll be cool."

Lucy nervously chuckled.

"Thank you. Now you can stay in here or you can go into the living room and hang out with my family." I paused. Maybe that wasn't a good idea. "They're good people and I'm pretty sure I can get my sister to make you some more food if you'd like." Lucy's eyes went wide at the sound of food. She carefully nodded. I escorted Lucy to the living room. Annie looked at me with concerned eyes. I did a quick round of introductions.

"This is Lucy. She needs my help," I began. I looked at my sister. "Annie, can you whip her up something a little more substantial that PB & J? She hasn't eaten in a bit."

"Sure, Benny," she said quickly. She gave the girl a quick once over as a look of concern crossed her face. "Lucy, Robby is going to grab you a towel. You go jump in the shower while I cook something."

Before Lucy could reply, Robby dashed to the towel closet. He was the roadrunner. All that stood in his place was a cloud-shaped Robby that slowly dissipated. Annie waved me over.

"What's going on?" she asked in hushed whispers.

"I don't know yet. She says she's in trouble and needs my help," I explained. "For now, I see a hungry, dirty and tired teenage girl. I'll start with that and go from there."

"You know I'm not your personal housekeeper for wayward children, right?" Annie said.

"Of course not, the housekeeper gets a day off." Annie smacked me. I grabbed my phone and walked to my bedroom. "I'm gonna call Rachael."

Rachael picked up after the second ring. "Hey, what up?"

"I need your help," I said quickly.

"Another case?" Puzo protested. "You know I don't work for you, right?"

"I need the *FBI's* help," I quickly corrected. "A teenage girl showed up at my door begging for help. She says if I didn't, she'd be dead in a week. She's afraid of the cops but I convinced her to let me call you specifically."

"I'll be there in thirty minutes," Puzo said swiftly.

"Also there is something I should warn you about," I quickly added. "My family forced their way into my house and are crashing at my place for a few days. This means my sister is here doing her sister things."

Silence.

"I'll stop by the armoury and grab a shotgun on my way out," Puzo added.

"Wanna play a video game?" Robby offered. Both teenagers sat on the couch in the living room as Alice waddled around, touching everything and laughing. Lucy shook her head at Robby's request.

"Video games are lame."

"Yeah, hella lame," Robby quickly added as quickly pushed the controller across the coffee table. Lucy pulled an iphone from her pants pocket. It was an older version and had a cracked screen. She tapped the phone a couple times before plugging in her ear buds. "Whatcha listening to?"

"Halestorm."

"Cool, cool, cool."

"You know them?" Lucy asked with sceptical eyes.

"Who doesn't?" Robby replied. Lucy shrugged and placed both buds in her ears. She vanished to the world of music. Robby subtly grabbed his phone and started typing. He was trying to make it look like he *wasn't* looking up Halestorm but he totally was. Lucy rubbed her wrist, happy that she was free of the cuffs. The first thing Puzo did upon arrival was remove them.

David and I watched all of this go down from the kitchen. I leaned over and whispered to my BFF. "When did video games suddenly become lame?" I jested.

"When he noticed the teenage bad-girl," David replied with a chuckle. "It happens to every boy. For me it was Tessa Holms. She was two years older than me, was in a do nothing punk band and always had a Mohawk. The rumours in school said she was freaky fun guaranteed. I asked her out thinking she was a sure thing. She wasn't and I got punched out. My Dad found out and lost it on me. Told me stuff like *you ain't a man if you act like that* and *I didn't raise you like that.*

"A couple days later I show up at Tessa's locker. I apologised and said that I had promised her a good dinner for our date and I needed to keep my word. She agrees, takes me to some super expensive place and pretty much empty out what little savings I had from my part-time job but we got to talking and found out we actually liked each other. We dated for a few months before she left for college."

"And she's still on your Facebook?" Annie asked as she walked into the room. David tried to stammer out a defense but Annie never gave him the chance. I decided to come to his rescue.

"Brie Danvers," I began. "She was a gear head. She worked on cars, smoked and could punch the lights out of anybody she met. She was the tomboy bad girl and I was head over heels for her but she wouldn't give me the time of day. I even took an auto-mechanic class in high school to try and fit in but I was too clean cut. I never got a shot. I even tried starting a fight with her friends to show her how tough I was. All that got me was my ass kicked and even more disgust from her."

"You were an idiot as a teenager," Annie laughed.

"Not much has changed," David added.

"Nikki Perlman," Annie said suddenly. I knew that name. I wracked my brain until it came to me.

"The rebel emo chick from high school?" Annie nodded.

"She was my bad girl," Annie said. "It was for like a hot minute in my experimental years. She was sexy and dangerous and I was obsessed with her. She would debate with teachers, was well read and liked stuff other then shooting and farming and in our high school that was unique. She was all powerful and bad girl like and she paid attention to scum like me."

"When you say *your bad girl...*" I asked.

"When you say *experimental....*" David quickly added.

"I mean exactly what you think I do. I gave it a try and it didn't stick." Annie smirked at the dropped jaws of David and I. "It wasn't for me. I wasn't into girls so we went our own ways but for those three weeks, I would have done anything to impress my bad girl."

"I remember that. You started dressing in all black and Dad was all Hank Hill *I'm worried about that girl.*" I paused. "I never would have expected *that* was the reason."

"You know," David said hopefully. "They say that things you didn't like as a child you may like as an adult. Have you thought about revisiting it with, say, you husband by your side?"

"Men," Annie said with a roll of her eyes. She walked out of the room. David quickly followed.

"I don't mind just watching."

Puzo emerged from the bedroom. She slid her phone into her jacket pocket and walked towards me. She politely asked Robby to leave and the kid reluctantly shuffled off. Puzo and I sat down near Lucy.

"Hi, Lucy. My name is Rachael. I'm a Senior Special Agent with the FBI." Puzo withdrew her badge and opened it up. She placed it on the coffee table and slid it towards the kid. Lucy picked it up and looked it over. "For many years I worked on missing children cases and endangered children cases. This means I spent a lot of time helping and rescuing boys and girls just like you. I want to let you know that I'm here to help."

Lucy nodded. It was amazing to watch Puzo work. She didn't talk down to Lucy. She talked to her gently but in an adult manner. Everything she did, from the order of her words to the simple gesture of trusting her badge to Lucy, was to build trust. She wanted to appear to Lucy as someone she could open up to and count on.

"You told Ben that your life was in danger. You said that you were going to die within the week. I'm here to make sure that does not happen," Puzo promised.

"Thank you," Lucy whispered.

"Now why don't you tell me what this is all about; why are you in danger?"

"It all started," Lucy said, "when I watched my father get murdered."

Chapter 06
Creeps, Murderers and Cannonballers

"My mom passed away a couple years ago. She was sick for a while," Lucy began. Her words were slow and still. "For a couple years it was just Dad and I. Then Dad died but I'm not allowed to talk about that." Her words trailed off. I wanted to press her for more but Puzo wouldn't let me. "Police showed up and took me away. They moved me away from Texas and I was put into a foster home. They told me it was for my protection.

"Foster care sucked. I lived with six other kids and we were all under the care of Mr. and Mrs. Owles. They were douches. We could do anything and they wouldn't care. Mr. Owles - he didn't like us using his first name - was a bit of a drunk and Mrs. Owles worked long hours. Shit kept getting stolen in that house and I had rarely been in a fight before moving there but either you learned how to throw a punch or you got beat down. Nobody in that house could be trusted. So when I was forced to bail, I didn't give it a second thought, I ran."

"What forced you to leave?" Puzo asked.

"The bad men started showing up," she said quickly. "I got out of school one day and there they were. I ran and they chased me down. I was able to...." He words trailed off as she stared at her hands. "I was able to escape them but when I got back to the house I knew I wasn't safe. I grabbed whatever cash I could find, bolted out the door and started running. All I could hear in my head was *Find Ben Thompson. He can protect you.*"

Puzo looked at me with a surprised look. She was thinking the same thing. How the hell did she even know who I was?

"Did you tell the Owles where you were?" Puzo asked. Lucy shook her head. "We should at least tell them that you're okay. Where are they located?"

"They're in the south end."

"Of which borough?"

"Of Chicago," she sheepishly said. My jaw hit the floor.

"How did you get from Chicago to here? That's got to be like 900 miles."

"I took a Greyhound and then I hitchhiked," Lucy admitted. I don't know how it did but my jaw dropped even lower. It punched through the floor and damaged the foundation. I cursed. This metaphor was getting costly. Metaphorical structural damage would cost a lot to fix. I'd need to be as rich as Auric Goldfinger to pay for this. Oh no, a simile! They always drove up the price. My floor was never going to be fixed, not in this economy.

Allegorical costs aside, I was shocked by what Lucy had just revealed. None of what she had just said could be considered an easy feat for a full grown adult let alone a teenage girl. The road was dangerous. There were creeps, murderers and Cannonballers out there. The streets were never safe.

"I was picked up within hours of getting into the city," Lucy continued. "They threw a bag over my head and tased me in the back. When I woke up I was tied to a chair in some building. I broke free, escaped and hopped on the first bus I found. Then I made my way here."

I stared in silence. What did I say after a story like that? Did I offer the girl a hug? Did I offer her a teddy bear? At that moment I realized I knew nothing of what teenage girls liked. My experience with hardship was with my Rangers brothers. For that you offer the guy a beer - or many - and you got him laid. Somehow I doubted that was the right path with Lucy.

"Can I see your back?" Puzo asked. "I want to make sure you're okay."

Lucy sheepishly nodded. She took off her jacket and tossed it on the coffee table. She turned her waist and lifted up the back of her tee. Puzo stepped forward and took a look. There were two puncture marks on her back. The skin looked mildly burned. Puzo looked at me and flashed a *WTF* look. I didn't know much about tasers but she did and she was knocked for six. She thanked Lucy and the girl lowered her shirt.

"Do you know where you were being held?" I asked.

"I don't know exactly," Lucy said. She started to describe what she'd seen. She was in a long room with several square pillars and a wall of windows. The room was painted in the generic white. Lucy didn't catch the building's number but she did know she got on bus #124

I rose from my chair and limped to my office, returning with my laptop. I placed it down and quickly started tapping on the keys. I first brought up the transit map and found the route of the #124 bus. Then I opened up Google maps and turned on street view. For the next twenty minutes Lucy and I followed the route. With each click of the mouse, the street would shoot forward a couple feet.

"There," she said suddenly with a point. I pivoted the camera. There was the Totleben Building. It was a six story office building. In the world of buildings, it was fairly new, only ten years old. It was a smaller building, sacrificing its air rights to make another nearby building taller. I opened up another tab and quickly googled the Totleben Building's address. I scrolled down until I found several post advertising office space for rent. It made sense. Nobody went into an empty office. I smiled as I typed. I felt like Hotwire. In reality I was nothing like Hotwire. My PC game was nonexistence compared to him. I was more like Hotwire's cat that he trained to use and flush a toilet.

"I need to know about your Dad," Puzo asked carefully.

"I'm not allowed to talk about it," Lucy snapped quickly. Puzo calmly apologised.

"I don't mean to be rude," I said slowly, "but what do you want from me? What can I do to help?"

"I need you to make sure I don't die," she said quietly. I nodded.

"I can do that, kiddo." I looked at Puzo. "I should check out the office space."

"I'll come with you." We both stood up and moved for the door. Lucy leapt up and ran towards us. She was frightened.

"You're leaving me here?" she said, a quiver of fear echoing through her voice. "You're supposed to protect me. I....she...you *have* to protect me."

"I want to do more than just protect you," I said calmly. "I want to stop whoever is trying to hurt you and I can't do that here."

"W...w...will I be save here?" she asked. I nodded. I called in David and Annie. I slapped David on the back. My slap was harder than it needed to be but that's only because David's a wimp and I'm a jerk.

"This is David. He is a Ranger. Do you know what that means?" Lucy shook her head. "Rangers lead the way. That means we are the biggest badasses that exist in the US military. We're stronger, tougher and better then Marines, Navy Seals and anybody in the Chair Force. If anybody tries to get through that door without a pizza, they have to go through him."

"Thanks, dude," David said, slapping my back. His strike was harder than it needed to be but that was only because I'm a wimp and David's a jerk. "It's about time you admitted I'm better than you are." I glared at him.

Lucy still looked hesitant. I moved to my sister and placed my hand on her shoulder. There was no way I was bro-

slapping her back. Annie and I had wrestled and fought many times as kids. I won each and every fight, no matter what Annie says. She lies. She always lies. I never lost to my sister, never.

"If David isn't man enough, then they have to go through Annie." Lucy looked skeptical. "Annie is a farmer's daughter who lived in a small town full strong arm football/farmer jerks who thought they were God's gift to women and did not like being told otherwise. She punched out half of her graduating class. To be honest, I'm more afraid of her than him."

Lucy smiled in relief. I grabbed my phone and keys and limped to the door. Puzo was right behind me. Lucy walked to the door and paused. Hesitation resonated in her face.

"Don't leave me now, leave me out with nowhere to go and the shadows start to fall," she cryptically said. "You sure I'll be safe here?"

"This is the safest place you can be," I explained. I grabbed my cowboy hat and gracefully placed it upon my head. "Now it's my job to make sure everywhere else is safe as well."

I opened the door, cane in hand, and dramatically hobbled outside. A smile beamed across my face. There was nothing cooler then when my life appeared like a movie. The phenomena happened from time to time and I called it movie-life. I got a dramatic exit and that was good movie-life. I got an epic one-liner and that was movie-life. A heroic swagger and the epic last line in the scene; that is what made movie-life great because nothing was more important than the last line in a scene.

"Did I hear somebody say something about pizza?" Robby asked in the distance.

Damn it, kid.

Puzo's cop car was the generic black FBI cop car. It looked sleek without being sexy. It looked like professionalism and silent intimidation all in one. I wanted to drive the Chevelle but Puzo said no. Actually she said yes but only if she could drive. We decided on her car.

"What'cha thinking, Puzo?" I asked. She had that deep in thought expression that I had seen from time to time.

"She's in Witsec," Puzo said eventually. "I'm not sure what the procedure is here but I think we need to call the US Marshals."

"Why? So they can search every gas station, residence, warehouse, barn house, hen house, outhouse and dog house? They'll just put up check points every fifteen miles." Puzo gave me a playful slap. "Why Witsec?"

"She saw her Dad get murdered and police moved her across the country," Puzo said quickly. "She's not allowed to talk about what she saw. She's in witness protection. The Marshals should be looking after her."

"But she's afraid of them," I replied. "She's afraid of cops."

"Maybe she's afraid she'll be forced to move again," Puzo said. "Maybe she blames cops. I don't know." Puzo shook her head. "Fuck, I feel bad for her."

"I...I need to know how she knows me," I said suddenly. "Someone told her to find me. They said I'd protect her. I need to know who is doing this."

"You and me both," Puzo said.

We pulled up to the Totleben Building. It was deep in commercial territory. There were few, if any, residential buildings around. This area was basically office building after office building with dozens of indoor parking lots to add to it. Dozens of support businesses surrounded the upscale buildings. There were corners stores, lunch time bistros, courier companies and row after row of street meat vendors. As we climbed out of the car I winced at the heat. Shit. Not removing the hoodie was a bad idea. Luckily, I spotted a hot dog cart. I smiled and hobbled over to it.

"What are you doing?" Puzo asked. "We're working."

"And I haven't eaten yet today. Do you want one?" Puzo said no as she shook her head. I looked back at the vendor. "Two please and a coke."

The vendor handed me two dogs and a red-can of coke. I slid the can into my hoodie's front pocket and I started decorating the dogs. First, I liberally coat the meat with relish. Then I put a line of ketchup followed by a swirl of mustard. I follow with a sprinkle of bacon bits. Nothing beats a good dog.

I hobble toward the building. Puzo and I enter. We saw a security desk with a guard sitting behind it, a large white guy with cracked skin and long greasy hair. Puzo flashed a badge as I looked through the building's directory.

"Third floor is empty," I say.

"Has anybody gone up there?" Puzo asked.

"Just a bunch of construction workers," he said with an indignant snarl.

"What are they working on?"

"I dunno," the guard replied. "I didn't check their work order."

"Then how do you know that they're construction workers?"

"A bunch of frick'n illegals speaking Spanish and carrying tools. What else are they?" Oh great. "They're the reason my brother and me went out of business. We were good, hardworking, American construction workers and small business owners but we can't compete with companies that hire illegals. That wall can't be built soon enough."

He was much worse than his hair. Puzo and I walked off as we heard the guard grumble *make America great again.* I rolled my eyes and took a bite of my dog. I smiled as my tongue felt the familiar feeling of meat-ish food passing by. My body savoured the food and *Hunger* was the most thankful. *Hunger* was a powerful force in my decision making. He ranked high, falling in alongside *Laziness*, *Sex Drive* and *Sleepiness*. But no force was as powerful in the Ben Decision Making Hierarchy as Desire to Re-Watch *The Expendables*. That entity was hella strong.

"You know those will kill you eventually?" Puzo asked. I blinked as a thought hit me. What if hot dogs were the cause of my death? Was that what the vision warned me about?

A couple years ago I had a vision of the future where I was dead. Alice and Robby were grown up and they were accompanied by a teenager named Clint - my future son. The vision said I had been dead almost ten years and I had given up my life to save everybody. The more I thought of it the more I hoped that my heroic sacrifice wasn't dying by eating a hot dog because that was going to be embarrassing, hella embarrassing.

Here lies Ben
Death By Hot Dog
NEVER Trust Street Meat

Chapter 07
My Visions are Running Google Translate

We stepped into the empty office and immediately I recognized the place. I had never been there before but Lucy's descriptions were dead on. The room was long. It was the type of room that would eventually have more walls inserted to make numerous offices and cubicles. Two of the walls were lined with square windows, each covered with newspapers. The walls were painted in the generic white that did little but cover up the wood and drywall. Eventually the white would be painted over with whatever colour the renter wanted but until then, generic white it was. A folding card table was set at one end with several folding chairs set out around it and construction equipment nearby. At the other end of the room was another lone chair.

I finished my second dog and let out a satisfied sigh. Damn if I didn't love the taste of meat-ish food.

I hobbled to the windows and took a look at the paper. Dozens of papers had been taped to the glass from the inside. They wanted to hide their operations but didn't want to paint the windows black. I glanced at the paper's date. It was only two days old. They hadn't been here long. I pulled off my gloves and ran my fingers across the paper. A shiver and a twitch and I vanished into the past.

Three Latino men were frantically taping paper to the glass. They called out to each other in Spanish. In the corner of my gaze, I spotted a figure cuffed to a lone chair. A bag was over their head. It was Lucy.

Reality returned. I called out to Puzo. "We're in the right place. They had her here."

I moved to the lone chair. It was a metal folding chair not unlike the type that Stone Cold Steve Austin would use to end a civilized debate. I took a deep breath and touched it. I fell back into the past. Lucy was just coming to. She was waking up to find that she was handcuffed to a chair, had a gag in her mouth and a bag over her head. Panic took hold and she let out a muffled scream.

From across the room a gaggle of Latino men, each wearing a thick leather jacket, huddled around the folding table and several construction equipment. One of them was quickly texting on his phone. The leather jackets struck me as odd. We were having one of the biggest heat waves in recent years and wearing anything more than a tee was just stupid. I could personally attest to that. I was still wearing my blue hoodie from first thing this morning and I was suffering for it.

"Boss says kill her," the man on the phone said.

The second man opened up a metal tool chest. He reached past the wrenches and screwdrivers and pulled free a small pistol. He screwed on a silencer and placed the weapon on the table. "Make it quick."

The five men stared at the weapon. Who was going to do the deed? Each of them was a trained killer, I could feel it off of them, but all of them seem to hesitate. The third man picked up the gun and cocked it. He walked over and leveled the weapon at Lucy's covered head. There was no shake in his grip. This man was very familiar with a weapon and he had killed before but as he held the weapon aloft, he found his finger frozen.

"Do it," the first man called out.

"She's a child," the third replied. "We don't kill children."

"She can bring down the boss," the second said. "If he goes down, so do we all."

"If you go to prison, who will look after your daughter?" The first man asked. "Think of your daughter."

"I am," the third said. With a sigh he lowered his weapon and returned to the table. He dropped the weapon. "She's only a few years older than Maricruz. Someone else has to do it."

Nobody else made a move.

Reality returned. I called over Puzo. She came over, holding several papers in her hand. They were written in Spanish. I told her what I saw.

"You understand Spanish?" I shook my head. "Then how?"

"I think my visions are running Google Translate," I said with a shrug.

I looked around the chair and spotted a piece of burnt metal. I knelt down for a closer look. It took a moment before I recognized what it was: a broken link of chain. It looked like a link of the chain that should have held Lucy's cuff together but instead of the bright silvery metallic look, it was burnt so black that I almost missed it all together. I reached down and touched the link.

A shiver and a twitch and I was back into the past. Lucy was still in her chair but the men had walked away. She was trying to move, she was trying to free herself but to no avail. Each time she tested the chain it held fast. Fear filled her mind, her body began to shake and the hairs on her arm stood on end. Suddenly an arc of electricity appeared. It started small, bouncing around the tip of her pinky finger, but quickly grew in size. It eventually leapt from finger to finger, growing with each hop. Lucy grabbed a link with her fingers and guided the spark towards it. A loud grinding sound accompanied by a bright burning light filled the room as the link snapped. It fell dropped to the ground. Now that her hands were free, Lucy had to move quickly. She pulled off the sack and tossed it aside. She quickly freed her legs and bolted for the door, grabbing her bag along the way. One of the men bolted for her, grabbing her by the arm. Lucy spun around and slammed

her fingers into his chest. A large series of sparks formed and a blast of lightning pitched the man back and into the air. He crashed into the ground, nearly a dozen feet away. Each of the men froze as they stared at her in fear. Lucy, however, just ran. She bolted down out the door and down the stairs.
Reality returned.

"She's like me," I said quietly. "Lucy has powers."

"Of course she does," Puzo said with an exasperated sigh. "Can you ever get a normal case?"

"I just solved the mystery of the murderous car thieves," I defended.

"Let me guess the murderer had the ability to make cars come alive and star in bad Disney films?"

"You know.....I never asked." I paused and smirked. "That was a very me comment. Are you beginning to sound like me?"

"Maybe."

"Am I sounding like you as well?"

"Depends, are you thinking about your actions and choosing the more logical choice?"

"Not even remotely," I said proudly.

"Then no, no you are not," she said with a shake of her head and smile on her lips.

Raymond Chandler was a successful American detective novelist. He died in 1959. He wrote a lot of books about noir detectives. In his books everything was dark, shadowy and everybody wore grey. This seems odd now but it was common in the time before colours were invented. He was famous for creating a method to get through writers block.

When in doubt, have a man come through a door with a gun in his hand.

This was forever known as Chandler's Law. So when suddenly three of the five Latino men entered the room, each drawing a pistol from within their leather jackets, all I could think of was: Screw you, Chandler. Monica deserved better.

I moved without thinking and ducked behind one of the few pillars. Puzo didn't get a chance to move. The three men approached with their guns leveled at her. She held up her hands and spoke firmly.

"I am Senior Special Agent Rachael Puzo of the FBI," she sternly said. "I'm ordering you to put down those weapons." Puzo got a string of Spanish in return. "I know you can understand me. You don't want to do this."

They weren't budging. I needed to save Puzo. Truth was Puzo wasn't some damsel who couldn't save herself. She often saved me. What she needed was something ridiculous and distracting and that was my forte. I reached into my hoodie pouch and grabbed the can of coke and instantly regretted it. I wasn't wearing any gloves.

"Not now," I pleaded as I fell into the past.

I saw the street outside of the Totleben Building and the hot dog vendor hard at work. He had a cooler of pop open and was shuffling warm ones to the bottom and putting the colder ones on top. He stood up and made a weird face. It was the same weird face everybody made before a sneeze. You look stupid, people eye you weirdly and only understand what you're doing when you expel a sneeze at 45 m/s. This time the hot dog vendor sneezed on the hot dogs. He quickly grabbed his tongs and rolled them over on the grill.

"What are you doing?" Puzo asked. "We're working."

No, oh no. Please no. I looked up and see myself walking towards the vendor, money in hand. Vision-Ben is going to buy a hot dog.

"And I haven't eaten yet today. Do you want one?" Puzo said no as she shook her head. Vision-Ben looks back at the vendor. "Two please and a coke."

The hot dog vendor looked down at the grill. There are only two dogs on the grill; the sneeze dogs. The vendor shrugged and took my money.

Reality returns. I felt like I was going to throw up. Never trust street meat.

I had to focus. I pulled the can free and pitched it forward. Puzo was standing in front of three men, each who had a weapon drawn on her. So when a can of coke slammed into the skull of Bad #3, dropping him and probably giving him a concussion, the other two turned in surprise. I ducked back behind the pillar and Puzo became *John Wick*. She stepped in, struck Bad #1 twice, grabbed his arm, twisted and threw him to the ground. Then she drew her firearm and pointed it at Bad #2. The entire thing happened in one smooth motion that took less than four seconds to accomplish. I was fast; David was fast; Puzo was faster.

"Put the gun on the floor, now!" Puzo yelled. Bad #2 didn't obey. He kept his gun aimed at her as he slowly started to walked towards the door. "FBI mean drop the *fucking* gun!"

She was being funny because FBI doesn't mean that at all. For those of you that don't know, FBI stands for Foxy Bodied Individual.

Puzo and Bad #2 were in a standoff. She could shoot him but not before he shot her back. What she needed was another distraction. The only problem was I was all out of coke. I needed to call on my vast Spanish knowledge if I wanted to reach Bad #2.

"El Chupacabra! El Chupacabra!" I yelled as I bolted out from behind the pillar. "Una cerveza, por favor!"

And that's the limit of my Spanish. Bad #2 doesn't move but he does glance in my direction. It's hard not to. There is some idiot with a cane and a cowboy hat dancing and screaming like a fool. I'd be insulted if he *didn't* glance.

The glance was all Puzo needed. She fired off a single shot and put a bullet into his shoulder. Bad #2 dropped to the ground and she was on him in a second, kicking the weapon away. As quickly as this all had started, it came to an end. Teamwork had prevailed. Puzo was Ricky Bobby and I was Cal Naughton Jr.

Shake and Bake.

I hate police stations. They are grimy and disgusting. They are cold and impersonal. FBI offices, however, have a higher budget and, therefore, are much nicer. I had been in Puzo's office a few times. She had a corner office, a nice view and comfy chairs. But the best part of her office was the hidden snacks she kept in her desk. Rachel and I had been together, officially and unofficially, for two years and in that time I learned an all important factor about her: my woman liked snacks. She always has a bag of M&Ms around the house. Hell, there is often so much M&M in her that she starts hanging out with Mekhi Phifer and Dr. Dre. I opened up B-Rabbit's desk and smiled. A bright yellow bag of peanut M&Ms stare up at me. I scooped them up and sat back down in my chair.

"Are you eating *my* snacks?" My eyes went wide. How did she always do that? Every time I tried to eat her M&Ms she'd know.

"We're a couple," I sad. "Doesn't that make them *our* M&Ms?"

"Not even remotely." She snatched the bag from my hand and plopped down in her chair. She sighed as she opened the bag and popped a few in her mouth. "I've got bad news."

Puzo put a small vial on the desk and slid it towards me. I picked it up and looked at it. It was filled with blue powder. It looked like Walter White had given up on meth and turned towards cocaine.

"This is a drug called Blue Cap," she explained. "According to the DEA the market for this drug is growing fast. The product is directly controlled by the Imperecedero Cartel."

"We just took on a drug cartel?" I asked in shock. Puzo nodded. This was....this was....this was....awesome! A drug cartel; I was taking on a drug cartel. This was movie-life. I get to be Arnie in *The Last Stand* or Emily Blunt in *Sicario*. As long as I could avoid the tire-fire death trap I would be okay.

"Stop smiling," Puzo snapped. "This is real life."

Lies. This was movie-life.

"Things are starting to add up. I think she saw her Dad killed by some cartel boss. That's why she's in Witsec." My smile vanished. Reality had just hit me like a ton of bricks and due to stupid tariffs, the cost of bricks had just gone up. Why did reality cost so much? "As much as I want to help her, the best choice is for the Marshals to look after her. They can move her somewhere safe."

"What's our next step?" I asked.

"I'm thinking you should go back home and look after her. We can go from there," she said. "I'm going to call one of my contacts in the Marshals and go from there."

The cab ride home sucked. I knew I should have driven. The entire ride I was silently thinking. I know handing Lucy over to the Marshals was the best choice but it still felt like a mistake. The kid came to me for help. I should help her but I couldn't protect her, not from a drug cartel. Perhaps she was better off with the Marshals. But she knew who I was. She knew I had powers.

As I entered my house I had made up my mind. The US Marshals were going to take her. I had done everything I could but the Marshals were better equipped to protect her than some gimp retiree. I took off my hat, ditched my cane and limped to the living room. David and Annie were making food as Lucy and Robby watched TV. Alice waddled around looking happy and content. I spotted Lucy sitting in my chair.

"You're in my chair," I said. "Out of my chair."

"Whatever, Sheldon," Lucy said with a roll of her eyes. She climbed out of the chair and plopped beside Robby on the couch. Robby did his best to contain his smile. Funny or not, he was happy that she was sitting closer to him.

"Uncle Ben," Robby said suddenly. "Lucy has the coolest last name." I blinked. I suddenly realized that I didn't know her last name. I looked at her. She sighed.

"Diamond," she said quickly. "My name is Lucy Diamond."

Chapter 08
Ain't TV Great?

My eyes went wide, my jaw dropped and my body froze. Any attempt to get my body to move proved to be a failure. This surprise had stunned my body into paralysis. Lucy was Lucy Diamond. She was my diamond in the rough.

When the diamond in the rough shows up, protect her.

Zoey's words rolled through my mind. She asked me to do three things and this was one of them. I had to protect Lucy. I had to look after her. I couldn't simply hand her over to the Marshals. If it was that simple then why did Zoey have to rip a hole through time to tell me that? That seemed excessive. It seemed more like a message sent through text and not through two psychic cowboys. At the very most, a message like this required Western Union to get a letter in 1885 and hold it for seventy years, two months and twelve days before delivering it.

I plopped down in my Lay-Z-Boy and shook my head. Now what the hell was I going to do? How was Cowboy Ben supposed to take on a drug cartel? How was I supposed to protect her and would I be putting the rest of my family in danger while doing so?

My mind raced a mile a minute. I couldn't figure out what to do. I needed clarity. I needed something calming. I needed a drink. I limped to the kitchen. Annie gave me a look as I reached past her and into the freezer. She gave me an understanding nod as I pulled free the vodka. I grabbed a tumbler, dropped a couple ice cubes into it and started to make my drink.

A Barbarosa is 1/2 vodka and 1/2 coke. I decided to make my variant. I came up with it a few years back but still hadn't named it. It was my magic drink, my Vesper. I just needed a name for it. I was really bad at naming things.

Ben's Unnamed Drink:
- 1/2 Citron vodka - adds character of lemon and lime with a note of lemon peel
- 1/2 Coke - Can or glass bottle. No plastic. Tastes better that way
- Ice - I like ice in drinks. I feel cool swirling around booze in ice.

"That type of day?" Annie asked. She spoke in a caring way and not a judgemental one. She understood the look. It was Dad's look. Dad's solution to a hard day on the farm was a nice drink. His solution to a *really* rough day was a shot of tequila, then a nice drink. His solution to a difficult problem was a stiff drink and a hard think. While I was good at drinking, I was very bad at thinking.

It was going to be a long night.

"What the fuck do you mean the Marshals can't take her?" Puzo was pissed. She was really fucking pissed. I hadn't seen her that pissed in a long while. Puzo had come home and told me the Marshals were mobilizing and would be here in the morning to pick Lucy up.

"I have to protect her," I said. "She's in danger."

We were arguing in the bedroom. I didn't like arguing in the bedroom. It felt like a conflict of interest to argue in the place we boned. It was like crapping where you cooked or birthing a cow in a slaughter house.

"No shit. She's made an enemy of the Imperecedero Cartel," Puzo snapped. "They are mainly based out of Texas and Mexico. They don't make their way up north; they are forbidden to. A different Cartel will go to war with them if they step into their territory. They are risking war to kill the kid. Do you understand the situation?"

"Yes, of course I do." Well, I did now. "But are the Marshals able to help her? Witsec is supposed to be super top secret. Unless you're Mary McCormack you don't get to know shit about the witnesses. So how did the cartel find her?"

"I know they have a leak," Puzo said. "But that doesn't change things. What do you think we should do?"

"We just have to protect her until...."

"Until what?" Puzo asked, "Until we take down an entire cartel? That takes years, Ben. What are you going to do, stand guard by her bed for years?"

"I have to do something," I defiantly declared.

"Why are you so insistent are ignoring reason?" Puzo asked. "What aren't you telling me?" I reached for my lucky ring and mindlessly played with it. The evening air was hot and muggy, even with the AC at full. The humidity was over-whelming but that wasn't the reason I was sweating. "Ben?"

"She's a diamond in the rough," I said quickly. "I'm supposed to protect her, Zoey told me to."

"Not again," Puzo said with an exasperated sigh. She shook her head and sat on my bed. "It's always her. It's always that fucking vision."

"Not this again," I protested. "I really don't want to have this fight, again."

"Neither do I but you're leaving us with no choice." Puzo lowered her gaze. "Every time that vision comes up, you lose yourself."

"I have to save Zoey," I protested.

"I know you do," Puzo said, softly this time. "I want nothing more than for Zoey to be safe. I've helped in every way I can but that vision has become an obsession for you. Every time it comes up, you start risking yourself and doing stupid things."

"I have to save her---"

"But you don't have to go to jail or die to do it," Puzo interrupted. "Five months ago I bailed you out of jail after you got caught breaking into a warehouse. I called in a big favour to get them to drop the charges. Shit, I probably broke a couple laws doing that.

"Now you want to keep a witness from the Marshals and take on a deadly and violent cartel because you were told to in a vision. Even with powers do you know how crazy that sounds? You don't even know if she's the diamond that Zoey was talking about."

"Her name is Lucy Diamond," I explained.

"No, it's not," Puzo corrected. "She made that up. Her name is Sally Condon."

I froze. Puzo grabbed her bag and her jacket and made for the door. "Where are you going?"

"I'm going home," she said shortly. "This place is too crowded for me."

"Wait..."

"Don't do anything stupid, Ben." Puzo said. "If you don't hand her over to the Marshals when they ask, you'll be arrested."

She leaned in and gave me a small kiss on the cheek before walking out of my bedroom. She walked out the door and was gone. I shook my head and limped for the kitchen. David was in the kitchen while Annie and the kids were in the living room. David handed me a drink.

"You okay?" he asked. I just shrugged. I limped to the front door and walked outside. Puzo and her car were already gone. I leaned against the porch's railing and stared out at the street. I closed my eyes and let the heat roll over me as I sipped my yet-to-be named drink.

"Hey." I expected someone to come and check on me but she was not on my list. I glanced behind me and looked at the violet haired child before me. She stepped beside me and hesitantly spoke. "A...are you okay?"

"I'll be fine, kiddo."

"W...were you two arguing about me?" she asked.

"What? Noooooooo." My words were exaggerated and drawn out. I didn't want to make the kid feel bad but I am a terrible liar. "Sometimes adults talk loudly and---"

"Don't treat me like a kid," she snapped.

"Okay, yes. We were arguing about you," I said after a pause. The kid was right; she had been through way too much to be treated like a child. Talking down to her wasn't going to be the answer. "We're debating the best way to protect you. Rachael wants to hand you to the US Marshals." Lucy stiffened. "They have more resources and they have numbers."

"They don't care about me," she said suddenly. "They just want me to risk my life so I can speak in court. They sent me to all sorts of doctors and shit just to make sure I'd be alive enough to walk into a courtroom. Then I started having really bad nightmares and they flew in another doctor to talk to me about them."

"Flew one in?" I asked. "How do you know that?"

"He gave me his phone number. It wasn't a 312 area code. It was a 212." I blinked. 212? That was my area code. She gave me her phone and I glanced at the name: Dr. Peter Balzary. I wrote the name and number down.

"What did you talk to him about?" I asked. She shrugged. "Did you talk to him about your fake name?" Lucy wouldn't make eye contact with me. "Why don't you tell me your real name?"

"It's Sally," she said quietly. "Sally Condon."

"Thanks for telling me," I said calmly. I took a sip of booze.

"Is Benedict Thompson really your name?" I nodded.

"Please allow me to introduce myself," I said with a smirk. "I'm a man of wealth and taste." I was lying. I really wasn't any of those things.

"I've been around for a long, long years," she finished, her face lighting up with recognition and joy. "Stole many a man's soul to waste."

"Pleased to meet you," I said.

"Hope you guess my name," she concluded. We smiled. Her grin was refreshing. All I had seen on her face was fear and sorrow. It was nice to see joy upon her face.

"Why the change of name?" She didn't answer. I took another sip of booze. "A couple years ago a bunch of men took Robby. They kidnapped him with a bunch of other children. We rescued him, obviously, but the kidnappers were trying to make the kids into children soldiers. They started by trying to get them to change their names. It was a way to dissociated them from their past."

"What did Robby do?" she asked.

"He never gave in. The kid's a fighter."

"I didn't know Robby was a badass," she said, impressed. "He acts like a dork."

"Life lesson: Dorks will surprise you, every time." She smiled.

Me: I need a location for Dr. Peter Balzary. He's a brain doc in the city
Hotwire: Give me a few.

I put down my phone on my Lay-Z-Boy armrest and looked around the room. Alice was in bed, asleep. Annie and David sat on one couch as Robby and Sally sat on another. The two were showing off their music collections. Each time Sally would show him a new band or song, he would stare at her with awe and wonder. Each time he showed her a band, she'd scoff and roll her eyes. I was worried that he would take offense but he seemed to absorb her suggestions like the college freshman staring in wonder and amazement at the world-ly and wise professor.

On the TV - on *my* TV - was an episode of some reality TV show that I was barely paying attention to. It was something about storage lockers and geriatric old men who bought stuff from them only to pawn them off. I hated reality shows. I also hated reality, so that could be the reason why. Reality never made sense to me. In movie world, the bad guys were obvious and bad things didn't happen to good people. In reality, a girl can lose both her parents in only a couple years. Reality sucked.

My phone buzzed and I picked it back up. It was an address from Hotwire. Dr. Balzary's office wasn't far. It was only a twenty minute drive from my house. I glanced at the clock. It was nearly eight at night. I smirked. It was time for some late night detective work.

I walked into the bedroom and made a line directly for my nightstand and pulled open the top drawer. In a small dish sat two ball-chain necklaces. One holds two oval tags, my army dog tags, and the other held three keys. With the conveniently placed pencil, I shoved the first chain aside. I don't like to touch my dog tags anymore, which is the reason I keep the convenient pencil close by. Psychic powers make reliving my military past more difficult than it has to be. Instead, I took the second chain.

I walked into my office and pulled a metal lockbox from my desk. The black box was roughly the same size as a case of pop, twelve cans. I quickly unlocked the box and removed my weapon of choice, my Beretta M9 pistol. I gave the weapon a check, refilled the magazine, and slid it into a holster. I clipped the leather holster to my belt and pocketed the extra mags. Last, but legally not least, I grabbed my firearm license and slipped it into my wallet. There were three firearms in my house. There was my M9, the surprise under my bed and the surprise under my back porch but of all them, the M9 was my favourite.

The M9 was the army's sidearm of choice for decades. I had trained with a M9 and spent many nights in the field sleeping with one by my pillow. When I was in Iraq,

I had a M9 and when my rifle jammed and the Elite Guard came over the wall, I reached for my M9. I've had my hands and finger on each and every inch of this M9. I knew it like the back of my hand.

My old drill sergeant used to say that a M9 was better than a woman because it came with a silencer. I have never repeated that joke in front of my girlfriend or my sister because I fear both of them.

As I put the lockbox back in my desk I paused. My eyes fell to a brown spot on the back of my hand. What the hell was that? Was it a birthmark? Had it always been there?

Dr. Balzary's office was in a three story building. It was the type of building that had all-hours workers on two of the floors so the building was open all night. A quick ride to the third floor found me standing beside the door to his office with a small bag slung over my shoulder. Dr. Balzary was a Psychiatrist whose focus was on PTSD and other trauma related mental disorders. A glance at the Samsung digital lock on his door also told me he was a tech-head. The lock was a sleek sexy black device with glossy digital keys, a card reader and a silver handle. It was the type of locks that rich people used because they wanted to look richer then normies. I pulled off my gloves and gave the handle a touch. I felt the familiar shiver and a twitch and fell into the past.

A lanky man, with balding hair and dressed in an expensive suit, talked on his iphone as he walked up to the door.

"Johnny," he said eagerly. "I'm ready to pitch my next book."

"You're doing another psychiatry book?" The voice on the other end said. "I'm happy to hear that. Your last one sold very well, for non-fiction."

"No, this one is fiction. I have a splendid main character."

"Okay, why not? Fire away."

"It's about a genius baseball player who quit after an injury and became a psychiatrist," Dr. Balzary said as he punched in the code and let himself into the office. "His name is Steel Hardy."

Reality returned. I shook my head and punched in the code. The door let out a beep and let me in. The office was fancy and immediately I felt like that I could not afford to be there. The furniture was expensive, the art was high end and even the chairs were real leather so fresh that if you press on it you'd hear a moo. The worst part was that this was simply the receptionist's office. I still had the real office to go.

I pushed into the inner office and the price of everything immediately doubled. The chairs were nicer, the desk was made from more expensive wood and the art was from names that even I recognized. I dragged my hand across his desk and fell back into another vision.

"That's when Steel learns that his girlfriend's brother is actually his arch-nemesis, Rock Magnus, and worse yet: Rock and Steel are half-brothers." Dr. Balzary walked into his office and plopped his briefcase down upon it. He walked to his safe and opened it with a touch of his finger. It popped open. Dr. Balzary withdrew several large brown files and plopped them down on his desk. "So then in the final fight, after Magus is about to detonate a bomb, Steel grabs a baseball and throws it, finally succeeding in the breaking ball that eluded him in the World Series all those years ago. The ball knocks the detonator out of Magnus' hands and saves the day. He runs into his girlfriend's arms. So what do you think?"

Silence.

"Johnny?"

"You're shitting me, right?" Johnny asked. "Please tell me that you're shitting me."

"I...I'm not," Dr. Balzary stammered. "Why? What's wrong with it? You're my agent, tell me."

"Dude, it sucks. First you have a convoluted main character. He's a World Series baseball pitcher and a genius psychiatrist? Were you watching too much *Anger Management*? At least in *Cheers* they made Sam Malone a bartender. Next, you have your girlfriend's brother be your brother as well? You realize you just made your main character commit incest, right?"

"I didn't say that the girl and Steel were related," Balzary argued.

"The audience will read that, no matter what you do. Then there's the name," Johnny said. "They all sound like porn stars, seriously." Johnny sighed into the phone. "Why do you wanna write fiction anyways? You're a psychiatrist."

"Jonathan Kellerman did it."

"Jonathan Kellerman had talent."

Reality returned. I felt bad for Dr. Balzary. He sounded so excited about his idea but it was just *so damn bad*. Also Johnny was right, my mind immediately went to incest. Whose fault is that, the doc's or mine and if so, what does that say about me?

I spotted the safe and hobbled over to it. It didn't have a keypad; instead it had a fingerprint reader. I smirked. This tech-head's obsession was going to cost him.

I've learned a lot from television; tricks with elevators and call centers, how to create a make-shift silencer and how to patch a tire but some of my shows get a little craftier in their lessons. One of my favorite shows, *Burn Notice*, used narration to give lessons on how to be a spy.

Michael Weston's Spy Lessons! Class Two: Cracking an old-school safe is pretty tough, but modern hi-tech security makes it much easier. Thing is, nobody wipes off a fingerprint scanner after they use it. So what's left on the scanner nine times out of ten is the fingerprint.

What this meant was with a little bit of tape, glue and various other office supplies I was able to copy the fingerprint on the scanner and use it to fool the scanner and unlock the safe. It opened with a happy beep. I smiled. Ain't TV great?

I pulled free the files and began to look them over. Why would a tech-head like Balzary have paper files? I opened one up and saw several doctor notes, most of which I couldn't read. I hate to be stereotypical but damn if this Doc's hand writing wasn't just the worst. I flipped through a couple pages until I spotted a familiar name: Croxallé.

Croxallé was a medical organization that belonged to the mysterious Visegar Company. It used to be KyroCorp and then something else before that. When one company got too public or made too much noise, it closed down and the Visegar Company opened another. They were one of dozens upon dozens of companies that Visegar hid behind. They were also responsible for dozens of experiments involving super powers. They also sent Jason to bang my sister and then dump her when she got pregnant.

Visegar were not my favourite people.
I tossed the two files into my bag. I wasn't originally going to steal them, stealing from a doctor was wrong and could bring down more heat than I wanted, but stealing from a Croxallé doctor meant I was safe - at least from the cops. Croxallé and Visegar had their fingers in more dirty shit than I did back in my farming days. They had enough clean projects to make themselves look good but that paled in comparison. In the world of fingers, only the tip of their pinky was clean, the rest was covered in the darkest and vile feces imaginable. In the event of a theft of sensitive material, they wouldn't dare call the cops for fear of exposing themselves.

For the record, there is no job as bad in this world that is as bad as shoveling chicken shit out of a coop. There were days when I was being shot at but at least I wasn't shoveling out a chicken coop.

I was about to close the safe when I spotted a digital recorder and a small box full of SD cards. Each of them had a patient's name on it. Balzary would switch out the SD card for each patient and record his thoughts. I thumbed through the cards until I reached Condon, Sally. I grabbed the recorder and Sally's SD card and tossed both into my bag. I closed the safe, cleaned off any trace of my existence and stood up. I spotted the Apple laptop on the table and debated grabbing it as well but changed my mind when I spotted an iPad on the bookshelf. I smiled and grabbed that instead.

Balzary was a tech-head. He had several apple products which probably meant he linked them all. He most likely shared data through one cloud or another. While I could grab the laptop and get Hotwire to crack it, the iPad had less security. Hotwire could crack that in hours instead of days. I shoved everything into my bag and did one final sweep before letting myself out, my bag full with stolen goodies. I was like the Grinch except without the lawsuit for theft of intellectual property. Merry Theft-mas everybody!

I headed across the street to the parking garage. I winced as I passed the price list. Why couldn't a doctor validate parking when you robbed them? Doctors were always trying to make an extra buck. I opened the Chevelle's door and tossed in my bag of stolen goods and then gently put in my cane. I was about to climb in when I suddenly heard a sound behind me. I paused and listened. It was a set of footsteps approaching. I smiled as my right hand dropped to the M9 on my belt. Twice today I needed my gun but didn't have it. This time I was ready. Fool me once, shame on you; fool me twice, shame on me; fool me thrice, I must be a Thompson.

"Hey there, hoss," The voice said. It was a Texas drawl, much like Sally's, but this one was male and much older with tired eyes. I pivoted around and drew my pistol. I aimed it at the approaching man only to find him pointing a weapon back at me. "Now, y'all best lower that weapon."

This man was dressed in cowboy boots, blue jeans, black blazer and had a white cattleman style cowboy hat. In his hand was a SIG Sauer P226 with a coyote brown frame. I hated the P226. It was more a Navy weapon. True, the Army *occasionally* did use a P228 but they were tiny guns that damn near broke in your grip. The real army used the M9. Hell, even those dumb ass Marines used a M9 and they barely knew how to tie their own shoes. Those that could figure it out often got medals for it.

"Do you often approach mysterious men alone while in a dark parking garage?" I said carefully. Suddenly I had a thought. I really hope I didn't just interrupt someone's late night dogging sex meet-up. "I mean guns are great for foreplay but I don't swing that way. It's cool if you do, I ain't judging."

"I ain't got the foggiest of what you're speaking about," the *other* cowboy said, "but if y'all put down that weapon then we could talk."

"That's a hard no, big shooter," I laughed. I stepped forward a couple paces to clear the Chevelle. The other cowboy took a couple steps back as well. "Why don't you put down your gun and trust me?"

"How about both of you drop your weapons." Both of us turned as a new voice cut through the tension. We aimed our respective pistols at the emerging form. The third man wore black slacks, black suit jacket and a blue plaid shirt with an azure tie. On his head rested a Stetson Bozeman cowboy hat made from wool black as midnight. In his hand was a Glock 22.

Suddenly I found myself in a three-way standoff with two cowboys. I blinked in surprise. This was an epic addition to movie-life.

Chapter 09
Invited to a Cowboy Gangbang

I remembered a time when I was the only cowboy in the city, assuming you didn't count the naked one that danced in Times Square. I stood out. I got the sexy looks from interested women and bored housewives who wanted to live out their Harlequin Romance fantasy. Then Van Cleef showed up and now cowboys were coming out of the woodwork.

"It's been a while since I've been invited to a cowboy gangbang," I said slowly, "but I am calling not it on being the guy in the middle."

"Y'all think you're funny," the *other* cowboy said. "But I ain't in the mood for foolin'."

"I don't think I'm funny," I corrected. "I *know* I am."

"Well I know that both of you are breaking a federal law by holding a gun to me," the *other other* cowboy said. He spoke with a hard O sound that seemed to stretch out. It reminded me of Fargo which mean this dude was probably from Minnes-ohhh-ta. "I'm a cop so both of you need to lower your guns."

Nobody budged.

"Shit, I'm also a cop. Y'all should lower your guns," the Texan said.

Nobody budged.

The three of us just stood there, keeping our weapons at the ready. Our bodies would shift as we moved our aim from one man to another but basically we remained in the ultimate cowboy-standoff. The differences between the three of us were noticeable. Mr. Minnesota was firm and steady. His arm never budged and he carried an air of dominance. I stood there, my Army training taking hold. My aim was solid but my body wavered. I had been resting on my poor leg for too long. Mr. Texas knew what he was doing. He held his gun with the proper grip and used the proper discipline but his arm had a twitch. It was almost if he had never fired before but that wasn't possible, not with his practised stance and grip.

"I'm reaching for my badge," Mr. Minnesota said. He pulled back his jacket to reveal a badge on his belt. A gold star looked up at us. "US Marshals."

Mr. Texas moved his left hand slowly as he reached into his jacket. He pulled free a leather case and flipped it open. A silver metal star glimmered in the faint light. "Texas Rangers."

They both looked at me. I laughed. "I'm not even remotely a cop." Marshal and Ranger glanced at each other for a moment. Suddenly both men turned their guns towards me. I gulped. "I'm going to grab some ID from my back pocket."

"Keep that hand slow, hoss," Mr. Ranger said.

"What am I going to do? Draw another gun?" I paused. "Actually, that sounds cool. I could aim at two people. Here's an idea. Why don't we each take a ten minute break? Then we'll come back with two guns apiece and we can go full on Woo like *Face/Off* or *Hard Boiled* or *Broken Arrow*?" Nobody budged.

"Fine, you philistines," I said with a disappointed scoff. I pulled free my private investigator's license. "I'm from SRG Security. I'm a PI."

"Since I outrank everybody here," Mr. Marshal said, "I'm instructing all of you to put down your guns. We can talk this out."

Ranger nodded and I followed suit. The three of us each holstered our weapons. I just smiled the biggest smile I had ever smiled. Ranger looked at me with a peculiar look.

"Whatcha grinning about, Dick?"

"I'm just did a gun standoff with Cordell Walker and Raylan Givens," I said with glee. My voice sounded like a kid a Christmas. "This is literally the happiest day of my life."

"What are you talking about?" Ranger asked.

"Well you see I don't get invited to many Cowboy Orgies so----"

"Forget I asked," Ranger said with disgust.

"I'm Jeff Arcel," the Marshal introduced.

"Drew Winnick," the Ranger followed.

"Ben Thompson." Each of us did a hesitant hand shake. Nobody was sure what to make of the threesome but at least the guns were put away and our pants were still on.

"You're a long way from home, Ranger," Arcel said. "Your jurisdiction starts and ends in Texas."

"I've got special permission," he replied with a huff.

"Special permission to be stalking my house?" I asked. Winnick frowned. "I saw you outside my house, why?"

"My investigation led me to you," he said sternly. "I'm looking for a criminal."

"So you followed me here." I moved my gaze to the Marshal. "You're here to check if Dr. Balzary has had any recent guests." He raised a quizzical eyebrow at me before smirking.

"You're that Ben Thompson," he said with a knowing voice. "You're the psychic."

I hate that I have a government file with that word written on it with a big red rubber stamp. You help the government find one measly little bomb and suddenly they know about you: psychic world problems.

"This brings the question of what you were doing here, Ben?" Arcel asked. I shrugged. "I shouldn't be looking for any breaking and entry should I?"

"Marshal, please," I said with a chuckle.

"That wasn't an answer," Arcel sternly replied. I am really bad at lying. I glanced at Winnick.

"Why are you following me?" I asked. "What is your

investigation and what do I have to do with it?"

"I'm looking the man who killed my fiancée," the ranger said suddenly. "She was murdered in cold blood and I ain't gonna rest until I find the vermin that pulled the trigger. One of the suspects vanished but recently resurfaced in this here city. You are labelled as a known associate."

I blinked in surprise. I had no clue what the hell he was talking about. I didn't know people. I barely knew myself. Who did I know that would be a suspect in a murder?

"I'm all for talking and sharing information," I began. I pulled two business cards out from my back pocket and handed one to each of the cowboys. "But three cowboys in a dark parking garage, in the middle of the night? If people see this they are going to have the same Brokeback Mountain thoughts that I did." Truth was I didn't want to be there anymore. The garage stunk. "How about we all get a drink at a nearby bar and talk about this?"

Arcel agreed but Winnick bowed out. He mumbled something about investigatory integrity and walked away. I shrugged. A quick drive of a dozen blocks and Arcel and I were seated at a booth in a bar. A Mets game played on the TV. They were losing. The Mets always lost.

"I got a report saying the girl's at your place." Arcel said. I nodded. "How did she come to be in your possession?"

"She showed up at my door asking for help," I admitted. "She won't tell me much but I am piecing things together." Arcel gave me a look inviting me to continue. "What I think I know is she saw the some boss of the Imperecedero Cartel murder her father. She got scooped by Witsec and put in Chicago in foster care. She bolted and ended up here. Then she got nabbed, escaped and came to me."

"How does she know you?"

"Still trying to figure that one out," I admitted.

"Why did she leave Chicago?"

"She said the cartel showed up at her school." Arcel nodded. He pulled free a notepad and wrote several notes. I took a gulp of my beer. "I know you guys are taking her tomorrow. I get that I just...." My voice trailed off as I searched for the words. As much as I wanted to save her I didn't know how. "She's skittish around cops."

"This is a careful situation," Arcel said slowly. "This case is a big one. We're talking multiple agencies involved: FBI, DEA and the Marshals. So much of this is hanging on her. We'll take care of her, I promise."

"I have one more question," I said slowly, "and this is a big one. This one will decide if I can trust you or nor, Raylan."

"I love that you know *Justified*," Arcel said with a chuckle. "But what's your inquiry?"

"Wayne or Eastwood?"

"Are you serious?"

"Yes. I am very serious," I said sternly. "I am super cereal right now."

"I meant is this seriously a debate?" Arcel clarified. "I'll always ride beside the Stranger. *High Plains Drifter* is my favourite movie of all time."

"Sally is in good hands then," I said with a smirk. The two of us shook hands and finished our beers. We said our goodbyes and I climbed in my car to head home, except I wasn't going home. I was going to see Hotwire.

Chapter 10
Shoot it! Shoot it! Shoot it!

I steered the Chevelle into the edge of the warehouse district of the city. The warehouse district is a weird one. It's on the edge of the business sector, it straddles the industrial sector and it's filled with sketchy looking men and women. I parked in front of a cold-storage locker rental lot. It was like those *Storage Wars* lockers you see on A&E except this one was colder and a front for an illegal business.

The first time I met Hotwire he was living in the loft above his nightclub. The club used to be a perfect hideout for my hacker friend; he'd run the legitimate business downstairs and run his slightly illegal one upstairs. The industrial sized AC unit installed in the club masked the intense heat signature from his massive computer system and kept him hidden away from prying police eyes. Then he got caught by Visegar looking into their stuff. Fearing for his life, he fled.

I hobbled to the building and clumsily climbed the stairs to the office on the top. This new business had some advantage that the old one didn't. It was a cold storage locker. It was a place full of massive fridges; this place was going to have massive electricity bills on top of his super computer system, not to mention the heat signature that would mask his servers from any prying law enforcement with a thermal camera. The place was remote, off the beaten path so to speak, so anybody who approached it wasn't doing so by accident. With an elevated office, and a scattering of cameras that I couldn't help but notice, Hotwire could spot anyone long before they reached him.

I grabbed the door and found it unlocked. I didn't bother knocking, I just let myself in. Hotwire already knew I was here. His place was essentially the entire top floor of the main building that had been converted into a four-bedroom apartment. In the main room was the holy grail of computer set-ups. Hotwire's desk was shaped like a C with a wall of six monitors, three towers and a massive cooling unit. Seated at the desk was the main man himself.

Hotwire was a man of contrasts. Hackers were supposed to look like Johnny Lee Miller or Rami Malek, not like Daniel Craig or Jon Hamm. Hotwire firmly fit in the second category. Hotwire, or Jimmy Wilcox, looked more like a playboy dynasty then a techno-geek. He had stylized black hair, a goatee and Italian suit three-piece suit.

"Hey, Cowboy," he said without looking up. "No hats indoors. How goes the hunt?"

"She goes," I said as I removed my hat. We bumped fists. I pulled up a chair and sat beside my good friend. His fingers were busy typing. I glanced at the screen and saw the studio for a 24 hours news station. "What are you doing?"

"This station is about to attack trans-rights with this massively bullshit news story. It's basically just lies, slander and hate speech," he explained. "The news anchor wants to run for office on that platform. I am in the middle of changing their segment to show said anchor in the throes of passion with several men courtesy of the videos on his phone. Then the station is going to discover that they just made several *massive* donations to several trans-rights groups."

"That's very generous of them," I smirk. Somebody once told me that in order to be a good hacker you had to have a loose definition of the words *legal* and *morals*. Hotwire had that in spades. "Wearing the White Hat today?"

"More grey then anything but yeah." He pushed back from his chair and called out. "Ian, watch the TV. This is going to be good."

Ian walked in and gave me a nod. We all watched the TV. The camera panned to the anchor as dramatic music played. "Good evening. Thank you for joining us today. A recent study finds that the average person spends three hours a week in the washroom. It is a basic human function that we all do. Is it too much to ask to be safe during that time? But are we safe? What are we letting into our washrooms? A new segment shows the dange----" The screen cut from the studio feed to the shaky video recorded from a camera's phone. The same anchor was on his knees before a several men. His mouth and hands were very full and very busy.

The three of us laughed. This was good, this was very good. Ian looked at his phone. "Twitter is blowing up. OMG. This is epic."

"Another bigot bites the dust," Hotwire said with a spin of his chair. He let out a whoop. I just smiled. It was nice to see him happy. It wasn't something I got to see very often. He lived a very difficult life. He was gay but couldn't come out due to family reasons, he was a cyber criminal with a conscience and to make matters worse, he kept ending up in my end of the weird. So to see a smile on Jimmy's face, even for a moment, was glorious.

"What's up?" Hotwire asked as his spin came to a halt. He fixed his tie as he climbed from the chair. He walked to the kitchen and got himself a drink. "Does this have to do with that Doctor from earlier?"

"Sadly, yes." I read Hotwire in. I told him all about Lucy, the doctor and the Imperecedero.

"A cartel?" Hotwire cried out. "Are you nuts?"

"She's fifteen and she's alone. What else am I suppose to do?" I turned to Burn Notice for my argument.

Michael Weston's Spy Lessons! Class Three: Fighting for the little guy is for suckers. We all do it once in a while, but the trick is to get in and out quickly, without getting involved. That's one trick I never really mastered.

"What can I do?" Hotwire asked. I pulled the iPad

from the bag and handed it to him.

"I need you to crack that and get into the Doctor's cloud. He works for Croxallé so I need to know what he knows." I grabbed a pen and paper and wrote down two names. "This is the US Marshal and a Texas Ranger I met this evening. I need to know if they are legit."

"I'll take care of it," Hotwire said with a smirk. "But you know a *please* every once in a while doesn't hurt, cowboy."

"I tend to hold off on pleases," I joked, "but I'll have to find a way to say thank you."

"I'm sure we can think of a way." A dirty grin crossed his lips. "How do you feel about being in the middle?"

"I'd be down for that," Ian added as he rolled his chair closer.

Damn it. I swore I called not it on that very thing earlier.

A couple years ago, Hotwire and I couldn't talk like this. We couldn't joke around like we were now. A couple years ago if you called Hotwire gay he'd take serious offense to it. Things changed when Ian came into his life. I don't know what it was that Ian did to the hacker but Hotwire seemed more content and at ease not only with himself but with the world in general. I had to find out exactly what it was Ian offered Hotwire and find a way to offer that to him as well.

Wait. No. I just rethought that. I'm not offering Hotwire *that* at all.

"You get a chance to look at the papers I sent you this morning?" Hotwire asked as he sipped his drink. He offered me one but I shook him off. The problem with driving a kick-ass Chevelle is you have to be sober enough to drive it.

"Yeah, I did. There wasn't much there," I said with an exasperated sigh. "It feels like every time we think we find something it just turns up dry."

"Visegar has been hiding for a long, long time," Hotwire reminded me. "We're not just going to stumble onto something."

"I know that but..." I trailed off. "I'm supposed to find her and I have no clue how. We're assuming its Visegar that has her. What if they don't? What if WhiteStar doesn't have her either? What if somebody all together different has her?"

Zoey; how was I supposed to find you when I didn't have the first clue as to where I was supposed to start? I couldn't just go around touching everything and everybody in the world until I found a lead. Somebody was bound to complain if I did that.

"We'll find her, I promise," Hotwire said. A small smile crossed his lips. "We're making progress. I recently damaged some of their security systems."

I raised a curious eyebrow. Hotwire flashed me a boastful grin. "Ever since the Robby incident I have been trying to find and dig into Visegar's system. Their defenses, however, are some of the best I have ever seen. Their firewall system would even use my own tricks against me and attack me with my own viruses. I had never seen a system like this before."

"Could it be some sort of counter-hacker?" I asked. Hotwire shook his head.

"They were too quick. Every time I meet this firewall, I hit it with something new. Sometimes it does nothing and sometimes I stun it but recently I hurt it and I hurt it bad." Hotwire was twitching with excitement. He was twitching so much that I expected him to have a vision of his own. "Their firewall didn't go down but it got slow and it left a different part vulnerable. It was like it retreated to protect the most important stuff. My point is, they are not unbeatable. We just have to keep chipping away until they fall." I frowned. Hotwire raised an eyebrow. "I thought you'd be happy at that news."

"I am, I promise," I said. "I'm just a little disappointed that it wasn't a counter-hacker. I was picturing some hacker-on-hacker duel where one of you wears VR goggles to fly through some 3D building to find data in a garbage file while the other is a magician using a ridiculously large glow-ing keyboard."

"Please stop quoting the end scene of *Hackers* to me," Hotwire said with a shake of his head.

"Hack the planet!" I yelled.

"Hack the planet!" Ian yelled. Hotwire glanced at him and shook his head.

"No," he snapped. "Just no."

"Mess with the best," Ian said in a slow, sexy tone. "And die like the rest."

Hotwire just stared at his partner for a second before hungrily biting his bottom lip. He tried to protest but he never got the chance. Ian continued his assault with another slow sensual quote.

"There is no right and wrong. There's only fun and boring."

"Okay, here is what's going to happen. I am going to lose the suit and sexually ravage my man. You have one of two choices, Ben." Hotwire said. "You can either leave now or stay and earn that thanks we were talking about."

I decided to leave. Hotwire and I were getting close. We were not getting that close.

It was late when I finally got home. It had been one long ass day. The apartment was dark except for an eerie glow that came from the living room. As I crept down the long hallway towards the room, I heard the sound of the national anthem followed by static. I was starting to get freaked out. This was basically how the TV scene went in *Poltergeist*. That movie freaked the living crap out of me when I was a kid. You know that horror movie you saw as a kid; the one you saw when you were way too young. It was always at some sleepover or when you begged your older sibling and they eventually caved. Either way the film scarred the crap out of you and scared you for life and when you went running to mom scared, you instantly threw either your friend or you older sibling under the bus. *Poltergeist* was that film for me. If I turned the corner into my living room and heard the words *they're here*, I was going to shoot something.

I turned the corner and stepped into the living room. "They're here."

Holy shit! Shoot it! Shoot it! Shoot it!

My heart raced and my body twitched. My hand dropped to my M9 and I tried to draw it from my holster but logic prevented me. It would be stupid to draw my pistol. Guns couldn't kill poltergeists. Thinking they would was a rookie mistake. Get it together, Dumbass. Nothing could defeat a poltergeist. Craig T. Nelson couldn't defeat the poltergeist and he was Mr. Incredible.

"You okay?" Sally's voice ripped through my fear and reason took hold. She was sitting in my Lay-z-boy, quietly watching the movie *Poltergeist* on TV. I sighed. What would be the odds of me walking in on the TV scene, on the very scene that scared me as a kid? The math is easy. The odds are 100% Why? Because the universe hates me.

I hate you too, Universe!

"You're in my spot," I said. Sally rolled her eyes and moved to the couch. I could see the blankets and pillows that Annie had laid out for her. I pulled off my gloves and plopped down in my chair. "What are you doing it up?"

"I can't sleep," she sheepishly said.

No shit! You're watching *Poltergeist*. You won't be able to sleep for a week. What are you, a sadist? I probably shouldn't say any of these thoughts out loud.

"Can I join you?" I asked. My brain exploded. Why would I ask that? Now I have to watch *Poltergeist*. I wasn't going to be able to sleep for a week.

"It's your house," Sally replied.

I stretched out my arms and accidently grazed a discarded black leather jacket with my bare hand. It was Sally's jacket and the moment I touched it I regretted it. I didn't want to see her past. I didn't want to forcefully peer into her life but fate gave me no choice. A shiver and a twitch and I fell into the past.

I was in a kitchen of some small home. There was a soft looking woman with gentle eyes and long spidery black hair. Her skin was subtly tanned. She wore ripped blue jeans and an ugly, torn and stained shamrock-coloured tank top that was obviously *hella* comfortable. On her neck was a familiar black leather choker with a metal heart in the center. She stood by the kitchen's island as she worked on a paper. Her green leather bag lay on the counter beside her. She had the same emerald eyes that Sally did.

This was Daisy Condon; this was Sally's mother.

The door suddenly opened and a man walked in. He wasn't a tall man but nor was he short. He wasn't a fat man but nor was he thin. He was, by every definition, average. His hair was brown, his face was square and his body was maintained. Every hair had a place, every whisker was well kept and his clothes were practical and not excessive. Nothing was extravagant, everything was sensible. The man allowed for one single exception. They were the Persol eye-glasses with a brown and clear finish.

The more I looked at the man the more I recognized the strong chin and solid features. I'd seen them on Sally. That meant this was Colin Condon; this was Sally's father.

"How was your day, honey?" Daisy asked as she walked over to him. She leaned in and gently kissed him on his cheek. Daisy smiled but Colin remained apathetic. "How was work?"

It was a gentle, romantic moment. It was like those touching movie scenes where husband and wife gently embraced each other, kissed and talked about----

Colin's hand shot out and grabbed Daisy by the throat. He spun her around and slammed her back against the wall, hard. The thud was loud and the entire wall shook. Colin's eyes narrowed as his grip tightened. Daisy's eyes bulged as she gasped for air. Reality returned.

WTF? WTF? WTF?

What the actual F did I just see? I bolted up in my chair and I looked around. I spotted Sally's green leather bag. It was placed by the coffee table. I also notice Sally's black choker near it. I reached out and touched the bag. I fell back into the past.

Colin pulled Daisy by her hair. He pulled her across the apartment until he reached the island. He cleared it off with a sweep of his arm, pitching the green bag and several papers onto the floor. He pulled the green tank-top over her head and yanked the jeans down to her ankles. He spun Daisy around and bent her over the counter.

"Do. Not. Move."

Daisy froze in place as Colin left the room. I zoomed in on the bare form of Sally's mom. I spotted several scars on her back. They were long and had been healed over, time and time again. What had caused such marks? Colin re-emerged a few moments later with a reed cane in his hand. Colin paused by his wife. He quickly raised the cane only to bring it across Daisy's bare ass. She screamed in pain. He pulled back and struck again, over and over. Each strike made a sadistic slap and left an impressive stripe. The ass quickly welted as the strength of the impact grew. With each strike, the cane struck harder and slowly moved up her back. Tears rolled down Daisy face as she cried out with each strike.

I pulled my hand away and fought to steady my breathing. What the hell type of man was Sally's father? I glanced at the choker and debated touching it. It was obviously Daisy's before Sally wore it. Did I want to see what image it brought me? I had no choice. I needed to see the next scene. I needed to know what type of man Colin was. He looked like a serial killer, quiet and meticulous, but he wore Eric Clapton glasses. With a sigh I reached out and grabbed the choker. A shiver and a twitch escorted me back into the past.

A sickening crack filled the air and I almost puked. It was sordid. There were cuts and welts all across Daisy's back. It reminded me of the Rorschach ink blot that was my chest. The only difference was I got it during service overseas and not by some abusive husband.

"Enough." Colin stepped back and dropped the cane on the floor. Daisy's legs gave way as she crumbled to the floor. Colin walked out of the room. He re-emerged a few moments later with a first aid kit and a large comfy blanket. He started by helping Daisy back up to her feet, then opened the first aid kit and withdrew several supplies. With a gentle and delicate touch, he meticulously disinfected the cuts and tended to her sore backside. Once that was done he carefully closed up the kit and reached for the blanket. Colin wrapped up his wife and lifted her into his arms. He carried her over to the couch and gently put her down upon the cushions. He grabbed the remote and turned on the TV.

"I...I...." Daisy's words trailed off. Her eyes were distant and her body was near-unresponsive. Somehow she found the strength to speak. "I....love it.....when.....you come home.....in that kind of mood.......sir."

A rare smile crossed Colin's lips. "What do you want, *Lilo and Stich* or *Beauty and the Beast*?"

"*Beast* first," she said, "then *Stitch*."

Colin held his wife close as he continued with his aftercare. Reality returned and I was left with a stunned look on my face.

I did not see that coming.

I thanked the darkness for hiding my surprise. Colin wasn't an abusive husband and Daisy wasn't some victim. They were a loving couple that were participating in a consensual act of love making. They were so different from the norm but it worked for them. Who was I to judge if it worked for them. I smiled. It was actually kind of romantic and, ironically, tender. Suddenly a horrible thought crossed my mind.

Sally wasn't wearing a choker. She was wearing her mother's submissive collar.

Nope. I'm not telling her that truth.

I glanced over at Sally. She was only half watching the TV. She was distracted and rightfully so given the day's events.

"What's on your mind?" I said with a soothing tone. Sally shrugged. "All this bring up memories and shit?" Sally nodded. "Do you want to talk about it?"

"Not really."

"Tell me about your Dad," I suggested. "I don't mean the bad stuff. I mean the good stuff. Tell me the stuff you love about your Dad."

Sally looked at me for a moment before speaking. Her words started out hesitant but the more she spoke, the more confident they became.

"Mom always said that Dad's brain was different the most people's," she began. "I didn't understand what that meant until I got older. Dad was a special type of person. He wasn't outgoing like other Dads and he wasn't all gooey and emotional either. Dad was quiet and stoic. Nobody ever knew how to reach Dad. Everybody thought he was weird but Mom figured it out. Mom fell in love with him and learned to decipher the Dad-Code.

"Mom told me that Dad didn't feel things like you and I do. She said that Dad didn't know how to feel. He didn't know how to like be happy or sad and junk. He was just always in a nothing phase. He always felt nothing. He never said he loved me and he never said he was proud. It wasn't sad, it was just life. I didn't know that was a weird thing until I got older. Mom taught him how to feel things."

That was what I saw. Sally didn't understand how but I did. The unique relationship they had was how they bonded. It was how Colin expressed his emotions. The room was dark but I knew Sally was smiling. I could hear it in her voice. She had very fond memories of her Dad. She was a Daddy's Girl but what else would you expect from a relationship when it was just them?

"When it was just Dad and I, we needed a way to communicate. We couldn't talk like Mom and Dad did so we found something else. Dad once told me that there were two universal languages in the universe: Math and music. He said that if we met aliens from another world, our musical notes would be the same and our math would be the same."

I didn't know that about music. It was nice to know that no matter where in the universe I went that *Uptown Funk* would still be a sizzling hot single.

Stop. Wait a minute, fill my cup, ET. Pour some liquid in it.

Sip you take; check you sign. Stretch you get, Yoda.

"Dad and I used music to get closer. When Dad was sad about Mom's passing, he'd sing *For the Longest Time* or *Tears in Heaven*. If Dad was happy and in a good mood then he'd sing *Happy*. When he was proud of me he'd sing..." She bit back tears as she tried to say the words. "He'd sing *Isn't She lovely* by Stevie Wonder. Everything was music between us; everything."

Suddenly Sally made sense. All of those cryptic words and weird statements, they were song lyrics. I spoke in movies and TV references. They were my primary frame of reference so they were my primary mode of speaking. Sally's primary frame of reference was music. That was why she spoke in song and thought in song. Sally was the music version of me.

"Dad even named me after a song," she said. "*Lay Down Sally*."

"Your Dad was an Eric Clapton fan," I deciphered. Sally nodded.

"He almost named me Layla but Mom wouldn't have it," she said with a snicker. "It was a song about being in love with another man's wife. She wasn't going to put that on me." I climbed out of the chair and plopped down on the couch beside Sally. She was still huddling in the corner of the couch, hugging a pillow.

"Lucy Diamond?" I asked. "Are you a Beatles fan?"

"I'm more of a Stones girl," she admitted. I liked her a little more. "Mom was the big Beatles fan."

"Moms always are," I said with a smirk. Sally smiled. I heard the sound of struggle as she tried her best not to cry. Yet despite her best attempts, the tears and sobs emerged. I looked at her and through the darkness tried my best to reassure her. "It's okay."

That was all it took. Tears and sobs poured out from the teenage girl. I opened up my right arm and she immediately took the offer. She cascaded into my chest and I wrapped my arm around her. I held her close as she sobbed and cried.

"Lay down, Sally, and rest you in my arms. Don't you think you want someone to talk to?" I said softly. I was *very* familiar with *Lay Down Sally*. I dated a girl name Sally way back in my player days and when you date a girl name Sally, you learn this song. "Lay down, Sally, no need to leave so soon. I've been trying all night long just to talk to you."

Chapter 11
Double Crap Sandwich

"Ben! Ben!" A screeching voice ripped through the silence. It was Annie. Truth be told my sister didn't screech but when you're woken up from a deep sleep by yelling, everything sounds like screeching. Needless to say, the banshee didn't stop. "Ben! She's gone!"

"What? I muttered as I sat up in bed. Annie was standing over me with a panicked look on her face. I shook the fog from my head and let focus take hold. "Who's gone?"

"Lucy's gone. I mean Sally's gone." Annie just sighed. "Whatever her name is, she's gone."

Now I was awake. I kicked my legs off the side of my bed and suddenly remembered I was nude underneath. Annie let out a sisterly cry of disgust and turned away. "Damn it, Benny. There are kids here."

"The kids are smart enough to not run into my bedroom," I defended as pulled on pants and a shirt. I limped to the living room and found the couch empty. The blankets and pillows were tossed in a pile and her stuff was all gone. I cursed and limped to the front door. As I reached the door, I closed my eyes and tried to focus. In my years of psychic activities I learned that my visions are a random as a cab driver's desires to obey the rules of the road. I also learned that if I focused, if I prayed and begged, I could focus my visions - slightly. My visions were like a light. Whatever it illuminated,

I could see. Normally it was like turning on a room light and seeing everything at once. With focus my visions were like a flashlight. I could aim it but there was still no guarantee that I could focus on exactly what I wanted.

Sally. Lucy. Sally. Lucy.

I repeated the two names, over and over, as I reached out and touched the wooden door. A shiver and twitch rolled through my body as I fell into the past. The fall wasn't a big one. I landed only an hour into the past. Sally walked to my front door. She was fully dressed and her bag was slung over her shoulder. She held her phone in her hand and was quickly typing. I zoomed in on the screen and saw the words *pawnshops near me*. Sally paused at the door and looked back.

"My bags are packed, I'm ready to go. I'm standing here, outside your door," She whispered. "I hate to wake you up to say goodbye."

Crap baskets.

What the hell was she doing? She wasn't safe out there. There was a cartel coming after her and the Marshals would be here soon. I ran to my room and pulled on a long sleeve plaid shirt. I clipped my M9 to my belt and grabbed my phone. I googled *pawnshops near me* and found that the closest open shop was a place called Howard's Pawn Shop. I grabbed my hat and cane and bolted out the door. Seconds later, the Chevelle roared to life and peeled out of the driveway.

My visions were closely tied to emotions. The stronger someone felt when they interacted with an object, the more pungent the memory was. This meant wedding rings and guns were some of the most dangerous things to touch. Take a wedding ring; be it a happy marriage or a troubled one, the ring is the catalyst of every emotion that union holds. Guns are just as bad. When you fight to defend what you love or when you fight to kill what you hate, everything you do with a gun is emotionally driven. Fear, love, hate, and honour. A gun reeks with it all.

So with my powers so closely tied to emotions, I had quickly learned to hate pawnshops. Everything in a pawnshop was filled with emotion and most of it was regret.

Pawning an engagement ring because the marriage had ended: regret and sadness. Pawning your jewellery to make ends meet: dejection. Pawning the last items of value of a passed relative: sorrow.

I hate pawnshops. Luckily, I wasn't in this one long. I entered the building and met the *illustrious* Howard. He was a fat, bald man who wore porn-style clothes. I walked in and he gave me a toothless grin as he stood up behind the counter.

"What can I do for you?" His accent was thick and everything about this man disgusted me. He just oozed slime and sordid. He reminded me of Jack Jeebs from *Men in Black*.

The pawnshop wasn't one of those high security joints with cages and bulletproof glass. It looked more like a regular store with glass display cases.

"I'm looking for a girl with violet hair," I said quickly. "Did she come in here?"

"Yeah, I remember her," he said with a lecherous grin. I felt ill to my stomach. "What's it to ya?"

"Did she say where she was going?"

"She asked about the nearest bus depot," he said with a shrug. "She pawned some shit for a ticket home. I gave her a good deal."

I pulled off my glove and touched the glass counter. I fell into the past. The clerk stood before Sally. Several watches and gold bands lay before him. They were not mine. They probably belonged to the Owles. Howard counted several bills as he put them down on the counter.

"I know a way you could earn a couple more Benjamins," Howard said to Sally. She gave him a suspicious look. Howard flashed a lecherous grin as he pulled down his zipper. "Don't get all prude on me now, girl. You look like you've tasted your fair share."

"Fuck you," Sally said. She grabbed her money and stormed out of the building.

I returned to reality and glared at Howard.

"Did she steal your shit? I ain't involved if she did but I'll sell your stuff back to you, cheap," Howard offered. I grabbed him by the collar and pulled him close.

"She's fifteen you sick fuck," I snapped. I grabbed him by the back of the head and slammed his skull down against the glass. "If you ever do anything like that again, I will rain down hell upon you. I will make your life hell."

"The fuck are---"

"She's fifteen years old," I snarled. I released him and hobbled to the door. I looked back at him with a look of anger and disgust. "I'll be watching you, Howard. Don't make me come back here 'cause I will. You can lock the door but I'll find a way in. I'll squeeze in your back door if I have to and you don't want the pounding that happens when I enter your back door."

I walked out, proud of myself. Fifteen seconds later I paused and thought about what I just said and groaned. That didn't sound anything like I had hoped.

I climbed out of the Chevelle and hobbled towards the bus depot. Even though I knew they were firmly in place, I double-checked my gloves. I did not want to accidently trigger a vision, not here.

There are places in the world that are emotionally super-charged. Churches rate high on the list, as do graveyards and funeral homes and so do airports, train stations and bus depots. It was the John Candy/Steve Martin trifecta. There was the overwhelming emotion of loss and sorrow with graveyards but nothing compared to what you felt at a travel depot. I felt the bittersweet goodbyes but nothing compared to the reunited scene when the separated met each other in the lobby. It didn't matter what was going on, anger, unhappiness and mistrust, it was all washed away and forgotten for that one moment when they get off the vehicle and see that special someone. That feeling of joy and relief when you're reunited with that person you care about. It was a moment of perfect and pure happiness and emotion and the visions that came from it were strong. It was like I was Anna Ferris screaming in the street and my visions were a speeding white car at the end of *Scary Movie*.

I pulled my long shirt up from my belt and draped it over my waist, hiding my gun from view. I had all the proper permits and licenses for my M9 but nobody likes to see a guy with a gun. I wasn't going after Sally without one, especially with a cartel on the trail, but it didn't mean I wanted to broadcast I was armed.

I stepped into the bus depot. The building, even for the morning, was full. There were dozens of people everywhere. I looked up at the board and let my mind race. Where was Sally heading? Was she going to Chicago? I shook my head. She had nowhere to go there. She had no family there and she hated the Owles. That left Texas. Would going back to Imperecedero Cartel territory be the safest place? But maybe she had some remaining family there. I pushed through the crowds as I hobbled towards the departure gate for Texas.

Despite the overwhelming heat, I carefully rolled down my shirt sleeves. My visions weren't triggered solely by the touch of my fingers. They were triggered when an object came in contact with any exposed skin on my body. I learned that the hard way when I placed my bare butt onto a public toilet. That was shit I didn't need to see, literally.

Psychic rule: avoid public washrooms and hotel beds. None of what you see is good.

I felt a firm hand clamp down on my shoulder. I spun quickly, ready to strike when I saw the familiar form of a white cattleman style cowboy hat.

"Drew?" I asked.

"What y'all doing here, Ben?" the Texas Ranger asked.

"I'm working," I snapped. "You're still following me?"

"No," he said firmly. "I'm following my suspect."

"Your suspect?" It hit me suddenly. "Sally is your suspect? What the hell?"

"This ain't got nothing to do with you, hoss" he sternly said.

"The hell it doesn't," I snapped. "You were looking for the guy who killed your fiancée. What does that have to do with Sally?" He tried to shrug me off but I didn't let him. I grabbed him by his blazer and pulled him close. Winnick may have been a cop but he was way out of his jurisdiction. "Tell me; now."

"My fiancée was Alexia Pike. She was a DEA agent," he snapped, slapping my hands away. "She be part of a task force that dealt with the Imperecedero Cartel. One night she went to meet with an old friend from her schooling days, a man named Colin Condon. That night she ends up dead. Colin was also killed and his daughter, Sally, vanishes. The case is restricted and ain't nobody is telling me shit. So when she pops back up, I go looking for her. I need to know what happened that night, hoss. I need to know who to kill."

Shit. I froze. I didn't know what to say. Drew Winnick lost his fiancée. Suddenly Marshal Arcel's words were starting to make sense. He said this case involved the FBI, DEA and the Marshals and now I knew why. The Imperecedero Cartel was a big drug running cartel that the DEA had been trying to break up. Some cartel big wig killed a federal agent which brought the FBI into the mix and the Marshals were holding everything together by hiding and protecting the witness.

This was a big deal and Sally was caught in the middle of it. No wonder she was afraid. The Imperecedero Cartel wanted her dead, and badly. Everybody wanted her for what she could do for them. Nobody really cared about her. I let my mind wander as I looked around the depot. A man suddenly caught my attention. He wore a black windbreaker. The man didn't look big but the jacket was bulky and filled out. I winced. I could feel his heat; I was overly warm with my sleeves rolled down. I could only imagine what he was like in a jacket. It made me think of the cartel men I faced yesterday. They were wearing heavy leather jackets and must have been dying in them. They were, at least, using the jackets to hide a gun.

Crap.

I looked the man up and down. He wore a ballcap, had fingerless gloves and solid black boots. He moved slowly and with precision. His head and his eyes constantly moved as he scanned the depot. He raised his left arm and whispered into his wrist.

Double crap.

"We've got trouble," I said suddenly. I pointed out the guy. "He's an operator. He's military special forces."

"They don't look like cartel," Winnick said.

I started scanning the depot for other operators. I spotted one in the distance and second nearly thirty feet behind us. I frowned. If there were three that I saw, then there were at least three that I didn't.

Double crap sandwich.

The reason I knew how operators worked was because I used to be one. Odin Squad was the best of the best. We took on the missions that others were lucky enough to avoid. The only problem was Cartel didn't work like operators. So who were these guys and what did they want?

"Follow me," I said quietly. We hustled behind the first operator. I lifted up the back of my shirt and quietly pulled my M9 free. Winnick drew his own weapon. I walked up behind the operator and shoved my pistol into his back. He stiffened. "Hi there, do you mind taking a left?"

My words were soft but he obeyed. Truth was the M9 was doing most of my speaking for me. We pushed him into a small utility closest. Drew moved quickly. He opened up the man's jacket to reveal a black tactical vest. It was one of those vests with dozens of pockets and Kevlar inserts. The operator carried a Heckler & Koch MP5K. It was a submachine gun that was compact and could hide under a jacket. He also had a FN Five-seven pistol. Drew dumped both in the nearest trashcan.

"He'll have zipties in his vest," I instructed. Drew quickly found some and zipped the man's hands together. I glanced at the operator.

"What are the odds you'll tell me who sent you?" The operator remained silent. I shrugged and pulled off my glove. "Fine. I'll do this the hard way."

A shiver and a twitch found me in a conference room with several laptops and a large computer screen on the wall. A man named Rhys Polson was on the screen talking to the room full of soldiers. Rhys never smiled. He wasn't the smiling type. He was the Operation Manager and this was one of his many teams. The screen flashed and a picture of Sally appeared.

"This is our target. When our contact calls in, we swoop in and apprehend her. She needs to be unharmed and alive. She is high priority and vitally important to Project: Whydah."

The vision ended. Some visions are like turning the channel to a TV show halfway through. You have no clue what's going on and have to figure it out for yourself. Others are like VH1's *Pop-Up Video* and I'm giving information throughout. When this vision was over I was left with one glaring fact floating in my mind.

These operators were a part of Visegar.

First the doctor and now a team of operators to scoop her up; what the hell did Visegar have to do with Sally? I pistol whipped the zipped man across the back of his head and watched him fall to the floor. Then I kicked him, twice. It was cathartic.

"What was that for?"

"Carthatic-ism?" I suggested. My answer sounded

like a religion for mental wellbeing. "Is that a word? I'm making it a word."

"I ain't got time for your dilly dallying," Drew snapped. "What's the play, hoss?"

"We got special forces here to take Sally. We need to get her out of here and fast. Help me and I'll see if I can get you a face-to-face with Sally." My mind raced. What were my options? I didn't want a shoot-out. There were civilians and cops. I didn't want anyone to get hurt. I looked up but Drew was already gone.

I limped out of the closet and looked around. I saw the Texas Ranger walking towards one of the uniformed officers with his badge out. The two talked quietly and I saw Drew pointing across to one of the other operators we had noticed. The uniform reached for his radio. Seconds later I saw several other cops moving towards the operator.

This could work. No spy would risk exposure or collateral damage if they didn't have to. I smiled. We could extract Sally without any violence or bloodshed. I smiled. It would be refreshing for once not have to----

Two gunshots rang out as one of the uniformed officer dropped to the ground. The operator raised his gun into the air and fired two more shots. That's when everybody started screaming and bolting for the nearest door.

I pushed through the crowds, feeling like a salmon swimming upstream, and I moved to the Texas departure gate. I spotted Sally in the distance. She was scared and moving for the nearest door. Good girl. Get out of there.

She didn't get far as a soldier's hand grabbed her and yanked her back. He held a gun to her side. Then he looked directly at me. It wasn't hard to figure out how he noticed me. When a hundred plus people are all running one way and an idiot in a cowboy hat is running the opposite way; he kind of stands out. He aimed the gun at me.

Shit. Now I was in a gun fight.

Chapter 12
I Even Have a Theme Song

Mr. Soldier fired off two shots in my direction and I dove behind the nearest locker. They were those dollar lockers that came with those stupid keys. They weren't very thick but they were big enough for my needs.

Hiding behind a locker felt very high school. I'd hide there when I didn't want the teacher to find me after I'd have just pulled some epic prank. Now, however, the consequences seemed a little more severe if I got caught. I peered around the corner and did a quick scan. Most of the operators were now visible. It was easy to tell them apart from the civilians: civilians were running for their lives and the operators were waving guns around.

I hate it when things are this simple.

I tagged six operators and gave each dehumanizing names. The leader was ordering his troops to take position. I called him Lt. Jerkface. The tall dude was Big. One solider cursed in Russian as he pulled his MP5K from beneath his jacket. I called him Rasputin. That left an idiot with a cocky swagger - BAMF - and the bad dude who had to shoot off early, kill a cop and start this whole gunfight. I called him the Two-Pump Chump. He seemed as stupid as Chicken-Head did, tied up in the utility closet. I called him Chicken-Head because he was the first to go down. The one that really caused concern was the blonde with spiky hair. He didn't have a

SMG. He only had a pistol holstered at his side. Why would Billy Idol show up to a gunfight and not draw his weapon? Oh my god, did he have a knife?

Two-Pump retreated backwards, his gun shoved into Sally's side. He backed up until he was near BAMF. I needed to do something but I didn't have many options. I was out-gunned and out-numbered. Shit. I needed somebody who was better at fighting than I was. I needed a real bruiser, somebody like Stelio Kontos but he was nowhere to be found. He was also fictional but that had never stopped me from relying on a person. You're always there for me, John Rambo.

I looked to my left and saw two uniforms and Drew Winnick but something was wrong. The Texas Ranger was behind some seats but he was crouched down. His coyote brown SIG was in his hand but his arm was shaking. I popped my gun out from behind the lockers and shot three bullets upwards. I used that as cover as I bolted across the floor. I wanted to do a dramatic slide across the floor and end up beside Drew but as I tried my slide came to a halt several feet away from cover.

Crap baskets.

Like a dog with an itchy butt I scooted across the floor until I ended up behind the same cover that Drew was. He looked at me and shook his head. "We're boned."

"Not yet we ain't," I said with confidence. I was lying. We were hella boned. "I need your help. She's in trouble."

"I know....but...." His voice cracked and his breathing got heavy. I had seen this before. I had seen this in myself. When I went overseas I saw some shit and did some things, neither of which I suggest. When I got back I was a bundle of nerves and a pile of wreck. Every time I got into a gun fight - admittedly it was more then I should - I would get the shakes and I would get anxiety. My heart would race and my hand would tremble. It would become difficult to breathe and my chest felt like I was John Hurt giving birth but I learned to deal. I knew that fear was normal. I just had to push through it. Doctors often suggested a radical new treatment called *talk-*

ing about it but that ain't the Thompson way. We use the tried and true method of *I'm not crying, you're crying* or the classic *what do you mean I should talk to someone? That's it, we're fighting.*

"We need backup," Drew said. He wasn't wrong but we didn't have time. Sally needed our help and she needed it now.

"One riot, One Ranger," I said, hoping the Ranger's motto would inspire him.

"I..." his voice trailed off. I growled. If the Ranger motto didn't work then I was going to have to use the big guns. I was going to have to quote one of the wisest men that ever existed.

"In the Eyes of a Ranger, the unsuspecting stranger had better know the truth of wrong from right," I began. "Cause the eyes of a Ranger are upon you; any wrong you do, he's gonna see. When you're in Texas look behind you 'cause that's where the Ranger's gonna be."

"You're an idiot," Drew said with a shake of his head. While that statement isn't *untrue* Drew had stopped panicking and his hand had stopped twitching. The power of Chuck Norris had won once again. "What's the plan?"

"Free the girl," I said quickly. "Then we get her out of here."

I looked around. There were several civilians, one uniformed cop bleeding out on the floor and two more uniforms huddled behind various cover. I scowled. I wanted to open fire but Two-Pump was still holding Sally.

"We need a better plan, hoss," Winnick drawled.

"Then wrassle one up 'cause I'm batting zero here," I mocked.

"This is the police," Winnick cried out loudly. "Y'all best be lowering them irons and letting the lass go."

"Like fuck we are," Two-Pump yelled.

"Great plan," I muttered.

"That was their one chance," he snarled. With a dramatic spin, Texas Ranger Drew Winnick popped up from behind cover. He snapped off two rounds from the P226. One bullet grazed Two-Pump's upper arm, forcing him to jolt his pistol away from Sally. The second bullet collided with Two-Pump's gun, knocking it free from his hand. I stared in shock. He just shot a pistol from a bad guy's hand. The Texas Ranger just full on westerned a baddie.

That was movie-life.

Two-Pump pulled Sally to the ground and rolled away as two of the Visegar jerks started to flank around us. I had Big on my left and Drew had BAMF on his right. As Big got closer I realized that he was beyond big. The man looked like he was approaching seven feet tall. Shit. When you're that big they definitely call you Mister. I popped up and let my M9 roar. Two shots flew towards Mr. Big but, somehow, I missed the giant. He ducked behind cover only to re-emerge seconds later with his MP5K in his hand. The SMG rattled off a flurry of 9mm rounds in my direction. I let out a squeal and dropped down. There has been some debate as to the origin of the high pitched female-sounding squeal. Yes, I will admit that the scream *sounded* like it came from my direction and my body but I promise you that it did not. I let out a *manly* grunt. The female scream came from Sally. It turns out that one of her powers is super ventriloquism and I will fight anybody who argues differently.

I rolled onto my back and leveled my pistol in his direction. Only this time I was aiming for his legs. I squeeze off two more rounds and watched as his knee exploded and his leg snapped like a chocolate bar. I learned much later that Mr. Big was deathly allergic to bullets. Who would have known? I rolled to my feet as he dropped to the floor. I hobbled over to his body and slammed my foot into his face. Mr. Big was out cold.

I looked over to see how Winnick was doing but he hadn't even broken a sweat. BAMF never made it close. He lay on the floor, bleeding from the neck in what could be a fatal wound if it weren't for the Ranger kneeling beside the man, holding a towel to the wound.

"Don't move and keep pressure on the wound," Drew ordered. "If you do that then y'all might just ride another day."

"We good?" I called out.

"We getting there, hoss."

I peered around the corner and spotted Rasputin and Lt. Jerkface. Two-Pump was still on the ground, holding Sally tight across his body.

"Get up," Lt. Jerkface snarled. He leveled his weapon in our direction. "We're pulling out. Get the girl out the back."

"Cops are on their way, man. We have to hold out for the long-run." Two-Pump panicked.

"We can't hold out," Rapustin snarled with his Russian accent. "We don't have the ammo or the secure position. We need to leave, now."

"Both of you, shut the fuck up," Jerkface snarled. "We have evac on the way. We need to move to the LZ and get the fuck out of here."

Shit. They were leaving and worst still; they were going to pull a Visegar vanishing act. That could mean anything. I had seen men who could go invisible by bending light and guys who could change their appearance. I don't know what a Visegar Evac would be but it wasn't going to be good for me or Sally. I needed to move and I needed to move now. I looked across the room and spotted a uniform looking at me. He had his service pistol out and was looking for someone to make a move. An idea was forming in my head. If Puzo was here I could pull off the good ol' Shake and Bake. So what did Cal Naughton Jr. do without Ricky Bobby? He became the Magic Man.

I signaled Drew and the uniform to give me a three second delay and then I bolted across the floor. I fired my pistol twice, trying to draw their attention. Both shots went intentionally wide. The three goons looked towards me and the standing two each raised their weapons to fire. That's when Drew and the Uniform popped up and opened fire.

Drew and the Uniform; it sounded like a TV cop show. Drew McBadBone is a highly decorated police detective who got framed for corruption and was fired. He is now a private dick solving crimes as he tries to clear his name. Officer Johnny St. Pressedsuit is a rookie cop fresh on the beat. He is a uniformed cop who is viewed as a straight laced, by the book cop but his dark secret is that he's a from a mob family and wants to protect his kin from inside the police. Now they are teaming up while secretly trying to betray the other. I even have a theme song.

Drew and the Uniform!
A pair of cops who take no guff.
Drew and the Uniform!
They're super strong and super tough!
Drew and the Uniform!
They once got hired by a unicorn.
Drew and the Uniform!

Okay, the song isn't great. I never said I was a singer or a songwriter. You try rhyming something with uniform. Things like that just don't come from a brainstorm. I can't just do thing all free form. No matter what anybody says, I'm not going to conform. Just because you are seeing my life doesn't mean you get to judge me.

Drew and the Uniform each raddled off round after round. Their weapons fire pulled the attention from me. Lt. Jerkface raised his SMG and just let loose. The explosion of returning rounds forced Drew and the Uniform back down behind their cover. Two-Pump snapped his head back towards my direction but I was nowhere to be seen

Magic Man: now you see me and now you don't!

I was hidden behind several chairs, creeping around to flank from behind. The closer I got to the three men the stupider I felt. This was a bad idea. This was a really bad idea. What the fuck was I doing?

You're being a Thompson. Oh crap. My brain had an opinion. Nothing good *ever* happened when my brain had an opinion. *You Thompsons are shit disturbers and dumbasses.*

You run head first into the lion's den to save some people you don't even know and why? Because you are good folk who just want to do good things. You're stupid folk but still good folk.

D...d...did my brain just compliment me?

I spotted Lt. Jerkface and Rasputin. They were returning fire in Drew and the Uniform's direction. Two-Pump was back on his feet. Sally was still held in his arm only now there was a blade in Two-Pump's hand and it pressed against her neck. He was slowly backing away.

"Freeze!" My words were stern as I held my M9 pointed at his back. "Let the girl go."

"That's not going to happen," he snarled. "You can't shoot me."

He was right. I couldn't fire without risking hitting Sally. If she could somehow drop to the floor I could fire but how did I signal her to drop without letting Two-Pump know?

"You're the cowboy gimp who should be staying out of the game but no," he snarled. "Here you are, risking your life for what, this bitch kid? What is wrong with you?"

"There are four things wrong with me. Let me list them off for you." I cleared my throat with an exaggerated cough. "One - Nothing wrong with me. Two - Nothing wrong with me. Three - Nothing wrong with me. Four - Nothing wrong with me."

Sally's eyes went wide. She grabbed Two-Pump's knife hand while she slammed her opposite elbow into his gut. Two-Pump groaned, his grip weakened and Sally let her body hit the floor. I smirked. I knew the girl would understand. All I had to do was speak her language.

I fired twice. Both bullets ripped into his vest and the operator toppled forward. Sally rolled aside as Two-Pump slammed into the ground. Chances were his vest had saved his life - not that I cared - but even with a vest two bullets were going to put him out of commission long enough for me to get away.

I grabbed Sally's hand and bolted down a narrow hallway towards the nearest door. It was the door into the employee's room. I gave the door handle a shake but it was locked. I stared at the electronic card reader and frowned. I couldn't psychically hack it but Sally could.

"I need you to zap the door," I said as I looked at her. "I need you to use your electricity powers to fry the lock. If you do that, we can escape."

"I...I..."

"I know you have powers. I was going to wait for you to tell me, it was your secret to tell not mine to reveal," I reassured her, "but we're out of time. I need you to zap it."

"I can't zap it," Sally revealed.

"But I saw you zap your cuffs," I said, confused.

"That's not how my powers work," Sally said. Sorrow and sadness appeared in her eyes and I felt like shit. Damn it. I looked around. The hallway was too narrow to shoot the lock; the bullet would bounce and almost definitely hit one of us.

"I have located them."

I spun around to see the blonde with spike hair standing before us. Billy Idol was blocking our escape. I didn't hesitate I spun around Sally and leveled my M9 at the blonde. I fired twice. Neither bullet reached him. Billy Idol raised his hand and let loose a nearly invisible tongue of flame that instantly melted the two rounds.

Crap baskets.

"I request that you do not do that again or I will burn you alive." His tone was calm and unnerving. The wheezing tone sent shivers down my spine. "Place your weapon upon the floor and surrender the girl."

"You need her alive," I said, trying to stall. "You can't use your flame to attack me."

"I have spent endless hours meticulously practising and perfecting my ability," Billy Idol said in his eerily calm voice. "I could burn the wings off of a fly without harming the rest of its body. I would advise you to take what I say as fact and extrapolate from it the miniscule difficulty I would have in burning you without harming her."

"You burn the wings off of a fly?" I mocked. "That is

hella serial killer, dude."

I stared at him and let my mind race. I had no options but surrender or call his bluff. I kept my M9 on him but stole a glance at Sally. She had a weird look of confidence on her face.

"We didn't start this fire," she said, clutching my arm. "It's always been burning since the world's been turning," I finished. I glance back at Billy Idol and gave him the signature Thompson smirk. I was calling his bluff.

I squeezed the trigger over and over, endless firing the rounds until I heard the frightening click that each soldier dreaded. It was the click that signaled the need to reload. I glanced up, hoping to see the body of Billy Idol lying on the floor but I wasn't that lucky. Billy Idol stood with a ball of fire in each of his hands. With his left hand he melted the bullets and with his right he fired the ball of flame towards me. I couldn't move, I couldn't dodge and I couldn't block it. I could literally do nothing but let this ball of fire hit me.

This was really going to suck.

I felt the heat approach, searing my skin from afar, like waving your hand over a lit candle. Sweat instantly formed on my face. Just as the ball of flame was about to strike me, Sally stepped in and let the ball hit her instead.

Chapter 13
Did I Go Out on a Cop Date?

I wanted to scream, I wanted to try and stop her but I found my body unresponsive as the ball exploded into a blinding flash of flash of flame and light.

Not again.

Sally.

Zoey.

The women in my life; I couldn't protect them. They kept dying. They would come to me for help and I let them die. Why would fate keep sending me people if I couldn't protect them? Hadn't fate hurt me enough? Why did it feel the need to strike me down, time and time again? Why did others get hurt in my eternal battle with fate? Why couldn't fate just strike me directly?

"We didn't start the fire," Sally's voice cut through the flame. How? "No, we didn't light, but we tried to fight it." Sally stood before me. The ends of her hair were slightly singed, her clothes were burned slightly but Sally was unharmed. Her emerald eyes had a crimson glow about them and a look of pride rested on her face.

It was the words of Billy Joel that saved her. Billy Joel was more than just a talented singer/songwriter. He was deity of great power and benevolence. All hail Billy Joel and his son, the Piano Man. The power of the Joel compels you.

"How dare you?" Pride turned to anger as Sally

glanced back at Billy Idol. The crimson glow in her eyes grew brighter as small flames formed in the palms of her hand. "You just tried to kill Ben. You tried to burn him alive. Why do all of you want to keep hurting me? What did I ever do to you?"

Pride turned to rage as her flames tripled in size and the glow in her eyes burned brightly. She stepped towards Billy Idol. He shook his head.

"Hold your stride, child," he wheezed.

"Rage," Sally muttered. "I feel it inside of me. The angrier I get, the brighter they burn and nobody has more rage then me."

"I have greater control of these flames than you do. You do not want to test your skill onto mine." Sally fired one ball of fire against him. Billy Idol tried to catch it but found himself pushed back by several steps.

"I have lost my mother, I have lost my father, I have lost my foster parents and now you just tried to take Ben from me. I have had unbelievable levels of shit poured on me and I'm still standing. My therapist said I needed an outlet. I need some way to let loose this rage. I think I just found it."

Sally fired the second ball and forced Billy Idol back again, only this time it was by even more steps. Sally instantly created two new balls. She roared now as she spoke.

"I am a teenage girl with fucked up hormones, massive amounts of trauma and just so much pent up rage." The balls of flames were each the size of basketballs. Then they quickly grew until each was the size of a beach ball. "To make matters worse, my cramps just started."

Sally flung both balls and watched as they exploded. Billy Idol was pitched backwards into the air. He flew nearly a dozen feet before crashing down onto the floor with a massive thud. Sally let a massive tongue of flame emerge from her hand. It looked like a flamethrower from one of Robby's games. The sprinkler recognized the fire and water stared to pour down from the room.

"Sally," I called out.

"They...must...pay," she roared, screaming between words. "Burn, burn, burn!"

"Lean on me, when you're not strong," I said calmly. Her head snapped around and stared at me. I continued. "And I'll be your friend. I'll help you carry on..."

Sally glanced at the operators and roared. She let out another burst of flame. Each of them recoiled. Sally panted heavily as she stared them down. "Last warning: run."

Lt. Jerkface waved his men back. Rapsutin, Jerkface and Billy Idol retreated. Sally waited until they were gone before raising her arms into the air. She let out another flame. The fire burned so bright that the sprinkler water evaporated before it even reached the flame. Then as quickly as the flame appeared, it vanished. The crimson glow vanished and her rage dissipated. Sally's legs began to wobble before they gave way. I was there to catch her.

"We all need somebody...." she panted as she fought to stay awake, "to lean....on."

That's when she passed out.

Movie-life is when I'm a part of an epic shootout. Movie-life is when I get clever one-liners right when I defeat the bad guy. Move-life is not when I have to stand around at the crime scene so cops can do their cop thing. Movie-life is not giving my statement thirty or forty times before they tell me to wait a little more to give my statement again.

Movies never showed this part of a shoot-out. The reason: it was hella boring. This was like the cancer sub-plot of *Creed*. It was very important to the movie but damn if it wasn't boring as shit. I want see Michael B. Jordan punch people, a lot. At least in the paperwork scene of *Hot Fuzz* we got witty banter, a guy with a gun and a massive explosion. I didn't get any of this.

"Hey, Cowboy." I looked over and saw the uniform

approach. I smiled at him. The cop is a dark-skinned man in his mid twenties. A wet towel hung around his neck. The majority of his uniform was still damp. He offered me a hand. I took it. "I'm Officer Chadwick Kani."

"Ben Thompson," I introduced. I look down at the kid. His shake was firm and strong. He was a tough kid and quick on the draw. "You're good under pressure."

"So are you," Kani replied. "You didn't have to stick around. I know you were here for the girl but you helped stop this from going from bad to worse. I respect that."

"I can't just let shit get worse," I said with a shrug. I looked past him and onto the other cops. "What did you tell the other cops?"

"I told them about the hostage situation, the kidnapping and how a couple of us did what we could to diffuse the situation." I nodded to a bench where Sally slept. Kani shook his head. "I don't know what happened with the fire but I'm sure as hell not telling that to my bosses."

"Why not?"

"I've been trying to get the boost to detective for a while now," Kani said with a sigh. "This will probably put me over the top. However, if I go spouting shit like the *girl had fire powers* then they'll never give it to me."

"Smart."

"That being said," Kani continued. "I'm asking you directly. What the hell is up with fire girl?"

"There are some people who have abilities," I carefully said. I expected a laugh or a look of disbelief but I got neither. "Some can shoot fire and others can go invisible, just to name a few. You don't look surprised."

"You walk the beat in this city and you see shit." It was a simple answer but I liked it. He reached into his pocket and handed me a business card. I handed him one as well. "I won't forget today. Give me a call if you ever need anything."

Did I just make a cop friend? Holy shit, I just made a cop friend! That was awesome but what was the next step? Did I go out on a cop date? Did we go see a cop movie on this cop date? Did I meet his cop parents? Was I moving too cop fast?

It took another hour before I got the good to go. I walked over to Sally and gently shook her awake. She groggily looked up at me. "Let's go back to my home, kiddo."

The Chevelle roared as it barrelled down the street. I glanced at the clock. How was it not even noon? I pulled over at a Rotten Ronnies and offered her lunch. Sally eagerly nodded. A couple minutes later and we each had a Big Mac in our hands. She hungrily wolfed hers down.

"Where were you going?" I asked. Sally froze. She looked ashamed of her actions. "I'm not mad, I'm just curious."

"I was heading home to Texas," she sheepishly said. "I....I don't belong here and I don't belong in Chicago. I'm a Texas girl. I was born that way and will always be one."

"Do you have any family there?"

"Mom has a sister," she explained. "Aunt Mary."

"Why weren't you staying with her?"

"Aunt Mary said she couldn't give up her life. She said I'd be safer with the Marshals than with her. She said....." her words trailed off. I gently encouraged her forward. "She said she didn't want to risk the lives of her kids by looking after me."

I silently cursed. Who the fuck did that? I would look after Robby and Alice without hesitation and I already knew that Annie was going to look after Clint when I was gone. I couldn't picture the family that wouldn't look after their own. Mine would live and die for each other. Why weren't more families like mine? Oh shit. My family was bat-shit crazy and high-functioning alcoholics. Maybe the world didn't need more of us.

"If you go home, the cartel will find you," I said. I

wasn't trying to scare her. I was trying to talk like we were equals. "You'll probably be killed."

"I'm probably going to be killed here," Sally retorted. "If I'm going to die, then I'm going to do so on Texas soil."

"I can see the future, kiddo," I began. "You will not die in Texas. One day you will die, we all will, but you will die with by the person that loves you the most. This person will cry at your loss and whisper how you made their life better buy being in it. You will die happy."

"You saw all of this?" she asked.

"Yes," I lied. "And it's not for a long, long time."

Sally smiled at me.

"I need your permission for something," I said, changing the topic. Sally carefully eyed me. "I have tapes from your sessions with Dr. Balzary. I need to listen to them but I'm not going to do so without your permission."

"Why do you need my tapes?"

"The men who tried to grab you today are not from the cartel. They are somebody different and they belong to the some company that Dr. Balzary works for. I need to see if he said anything that can help me protect you."

"You could have just listened without telling me," she said.

"I could have but I'm not. This is your life and your past; I'm not going to sneak into it. I will only go if invited."

Sally nervously munched on her fries. She eyed me suspiciously. "H...h...how did you know I had....powers?" She whispered the last word.

"I saw it in a vision when I was trying to find out who was chasing you."

"Why didn't you say anything?" Sally asked in her drawl.

"Because coming out from underneath the cape is a big thing," I said. I just came up with that saying. I'm hoping it catches on. "It's not my right to out you. If you wanted to tell me, I was going to let you. If you decided not to, I was going to let that slide as well."

Sally smiled again. She gave me a nod. "You can listen to them."

I smiled at her.

"Tell me about your abilities," I suggested.

"I absorb different things and then I can shoot them out," she explained slowly. "You saw me absorb fire. Then I can shoot it back out."

"If you don't absorb it you can't create it?" Sally nodded. It made sense. She got zapped by a taser and then was able to zap her way out of the cuffs but she didn't have enough electricity in her to zap the lock.

"I've absorbed ice, fire and electricity," she said.

"What about wind or nuclear?"

"Wind is difficult, it's too fine to easily absorb and I don't really know about nuclear. I haven't had much exposure." We both chuckled.

We continued to eat. I glanced up as a McEmployee walked by. He was a teenage boy sent to clean the dining room. He glanced at Sally and gave her the type of smirk that only meant one thing. Sally blushed and played with her hair. I fought the urge to put my fist through his face.

Weird; where did that reaction come from?

The scariest sight I have ever seen was Puzo and Annie standing at my doorway as I pulled in. Neither looked happy with me. I paused and looked over at Sally.

"Want to see how quickly we can drive to Texarkana?" I said suddenly. Sally just gave me a confused look.

"Texarkana, Texas?" she asked. "I thought it wasn't safe to go there?"

"It sure as hell isn't going to be safe for me here," I gulped. "Also we have to make you watch *Smokey and the Bandit.*"

"That's one of those boring car films, right?"

"It is an *amazing* car film," I corrected.

"Those are so boring. Like those fifty films where that old man boxes." Was she dissing Rocky? She wouldn't dare.

Marshal Arcel came out from my house and I felt a little safer. At least they could arrest a FBI lady when she tried to shoot me. With I sigh I climbed out of the car and walked towards the house. I leaned in to kiss Puzo but she pulled away. It was the kind of motion that said she was pissed at me and a kiss wasn't going to cut it. It was a subtle look. Annie, however, went for a less subtle approach.

"What the fuck are you doing getting into gun fights?"

I gulped. Things just got worse for me when Annie got mad. I glanced at Sally who just shrugged. She slipped past the two women and walked towards the Marshal.

"How goes, Mr. Arcel?" she asked as she walked into my house.

"Not bad, munchkin, you?" he replied as he followed.

"Been better," Sally said with a shrug. She glanced back at the doorway and at me. "They seemed pissed. Is Ben going to be okay?"

"I honestly don't know," Arcel said. "But I'm sure as hell not getting involved."

I flashed Puzo the Thompson smirk, the one I'd seen my father use to get out of trouble hundreds of times, but Annie wasn't having any of it. "No, no. You are not Dading your way out of this."

"Your sister's right," Rachael said. "This is serious. What the fuck happened out there?"

"I...I....I don't know. She got in trouble and I tried to help," I replied. I let out a sigh. "Sally is in more danger then we originally thought. She's being hunted by Croxallé as well."

Puzo's lip tightened. She shook her head and turned to walk inside. She paused and turned back. She silently hugged me. We held each other for a moment. She was still mad at me but she was happy I was safe. Puzo walked indoors. This left Annie and I standing at the doorway. She just looked at me with that stern older sister glare. Eventually her glare cracked and a look of relief crossed her eyes. She wrapped her arms around me and simply hugged me. I held her close. We just stood there, silently hugging each other.

''Stop doing this,'' she pleaded. "You have to stop risking your life. I almost lost you once. I can't go through it again."

"I'm sorry, Annie. I'm sorry."

Rachael, Sally, Arcel and I all retired to my office. I pulled in extra chairs so everybody could sit down. Arcel walked up to my murder-board and gave a low whistle. "Do I want to know what all this is about?"

"It's a missing person's case," I said quickly, hoping he'd drop the subject. He paused over the Malpaso pile. Eventually he lost interest and sat down.

"The way I see it we have two separate issues involving Sally," Arcel began. "The first is the cartel and the second is this Croxallé issue.

"The cartel has a mole in my organization. I set up a safe house through our Witsec channel but the house got hit by cartel men."

"Are we in danger here?" I asked. Arcel shook his head.

"I haven't put you or your house into the system yet and now I don't plan to. Right now, I'm the only person in Witsec who knows your location and I plan to keep it that way."

"What are you doing about the mole?" Puzo asked.

"Witsec has procedures to weed them out," Arcel assured. "We'll be fine. What I need is to know what this whole Croxallé thing is about."

"That's a classified investigation," Puzo said. Both cops did the federal stare. Each were about two seconds away from whipping out their federally issued dicks and measuring them to see whose was bigger. I have seen Puzo naked and watched her wield that FBI badge like a broadsword. My guess was her dick was bigger. "I'll show you mine if you show me yours?"

Wait, what? Did she actually just say that?

"Sure, what do you need to know?"

"What happened with the cartel?"

"I'm not allowed to talk about that," Sally abruptly said. Arcel looked at her and smiled.

"It is okay, Sally," Arcel assured her. "We can trust her. May I tell her?"

"I guess," Sally said, stealing glances at me. I gave her a smile and a nod. She seemed to relax slightly.

"Colin Condon was a supply officer for a trucking company called Wingham and Finch. His job was to calculate gas usage per trucks based on their weight and find better ways to load and supply the company's trucks. He was very good at his job and made decent bank for it."

"Dad didn't care about the money. He liked the job, he liked the numbers and he liked the challenge," Sally added.

"His unique views of the task at hand help make Wingham and Finch one of the most profitable trucking companies in Texas," Arcel continued. "Then he noticed that his math wasn't adding up. Trucks were heavier than expected at weighing station. This meant that somewhere between departure and arrival, the trucks were making two unscheduled stops; one to pick up something and another to drop it off. Then he found evidence that the trucks are being used to smuggle drugs into the US.

"Colin contacted an old friend of his. Her name was Alexia Pike and she works for the DEA. Pike began an investigation into Wingham and Finch and Colin was her inside man. The two uncover that the Imperecedero Cartel is using trucks to smuggle a new drug call Blue Cap into the states."

"What does this drug do?"

"It has a weird numbing effect on the body. You'll

start hallucinating, you won't feel pain and it'll seem like you have endless energy. However, it is highly addictive and can cause seizures, violent behaviour and there is a higher risk of suicide while on it."

Arcel reached over and took Sally's hand. They both took a deep breath before he continued. This was the bad part.

"Pike was over at Colin's house preparing for the next few days of their investigation when the cartel stormed the house. They were being led by Ismael Salazar. He killed both Colin and Pike. Sally was hidden at the time and saw the whole thing. We've arrested Ismael and are awaiting trial. He got bail with bribery and blackmail. Now the cartel wants to get rid of our witness."

"They're afraid he'll crack," Puzo finished. Arcel nodded.

"The Imperecedero Cartel is run by Guzman Salazar. Ismael is his youngest son. Cartel intel says Ismael know *everything* but he's kind of a fuck up. He likes to party and screw but is struggling to impress Daddy while he's state-side. If he turns states' evidence then we could almost dismantle the Imperecedero Cartel."

The room sat in silence. Puzo and Arcel did their cop thing. Puzo began to explain about the Croxallé investigation. I glanced at Sally. She was sitting on the couch, curled up in her own arms and huddled in the corner. I limped over and plopped down beside her. We silently looked at each other for a moment.

"You watched all that happen?" I asked, breaking the silence. She nodded. "I'm sorry. I know what that's like. I wouldn't wish that on my biggest enemy."

"What do you mean you know what that's like?" she asked with curious eyes. I gently patted my bum leg.

"I got this overseas when my humvee ran over a bomb," I said. "I was knocked out of the fight and good friends fought to keep me alive. I watched a bunch of them die trying to save me."

Silence.

"I'm sorry you had to go through that, Ben," she said softly. "How did you get over it?"

"I'll let you know when I figure it out," I honestly replied. I pointed to Puzo and Arcel, still chatting to one another. "But being around people who want to help is the best thing I can think of and those two want nothing more than to help you."

"This is why I hate our system," Arcel said with a sigh. "If we had known there was an investigation into Croxallé we would have suspended our contract with them."

"What did they do with you?" I asked, suddenly interested in their conversation again.

"We clear several doctors to help in certain situations. We wanted to give Sally a check-up before moving her into foster care. We used one from Croxallé. They came and gave Sally a physical before we whisked her out of Texas.

"Two weeks later Sally reported having severe nightmares. It's not uncommon for trauma victims and those who have witnessed a horrible crime. We flew in a psychiatrist to talk with her."

"Dr. Balzary," I added. Arcel nodded.

"He was also from Croxallé," the Marshal concluded. "Now the question is why do they want her and since when do medical companies have military goons?"

I looked at Sally. "Do you know what Project: Whydah is?" She shook her head no. I looked back at Puzo. "They want her because she is important to some project."

Arcel opened his mouth to ask how but paused. He slowly closed his mouth and gave me a weird look. It was a glance I was very familiar with. It was the *psychics are weird* look.

"So what's the next step? What's the next plan?" Puzo asked.

"I'm keeping her here," Arcel said. "Until further notice, you're in charge of her, Ben."

Sally's, Puzo's and my eyes each went wide for vastly different reasons. The three of us looked at each other in shock. I was in charge of another life? Was this a good idea? Was this a smart idea? I glanced at Sally. She stared back at me with a confused look upon her face. Puzo was the first to speak.

"This is a really bad idea," she said. "Ignoring the fact that Ben is the last person who should be looking after a kid--"

"Fact," I added.

"--And I mean positively the absolute last," Puzo continued.

"Hey!"

"The cartel may not know where she is but Croxallé does," Puzo said. "Ben has tangled with them before. They know exactly where he lives."

"That's where you come in," Arcel said with a grin. "I can't put a man on the door without signaling my mole. So I need the FBI to quietly put a guy or two on the door."

"Why don't we just bring her into our FBI offices and put her into lockdown?" Puzo asked. Sally suddenly recoiled back into her chair. Puzo eyed the teenager and frowned. She suddenly realized what Arcel was trying to avoid. "You've spent a lot of time in police stations, haven't you?"

Sally quietly nodded. The kid had seen enough white walls, both municipal and federal, to last a lifetime. If she had any chance at growing up normal she needed something different. She needed a life. She wasn't going to get one for the next couple days but the least we could do was cut the kid a break. We could try and do for her what life had not.

"I'm worried about you," Puzo said to Sally.

"Sally, I understand why you left foster care but why come here?" Arcel asked.

"It was a voice in my head," Sally began. She bit her lip as she tried to formulate her words. "After I moved in with the Owles, I started getting nightmares. They were horrifying. I saw monsters in the darkness, I saw pregnant women in cages and I saw----" her words trailed off. She looked at me and I nodded. With a deep breath she continued. "I saw Dad die, over and over. But there was also a woman in my mind, a woman made of fire that burned through the darkness. She was there at the darkest and she would protect me from the worst of the worst. She would whisper to me and keep me safe."

Puzo glanced at Arcel and gave him a quizzical look. He just shrugged.

"When the bad men showed up at Owles' place, I panicked. She had protected me from the evils in my mind. She couldn't do anything about those that lurked in the real world. She told me to run. She told me *Find Ben Thompson. He can protect you.*" She looked at me. "Ever since I've been here, I haven't heard her voice."

Silence.

Nobody knew what to say to that. How do you argue with something like that? How could you? Arcel glanced at Puzo. She nodded.

"I'll put someone on the door," she said as she climbed to her feet. "I don't like this plan." Puzo dug her phone from her pocket and walked to the door. She paused before exiting and pointed to Arcel. "Clean up your house."

Chapter 14
You Can't Just Spring Age-Play on Someone

My phone buzzed and I quickly grabbed it. Hotwire had messaged me. Puzo was gone, she was taking care of FBI stuff, and Arcel had hung around enough to make sure that Sally was okay before leaving with a tip of his hat. This left Sally with my family.

Hotwire: I got that search done. You want me to send the files?
Me: Summarize?
Hotwire: Lazy
Hotwire: Deputy United States Marshal Jeff Arcel. Works for Witsec. Kind of a sketchy record. Likes to bend rules. Has a couple citations in his past for force. High number of shootings. Big hospital debt due to sick mother who passed.
Hotwire: Ranger Drew Winnick. Legacy. 4th generation Ranger. Crack shot. Great record. Texas Celeb. Deadly with a gun.
Me: I saw that first hand. Shot a gun out of somebody's hand.
Hotwire: Dozens of awards from shooting competitions. One of the highest ranked officers for shooting in the country.
Hotwire: She doesn't lube.

Me: Sorry, what?
Hotwire: Lose. Fucking autocorrect.

I laughed for a moment before pausing. How often did Hotwire use the word lube that autocorrect suggested it? The moment I had that thought was the moment I regretted it. I didn't want to know the answer to that.

Me: I owe you. Thanks.
Hotwire: Be careful around Winnick. File says that the Ranger has been suffering since their SO's death.

I rolled to my chair and plopped my phone down. I grabbed Dr. Balzary's recorder and slipped in the first SD card. Leaning back, I pressed play and was greeted with the Doc's voice as he introduced himself to Sally. Hours passed as I listened to Sally's sessions. I heard her talk about losing her dad and of how scary it was to watch it happen. She talked about struggling with surviving while both her parents had died. She talked about wishing it was her who died and not them. She talked about joining them.

I had to pause for a while. The sessions were hitting a little too close to home for me. I had gone into therapy after getting out of the army. I was a mess. I had watched my friends die and wished it had been me. I felt guilty for surviving. I felt guilty that I was alive and they weren't and worse still, that I wasn't doing anything worthy of this extra time I had been given. It took time for me to learn that it was okay that I survived and that it was a good thing. My doc had told me I would heal in time; that I would find something in my life to make it worthwhile.

I didn't stay in therapy for more than a couple months. While I understood its purpose, I could never benefit from its methods. My brain-doc wanted me to do things like journal my emotions and talk about my emotions and actually have emotions. Truth be told, I found greater therapy in doing stuff than talking about it but that's the Thompson way. It may not be the best way or the healthiest way but it was our way and we were still standing.

The first person to make a *not without a cane* joke after that gets a boot to the head.

After each session, when Sally was gone, Dr. Balzary would talk into the recorder before packing up and flying out of Chicago. They were mostly his thoughts on the day and on Sally. Dr. Balzary was a wordy som-bitch and he loved the sound of his own voice. Most of these post-session rants were mundane but a few caught my attention.

I'm beginning to find my stance on Sally changing. I am a psychiatrist and I am loyal to my patients but the company has always come first. I was to examine Sally to make sure that there were no ill effects of the implanting process but I am growing to care for her in more than a clinical sense.

I originally argued against implanting literal thousands of terrabytes of data into Sally's mind. With the recent crippling attacks on our digital systems and the raised threat by WhiteStar, our usual digital transfer and courier methods are not secure enough for such cross-country transfer. But to use her was just a bad idea.

Psychically implanting data into any person is difficult and comes with risks, but to do it to a girl who is suffering from trauma and PTSD, it's almost unthinkable.

I question if I am being clear headed about the situation. This is a practiced process. We inserted the data into her head back in Texas during a physical and then slowly withdrew it in Chicago. I have slowed the withdrawal, taking less and less at each of our sessions, but was that for her benefit or mine? Is it because I care for this girl and I don't want to risk her health?

What the actual fuck? Psychic implanting? Was Croxallé using Sally like some sort of data courier? I tapped the next track button and listened.

There are several dangers in psychic implanting, especially when we insert a completely different personality onto an existing one. I saw an agent have a mental breakdown when he discovered the implanted personality was not his own. I met one undercover agent who had dozens of personalities placed upon him over the years that he now had identity issues and was struggling to decipher which memories were his and which were not. But this new symptom of Sally's is something I have never witnessed before.
She has developed a personality inside of her mind that she refers to as the burning lady. I would normally attribute this imaginary friend to the trauma Sally has undergone, but this is different. The burning lady tells Sally thing that she did not already know. Sally now knows names and places that she didn't before, all because the burning lady told her. I hypothesize that some of the implanted data has seeped into her consciousness and the burning lady is a fabrication that her mind concocted to process this information. More investigation will be needed.

Could that be how Sally knew me? Was Croxallé sending data about me and somehow it was leaking into her consciousness? I've kicked up shit before and was quite good at it. Croxallé would probably have a warning or two out about me or at least my fragile ego hoped. I tapped the next session.

This is beyond what I have ever expected. The burning lady is not Sally's fabrication, it is a second personality layered into her mind but how? Somebody tampered with the psychic implantation back in Texas but to what end? They put a new personality into Sally's mind - albeit not a full one, just enough to guide her. They didn't put the personality on top of the old one, replacing it or covering the original, they put it in the back of her mind to protect her, like a guard dog protecting a master's chair.

She has also started mentioning a cowboy in her dreams. At first I passed this off. She is a Texas girl stuck in the most anti-Texas place we could think of. Dreams of cowboys could just be her brain processing her longing for home. Now, however, I think differently. She's mentioning things that happened to a specific cowboy, like war and injury. Her dreams are set in the Civil War but this cowboy is beginning to sound familiar. It's beginning to sounds like someone from modern times.

Who is the burning lady and why was she sent to protect Sally? What is the child's importance? Who did this? Who had the ability? Worse still, the personality seems to be preventing the withdrawal of specific information. Key aspects of Project: Whydah are trapped within her mind. The company will not allow this. They need what is in her mind and they may have to take more intrusive or violent methods to extract it. I fear for the child's safety.

And I finally had some answers. I had a shit ton more questions but at least I had a couple of answers. There was information in her brain and Croxallé - and by extension the Visegar Company - wanted it out but somebody was stopping them. Who was fucking with Visegar on such a level? I mean, I am psychic but I'm a whole different type of psychic. This type of inserting and withdrawal of knowledge had to be some crazy red-headed level of psychic. Were they good like Oversight? Where they bad like Polaris? Or did I just stumble across the fourth faction?

In the meta conspiracy there were three factions. First

was Visegar. They were big, bad and loved doing experiments to force change. The second was Polaris Industries. They were strong and manipulative. Then there was Oversight. They were a government-esq operation that kept an eyes on the other two, doing their best to intervene when possible in order to keep the meta-secret hidden and protect the human populace. So who was Sally's guardian angel? I listened to the next message.

Supplemental Message: I received a call from the company. Sally has vanished. She departed from her foster care. A retrieval team is doing their best to find her. The team leader showed up at my office for information. He advised me of the situation and asked if could provide any additional insight. He asked where she would go to. I couldn't give him an answer. I'd like to think that she'd come to me but logic says otherwise.

I long for the moment that Sally comes to me for help outside the nature of our professional relationship. I long for the moment that she could feel secure enough to trust me. I don't believe foster care is the best option for her. Perhaps I could offer her more, for her as a child and, perhaps......

I dislike this retrieval team's leader. He has the same demeanour that most Ops agents do. He is rough and crass but this one has something different. He has a look about his face that shows great loss. It was like physical parts of him were ripped from his soul and he just became sour because of it. His name is Leo Anderson. While I suspect that he'd be an excellent case to study I hope never to see the man again.

Leo Anderson? My Leo Anderson? Shit. Corporal Leo Anderson was one of the four member team known as Odin Squad. We were a highly specialized Ranger unit that did the toughest of the tough missions overseas. The unit was dissolved midway through the war and we were shuffled to other units but no matter where we were, we were still Odin. So what the fuck was Leo doing with Croxallé? Jack's words came rushing back to me. Leo got out. He went private. He was now working for the enemy.

Crappity, crap baskets!

I grabbed my phone and dialed the number Jack gave me. The phone rang several times before Leo answered.

"Hello?"

"Leo, you old som-bitch," I said in a highly fake and overly eager tone. "How you been?"

"Ben?" Leo stuttered his response. He was surprised to hear from me. It was a fair reaction; I was literally doing the dumbest thing possible by calling him directly. "What up, Hop-a-long?"

"Not much. It's been a busy day stopping your team from kidnapping and torturing a teenage girl." I cut right to the chase. No time for bullshit. "How is your team?"

"Somehow they all survived."

"Yeah, that was accidental," I laughed. "So what the actual fuck are you doing trying to kidnap a teenage girl?"

"I'm doing my job," he replied. "What's your excuse for getting involved? Oh wait, is this another wacky *Ben doing the dumbest shit* moment?"

This was the mind game. Each of us was trying to rattle the other first. Leo forgot who he was dealing with. I was not going to be rattled, not now and not ever. I am Ben Thompson. I am unrattleable.

"Or is this a *womanizing Ben doing crazy things for a girl* bit?" Leo asked. "I didn't know you liked them that young."

"Fuck you."

Shit. He rattled me.

"I can't walk away when someone's in trouble, you know this," I sighed, "Especially when she's a teenage girl."

"You can't walk at all."

"Fuck you."

Shit. He double rattled me.

I am really bad at this game. I'm sorry for my earlier boasts. I don't know what I was talking about. I get rattled real easy. I get rattled when minute rice takes ninety seconds. I get rattled when Rocky get beat by Clubber Lang and I've literally seen the film eighty-seven times. I once got rattled by the sound of a literal rattle.

In my defense of the last example, the Army Bunny I was hooking up with pulled out a rattle and a pacifier during sex and started acting like a baby. It was off putting. Seriously, you can't just spring age-play on someone.

"Give me the girl," Anderson ordered. "She'll be okay. The company will take care of her. You have my word."

"Not going to happen," I said. "You'll just have to come to my home and get her."

"I don't know why Oversight thinks that you're important but they've labeled you as protected," Anderson revealed. "But just because I can't move against you at your home doesn't mean I can't drop you out in the field."

"I'd like to see you try," I mocked. Before I realized what I was doing I slipped into story. "Remember the time you and I were at one of the CIA's secret bases dropping off a prisoner and you tried to make time with the woman in the burqa but she turned out to be a dude in disguise and you let him into the base?"

"We doing stupid stories?" Leo asked. "Because that's a fight you can't win. I have more stupid Ben stories than almost anybody."

Shit, what was I doing? He was the enemy but I was talking to him like we were old friends. In truth, that's was what we were. We were old friends who had fought together in the past and now ended up on opposite sides of the battle.

"How are you, Ben?" Leo asked suddenly. His voice was less orderly and more sincere. "I've been hearing shit about you."

"I've had a rough go but I'm getting there," I admitted. "The office did a number on me but I got a new office now."

"All things aside, Ben, you're still my brother," Leo admitted. Rangers were always brothers until the very end. "I'm glad you're okay."

"Thanks, man."

"You got out of the game, you retired. Do yourself a favour and stay out before you get hurt."

Then he hung up.

"Your movies suck," Sally said abruptly. She stood before my DVD and Blue-ray collection looking at the physical copies I kept. I'll admit that most of my screen time came from Netflix and Hulu and the like but when it came to those special films, those films I adored more than any other, I bought them in the physical and displayed them with pride. "What is your obsession with this Stallone guy?"

"Sylvester Stallone?" I defended. "He's the greatest actor of all time." My eyes sparkled and I nervously played with my hair. It was at that moment I realized that I might have a crush on Stallone.

"You mean the guy from that *Spy Kids* movie and *Antz*?" She rolled her eyes. "A grown man shouldn't be into lame kids films."

My jaw hit the floor. Annie and Robby stared in a shocked silence as David burst out laughing. Alice laughed too but she really didn't get the joke. She was laughing at my jaw-dropped funny-face.

"He does more than kids films," I defended quickly, speaking a million words a minute. "He did *Rocky, First Blood, The Expendables* and--"

"*Rocky* is the boxing film, right?" I nodded eagerly, hoping we'd found mutual ground. "I never saw it."

That's it. I quit. I gave up, right there and then. The younger generation is damned. Oh god, I sound so old when I talk like that. Wait. I'm not old. I'm still hip. I'm lit, y'all. I'm lit.

As my mind broke in several places, while David laughed endlessly at my expense, Annie rolled her eyes. "Pick a film to watch. Just because we're not at home doesn't mean it's not movie night."

"*Smokey and the Bandit*!" Robby cried out.

"No, no, no." Annie put her foot down. "Ever since Ben showed you that movie it's been all you want to watch. I love me some Smokey but I need a rest, kiddo." Annie turned to Sally. "What's your favourite film?"

"I...I don't really have one," she muttered. "I like things like *School of Rock* and *Means Girls*."

"Both good picks," Annie said. "Which would you be in the mood for?"

"I...um." Sally's voice trailed off. She was still nervous around us. It made sense, she only knew us for a couple days. Everybody else in her life had either died or let her down. I understood why she had her shields up around us. She didn't want to get hurt again. "Can we watch something else?"

"Sure, whatcha thinking?"

"My mom used to watch her favourite film with me, over and over. I kinda miss that film. Can we watch it?"

"What is it?"

"*10 Things I Hate About You*."

I groaned, David groaned, Robby groaned and Alice said the words fwoosh over and over. Annie's eyes just sparkled. Annie would say her favourite films were things like *High Plains Drifter* or *Dirty Harry* because she was a farmer's daughter. She always wanted to be seen as rough and tough but deep down she was a girly-girl and we all knew it. Annie loved chick flicks like *Pretty in Pink* and *She's All That*. However, there were two films she adored above all others. *Empire Records* and *10 Things I Hate About You*. We had all seen *10 Things I Hate About You* seventy-three times. A patter of excitement bubbled across her face and into her voice.

"I love that film. I adore it. The boys won't watch it with me anymore."

A smile crept across Sally's face. Annie patted the space beside her with her hand, inviting Sally to sit beside her. The teenage girl hesitated at first but eventually agreed. We all sat down and began our seventy-fourth watch.

Chapter 15
Captain Well Endowed

A frantic bang on my bedroom door startled me awake. It was early in the morning. I looked around and found myself in my bedroom, topless but still in jeans. My phone was by my side on the bed. The last thing I remember was sitting on my bed, with my legs stretched out, glancing at my phone. I was staring at it hoping Puzo would respond to my goodnight texts. She hadn't. I fell asleep waiting.

Bang. Bang. Bang.

I leapt up and limped to my bedroom door. I pulled it opened and found a dressed Sally frantically staring at me. Tears were welled up in her eyes but they didn't dare roll down her face. Sally forbade it. She went to speak but her eyes went wide as she saw the smattering of unsightly scars that adorned my chest.

"Arcel," she said, quickly regaining her motivation. "He's in trouble."

She shoved her phone towards me. There were three imessages on the screen. The first was a message that simply said *come alone or he dies*. The second was a map location and the third was a small video. I tapped the screen and the video came to life. The camera panned across an empty room to fall on Marshal Arcel on his knees with his hands cuffed behind his back and the barrel of a gun pointed to his head.

"Tell her to come or you die," A latino voice said.

"Fuck that," Arcel spat. He looked up at the camera with a stern look. "Don't come, I'll be okay." A pistol slapped him across his face.

The video ended. I looked at Sally. The tears looked heavier than before but still they did not fall. Sally's strength was wavering but those tears would not fall. "Help him, Ben."

"How?"

"I'm going to save him."

"It's too dangerous," I protested.

"I don't care," Sally snapped. She looked at me with stern eyes. "I can't lose him. I'm going. Are you coming with me?"

There was a moment of silence but I eventually caved. There was no changing her mind. If I went with her then I could protect her. I grabbed a Rolling Stones shirt and quickly pulled it over my sweaty chest. I sighed. I didn't know what was going to kill me first, Sally or this heat wave. I reached under my bed and pulled out a shotgun lockbox. I kept two firearms inside the house. There was my trusty M9 and my American made Remington 870 shotgun. There was also a surprise under my back porch but that was technically *outside* the house, so there.

The M9 I could use without my gloves. It was a psychically clean weapon. My shotgun was not. If I touched it with my bare skin I was a greeted with an image of my own past, an image I had tried to forget. It was a time when I was so low and saw no way out but to Cobain. I don't ever want to see that image again. My shotgun was properly secured in a long lockbox that could only be opened with a six digit number. I knew the number and so did Annie. It was the date our mother had passed away. I lifted up the box and placed it squarely on the center of the bed. I wasn't going to take the shotgun with me; I was leaving it for David and Annie, just in case.

I grabbed my M9 and shoved as much ammo into my pockets as possible. I grabbed my phone and cursed. It was dead. I couldn't call for help. Fuck. I grabbed my keys, a lighter and my hat and limped to the door. Sally pulled on her jacket and reached into the pocket, withdrawing a pocket knife. It was an Ontario RAT pocket knife that folded in half. It had a 3.5 inch blade with a five inch pink grip. She flicked it open and checked it over before closing it and returning it to her pocket. She looked up at me.

"Pink?" I asked.

"Fuck you, pink is cool."

Our conversation ended there.

The Chevelle roared to life as we peeled out of the driveway. We only made it three blocks before a Crimson Silverado pick-up truck squealed to a halt before us, blocking our path. I slammed on the breaks. The truck door opened and Winnick emerged from within, his coyote brown P226 draw and pointed at me. My hand dropped to my M9, ready to draw it if need be.

"Where are you going with her, Ben?" He called out.

"We decided to get our hair done?" I suggested. There was literally no good answer to where I was going with a teenage girl at 3 am.

"I was promised a chinwag with her and now you're speeding off in the middle of the night." Drew shook his head. "That dog don't hunt, hoss."

"Arcel is being held hostage. They want Sally. We're going to help him," I said. "We could really use the back up."

"I ain't caring 'bout that," Drew scowled. For a moment he didn't move. It was like he was debating with himself. After a moment he lowered his gun, ashamed by his previous words. "I ain't about to let a lawman perish, either. What's the play, hoss?"

The address the cartel sent was an abandoned store front in a quiet neighbourhood. Above the building was an old forgotten sign that said *Pirates Rum*. There was a Moneymart on one side of it and a sketchy corner store on the end. Across the street was a low-end strip joint. We were in a classy neighbourhood.

"You sure about this?" I asked. Sally nodded. "Then let's do this."

Sally and I climbed out of the car and crossed the block and a half towards Pirates Rum. I saw two Latino men standing on the roof and one by the door. Each were wearing a large leather jacket which obviously hid their firearms. The man by the door spotted me and reached into his jacket. I already had my M9 drawn. I quickly raised it and pointed it at him. He froze.

"Hi, I'm here to drop my daughter off at a play date," I said in my best housewife voice. "Draw the gun with your left and toss it on the ground." The cartel man did as he was told and tossed down a pistol. I kicked it into an open sewer grate. "Now open the door for the lady like a good gentleman should."

The cartel man scowled as he opened the door. Sally flashed the man a nervous smile. "Much obliged."

"See, Sally. You should always date a gentleman," I said as we walked in. "If he won't open the door for you, who knows what else he won't do."

We entered the store. Abandoned shelves were everywhere and metal pegs hung from the wall. In the middle of the room was Arcel, on his knees. His mouth was gagged with a dirty rag. Several cartel men stood around him, each with a weapon drawn.

"Throw down the gun," one ordered. I shook my head.

"Nope, that ain't gonna happen." I called on every inch of swagger and confidence I had and I pushed it forward. I was going to need every ounce of Confident Ben to pull this off. I was going to have to drop to my knee and milk Confident Ben dry. Crap; phrasing. "How about each of you throw down your guns and surrender calmly."

Every man with a gun pointed it at me. I stepped in front of Sally. "If you shoot me, she runs out that door and vanishes. You'll never get her back, never. Now let Arcel go."

"Some would call this move of yours stupid," A new voice. A Spanish man emerged from the back room. He was better dressed then the goon. He had on an expensive shirt, had well kept hair and a charming smirk that rivaled my own. "I think it to be very brave, el vaquero."

"I don't know what that means," I said honestly. "I don't speak Spanish but I am assuming you just called me Captain Well Endowed."

"It means cowboy, idiot," Sally said with a sigh.

"You speak Spanish?"

"I was born and raised in Texas, of course I speak Spanish." I learned something new today and the sun wasn't even up yet.

"Well if you're so impressed then why don't you release the US Marshal and we can each go our own way."

"Is that a US Marshal?" The new man said with obviously fake surprise. His acting was horrible. He wasn't even trying to make his surprise seem realistic. "I learned of a situation and I am here to offer my skills."

"Who the fuck are you?"

"I am Ismael Salazar," he said with a smirk. "I am an upstanding member of the Latino community. My family and I are looking to expand our outreach programs to the suffering cities of your nation."

"You know that only works if you have something to offer the nation," I said. "Unless Mexico is hiding a super secret city of technology, then I ain't calling you T'Challa."

"As for what is occurring in this dwelling, I know nothing about it but I am offering my skills as a negotiator to bring this vile situation to a peaceful conclusion."

"I want the Marshal," I said quickly.

"And they want the girl," Ismael replied. "How about

we trade and then you can be on your way, el vaquero"

"No deal," I said. "In fact I was planning on double-crossing you."

"You were? That is very bold of you. How were you going to do that?"

"Well did you know in that the amount of flame needed to make a flame bright enough to blind everyone here for just a moment is staggeringly large? It would take the same amount of flame equal to 3000 lights from a cheap BIC lighter." I held up my now empty lighter and tossed it to Ismael. He caught it and glanced at the plastic lighter, confused. "I bet you wondering what this has to do with me betraying you."

"I am curious, el vaquero."

"Well the secret to my betrayal is the very girl you want." Sally's eyes glowed crimson as she raised her hands and I closed my eyes, tightly. Fire erupted from her palms with a burst of blinding light. Several screams of agony filled the air as the bright -albeit short - burst of light robbed them of their sight.

I opened my eyes and bolted towards the nearest goon and slammed my pistol into the side of his face. I heard a crack and the man dropped. The back door kicked opened as Drew marched in from behind. In his hand was a Remington 887 shotgun. The weapon roared loudly. He moved in from the rear just as the cartel men started to regain their vision. Drew dropped two men before they had a chance to fire back. The Ranger fired quickly as he bolted to the side and dove behind cover. Everybody scattered, trying to find one form of cover or another. Ismael bolted towards the nearest door.

"Go!" I yelled. Sally made for the front door as I bolted for Arcel. One goon moved to stop me but I dropped him with two rounds before he had the chance. I grabbed Arcel and pulled him to his feet. We moved to the door. My pistol rang out again and again as I fired behind me. Seeing that Arcel and I were safely away, Drew backed out from the same door he entered.

The attack was quick, it was dirty but it got the job

done. I pulled Arcel towards the Chevelle. In the distance I could see Sally standing beside my car, eagerly watching us approach. Suddenly two bright lights filled the night air as a pair of headlight flicked on. A van came to a screeching halt beside the Chevelle and the side door opened. Four men jumped out, four that I recognized: Rasputin, Billy Idol, Lt. Jerkface and Two-Pump.

Billy Idol and Two-Pump grabbed Sally. They lifted her up and tossed her into the van. Rasputin and Jerkface each raised a weapon towards Arcel and I. Time seemed to slow as I ran through my options.

I had none.

Fuck.

I limped toward the MoneyMart and fired twice into the pane glass window. Arcel and I jumped through the window and smashed through the glass just as Rasputin and Jerkface opened fire. Their bullets barely missed us as the glass shattered and fell all around us. An alarm filled the air as we hit the floor. I scrambled to my feet and peered out the window. The van sped off.

Fuck. That.

I climbed out of the MoneyMart and bolted for the Chevelle. I couldn't lose the van. If I did, then I lost Sally and possibly for good. I fired up the engine and slammed my foot on the gas. The tires squealed as the Chevelle shot forward. The van in front of me was getting away. It smoothly took a corner; I sped forward and tried to take it as well.

Driving is easy. Precision driving is not. I learned how to precision drive back in my ride or die days of the Rangers. I was never the best at it and worst still I hadn't kept up with it. I took the corner but sloppily. I slid across the street and collided with a trashcan, sending it flying. I gulped. Precision driving was not a bicycle. You didn't just get back up on it. You had to practice it. I had not. I was trying to be Vin Diesel but at this rate I was just going to end up like Paul Walker.

I needed help and I needed it quickly. I wasn't going to catch them with my skills alone. It wasn't that this car couldn't keep up, Jason built her with power. She was simply a viciously beast caged in my hands.

Jason.

I used to hate the guy but now I respected him. His life had not been easy. He had been a victim of a horrible system and was forced to wrong under Visegar's control. He died a hero and I'm not ashamed to say I missed the guy. The Chevelle was his. He gave it to me to look after until Robby was old enough and skilled enough to respect the car. Robby, Jason and Jason's father: it was a legacy car.

Suddenly it hit me. There was someone who could help me drive: Jason.

I awkwardly pulled off my gloves with my teeth and gripped the steering wheel. I felt my heart race and my chest heave as my breathing became laboured. I focused on the thought of losing Sally. The thought of having another friend die because of me. I felt fear, anxiety and nausea all building up. Then I let them overwhelm me.

This was a technique to super charge my powers. It was dangerous, especially when you hadn't properly named the ability something cool (Power: TBA is what I call it), but it granted me an unparalleled level of access to the past.

I felt like a boxer getting severely beaten in the ring. I was trapped in the corner, receiving blow after blow from my opponent. Each punch shattered my strength and weakened me. Each blow crippled me just a little more. Each strike caused my fear to rapidly grow. Fear and I have never been on good terms, I am Yankee to its Red Sox, but when I let it go unchecked it would became stronger than I ever imagined and go do something incredibly stupid like win the 2004 World Series. It was at that moment, when I felt like my body was about to shut-down, that's when I grabbed the shifter.

Every inch of my body shivered and every muscle and nerve twitched. I looked like I was having a seizure. It was like the past, present and future were all combined into my boxing opponent and I just gained Rocky strength. With all the power in my body I swung and connected with a powerful haymaker.

My vision was like a water slide and the waves were forcing me along. I could see the enclosed slide all around me, except the sides weren't made out of the same ugly orange material as the rest; they were made from fractured moments of the past. I saw the Chevelle being built, I saw Jason's father waxing the hood and I saw endless hours of Jason's driving it.

I don't know if words could explain what this moment felt like, or if there was anything in movie-references that could compare, but I felt like Barney Ross listening to Tool. Mickey Rourke is giving an epic speech about the death of a soul and Barney is standing there, being swallowed by a moment of pure truth.

The only names I've come up with for my ability, as lame as they sound, are the Clarity Channel, Psychic Passageway or Super Subway. None of those were any good, but whatever I decided to call this slide, it was giving me access to everything in every point in time for the Chevelle.

Amid the slide I saw what I wanted. I saw an image of myself currently driving the Chevelle and I saw a different image of Jason learning how to precision drive. In the past if I touched an image I would fall into that moment of the past. I would feel everything of that moment and be completely immersed. The only problem was I was essentially useless in the present while in the past. That would be insanely dangerous while driving. I would end up wrapping myself around a telephone pole Harrison Ford style but knowing my luck I would end up with more than just a rugged chin scar. I was left with only one option: try something very stupid

The Benedict Option

I reached out with both hands. With one I pressed the current image of me chasing after Sally and with the other I touched an image of Jason learning how to precision drive. Suddenly I was there, between two points of time. I wasn't some cosmic voyeur watching the past; I was actually Jason participating in it. I felt what he felt. I saw what he saw. I vomited what ---- you get the idea -- all while still driving the

Chevelle.

We were behind the wheel as Jason's father - our father - taught us. His name was Roy Daggett. I had fallen into a father-son moment and I felt the joy teenage Jason felt as we learned how to properly drive.

We kept one hand on the wheel and the other on the shifter. Roy shook his head. "Keep your hands on the wheel, boy. You can't feel a car if your hands ain't on her. Don't grip the shifter until you are absolutely ready." Roy ran his hand over the dashboard. "There ain't nothing more important when you drive a car than to listen to the girl. She will speak to you through that wheel. You just have to learn how to listen."

I took my hand off the shifter. I gripped the wheel with both hands and tried to pay attention. I needed the beast that was the Chevelle but she didn't want me. I wasn't worthy of her.

We slammed the shifter into third gear as we sped up. Roy rolled his eyes. "This is a car, not a hammer. Treat her like a woman and be gentle with her." Roy suddenly let out a wicked smirk. "Unless she likes it rough like your momma."

We cringed at that.

I shifted gently into third as the Chevelle reached 30 mph. I spotted the van in the distance. It took another corner. I pressed the accelerator further down and quickly shifted into fourth. With each move I did I could feel the experience of Jason flowing into me.

"Pay attention, boy," Roy said sternly. "You're going to learn to take a corner. This is called the Heel-Tow Downshift." We looked up and eagerly listened. "You'll be steering with the left hand, shifting with the right hand, clutching with the left foot, and working both the brake and gas pedals with the right foot -- all at exactly the same time."

We stared in shock. How was that even possible? Attempt after attempt flashed before my eyes. I got a montage of experiences. We tried the maneuver over and over as the theme from Rocky played in the background. This was our montage. This was our Apollo training Rocky to fight Clubber Lang moment. With each attempt, we got a little better at the Heel-Toe Downshift until eventually we did it, until we mastered it. Roy glanced at Jason and gave him an appreciative nod. It was a Dad moment, silent and still. In Rocky terms, it was the hugging in the water moment.

I lifted my right foot from the gas pedal and pressed the brake. Just before the braking was done, my left foot depressed the clutch and my right hand began to the downshift. My right foot eased up on the brake as the car approached the turn-in. I rotated my foot so the heel was above the corner of the gas pedal. As I shifted through neutral my right heel revved the engine quickly with a push of the gas. As my left foot released the clutch, the right foot rotated off the gas as it completed the braking with a smooth release. Not one to stay in one place, my right foot leapt to the gas pedal as I sped around the corner, gradually applying pressure to accelerate myself out of the turn. I had just successfully done the Heel-Toe Downshift and the entire move took just over half a second.

The Chevelle roared in my hands. The beast was finally being freed and I could hear her purr through the wheel. I could feel her and she was ready to play.

I shifted back into second and then into third. The beast dashed forward. We saw the van and quickly closed in on it. We pulled alongside the van

"There ain't nothing worse in racing than a man who can't accept he's lost. When someone has bested you and is passing you, you let them," Roy said sternly. "But if some worm won't let you pass and is risking your life because of it, you take that som-bitch down and run him off the road. Driving is about looking out for yourself above all else."

The van swerved to left, trying to run me off. I steered to the left to avoid him. The van retreated back to the right before veering to the left to strike me one more time. The Chevelle roared and I heard her, loud and clear. We were taking this asshole down. I slammed down on the gas, shifted to fourth and with a burst of unmatched power, the beast shot forward. We quickly passed the van but the beast was not satisfied. She was insulted. How dare this van try to strike her? How dare this van think it could compare to her? She wanted revenge. She wanted to teach the van a lesson.

We swerved towards van and cut it off. The driver panicked and jerked the wheel to the right. The van swerved to the right and crashed into the side of a building. I slammed the breakes and slid into a sexy sliding halt. The beast roared once more.

The beast was satisfied.

"There is one lesson above all else that you have to know about racing." The words started coming from Roy but eventually they morphed into our words. Reality blinked and we were no longer behind the wheel. We were in the passenger seat, where Roy once sat, and in our place was an older Robby. We were imagining teaching Robby in the same fashion as we had. "Respect the car. She is useless without you and you without her but mistreat her and she will mistreat you. You and her are one."

Chapter 16
She'll Live Her Life Like Superman

Reality returned to normal as I climbed out of the car. My M9 was drawn and I was not holding back. I limped forward, keeping my finger on the trigger and my barrel aimed at the car. I was ready to kill.

"Sally!" I yelled. Confident Ben was gone. This was Angry Ben. I was tired, I was sore and I was really done with the whole getting shot at thing. Enough was enough. "Sally!"

I heard a door open and saw Rasputin climb out. I fired twice and put two rounds into his chest. Rasputin fell backward and crashed into the ground. I heard a groan, he was wearing a vest, but he was still down for the count. I glanced at the driver's seat and saw Chicken-Head seated behind it. His hand slowly moved to the gun on his vest. I aimed at the window and fired through the glass. He stopped and raised both hands into the air. I saw Jerkface stick his head out from behind the car and I popped a shot off at him. He ducked back as my 9mm round dinged off of the van's side.

"Let her go!" I ordered. How did Visegar find us? I forced the question out of my mind. I was here to save Sally and nobody was getting in my way.

Two-Pump stepped out of the van with Sally in his right arm and a gun in the left - his weak hand. He was still feeling the effects of Winnick's earlier shot. I glared at him. We'd already done this dance. It didn't go well the first time and it wasn't going to go any better this time.

"Don't move or I'll shoot her," Two-Pump called out. He pressed the gun to her head.

"You can't kill her, you need her," I replied.

"I need her alive," he smirked. He pressed the gun against the middle of her spine. "I can make sure she never walks again." He moved the gun higher up her back. "I pull the trigger here and she can't use her arms." He moved the gun to the top of the spine. "Here and she'll live the rest of her life like Superman did. I have to make sure she's alive, I don't have to keep her from harm."

Red flared up in me. I wanted to make him suffer. I wanted to kill him but I couldn't. I didn't have the shot. Sally, however, wasn't going to let this slide. She slowly dropped her left hand to her jacket and reached into her pocket. I tightened my grip on my pistol. I'd only have one shot at this.

Sally pulled the pink knife from her pocket and stabbed it backwards into Two-Pump's leg. Two-Pump screamed but Sally didn't let up. She slammed her left elbow upwards into the side of Two-Pump's face. She wriggled out of his grip and bolted towards me. The girl was good, very good. Two-Pump fell to one knee but his gun never dropped. He raised it towards Sally and readied his shot. Time seemed to slow as fear crossed my eyes. He was going to shoot Sally in the back. I tried to line up a shot but Sally was running directly at me. She was blocking my shot. There was nothing I could do to stop Two-Pump.

Gunfire.

Sally ran into my arms and I held her tight. I expected this to be a goodbye hug, the last thing we did together before she bled out in my arms. But Sally didn't fall. She was okay. I looked past her and saw Two-Pump on the ground, the gun missing from his hand.

"Again? What the fuck?" I looked in the distance and saw Drew Winnick. I blinked. He did it again, he shot a gun from a bad-dude's hand but he did it from almost a block away. Who the fuck was this Ranger?

Drew stood beside Jeff and both had guns out. They opened fire on the van. I grabbed Sally and pulled her towards the Chevelle. "Run."

"No shit," she yelled.

I heard the Visegar men scramble as we bolted across the street. Some were grabbing guns and firing back. Others were scrambling to get out of there but one did something different. Chicken-Head leapt from the van and chased after us. He paused as he raised the weapon in his hand. It wasn't a pistol but it was a taser. He fired and two electrodes slammed into Sally's back. Electricity ran through her body, up her hand and into mine. We both twitched and screamed as we got a powerful zap but the pain lasted only a second. Sally released my hand and stood still. She allowed the electricity to flow into her. She was absorbing it. I glanced at her eyes. They weren't crimson like when she absorbed fire. They had a canary glow. She turned around and faced Chicken-Head.

"No, not again. Not again." Frantic fear echoed through her voice. I scrambled to my feet. My powers were based on emotion. Blasters were the same. The strength of the element that they conjured was based on the emotions they had: the stronger the emotion, the stronger the blast. For fire the emotion was rage. For electricity it was fear. Sally was afraid, she was frantic and her mind was all over the place. She couldn't focus, she couldn't calm herself. She was just afraid.

She thrust her palms outwards and fired a large blast of electricity. It collided with Chicken-Head's chest and sent him flying backwards, crashing into the van. Everybody paused and looked at her. Arcs of electricity leapt across her body as bolts fired from each finger. Sally fired into a transformer and caused it to explode. The block fell into darkness as lights instantly shut off. Sally let off another big blast into the air, causing a loud thunderous sound to echo outwards, before falling to the ground. I grabbed her and held her close. I raised my gun towards Jerkface and his crew but nobody moved forward. Suddenly, I heard the sound of a new van approaching from the rear. I looked behind me only to see a canister bouncing along the street. I recognized the canister. It was a flash bang grenade. I rolled atop of Sally, hoping to protect her, and covered my eyes.

The flash bang went off. Even with my eyes closed, the noise was enough to disorientate me. I lay atop of Sally, not moving. I lay there for several minutes before my hearing returned. Looking up, I saw the street we were on was nearly empty. Drew and Jeff lay in the distance, on the ground slowly recovering. The original van was on the street, abandoned, but the Visegar goons were nowhere to be seen. The second van was their extraction team. Visegar had fled.

I rolled off of Sally, fighting for balance, and saw her shaking and convulsing. She looked at me with worried eyes and cried out. "I don't feel well, Ben."

Sally was having a seizure.

I needed help and I needed it quickly. I knew the one person who could help me but it was a risky idea. It was a dumb idea but it was my only option.

The Benedict Option.

Fifteen minutes later the three of us were standing at the doorway of Doctor Christine Hammett, a Croxallé doctor. She opened the door, groggy and tired. She looked at me, confused and with a taser in her hand. "Ben, what are you doing here?"

"I need your help," I said as I pushed my way in.

I sat in a very pink living room staring at pictures of fields of flowers and rocky coasts. This was literally the pinkest room I have ever set foot in. The walls were pink, the furniture was a lighter pink and the shelves and picture frames were a third, different pink. I was told later that the walls were *rose*, the furniture was *pink lemonade* and the shelves and picture frames were *ballet slipper* but that all sounded like fancy words to say the same thing.

Jeff and Drew sat in the room beside me. There was an awkward silence as we waited. Drew was on his phone and I was busy losing myself in a sea of pink. A sea of pink was better than a red river or was that what they called it when it tapered off? Jeff looked at us both before speaking.

"I owe each of you a big thanks," he said. "I didn't want you to bring Sally but thanks for getting me out of there."

"From what I hear it, be the girl you best be thanking," Drew said. Jeff looked to me and I nodded. "She's a bit of a spitfire that one or should I be calling her a bundle of energy instead?"

Electricity humour; what a shock.

"Yeah, I kinda have a couple questions about that as well," Jeff said. They both looked at me. I blinked and feigned surprise.

"Oh...right. Yeah....Wow. She fires electricity. That is.....wow.....colour me shocked." I am very bad at lying.

"Spill, hoss."

I sighed. This was going to be twice in twenty-four hours. This was way beyond my limit for reading people into a global conspiracy. I told them about the Lycotta gene, I told them about powers, I told them about Visegar and Polaris and I used small words the entire time. The small words were not for the benefit of Jeff and Drew. It was for me. I am not a smart man.

Silence.

Jeff let out a low whistle. Drew shook his head.

"Every inch of me says that ain't true," Drew began, "but I just seen what the lass did with my own two eyes. I'm going label myself as conflicted. That would explain all the flame at the bus station."

"Psychics and electric girls," Jeff said. "What else is there?"

"I've seen invisible men, eye-lasers, super healers, telekenetics and a shape-shifters," I said. "I don't know what the limit is."

"And Visegar, one of the people that want Sally, put data into her head and now want it out?" I nodded. "And who is this Doc?"

"Christine? She's a friend. She specializes in people like me."

"So how did Visegar even find us, earlier?" Jeff asked.

"I've been wondering that myself," I said slowly. "Pretty much everybody who knew where we were is in this room right now."

"Pick your words carefully, hoss," Drew said. "We all just threw down together and I'm just starting to like y'all. I ain't ready to be tussling."

"That's what bothers me," I said. "None of us has a motive. Jeff doesn't want Sally in the hands of Visegar. He needs her alive to testify. Drew doesn't want Sally in their hands either or he's never going to find out more about the death of his girlfriend."

"Fiancée," Drew quickly corrected.

"So you're saying that this just leaves you?" Jeff asked. I paused. Was I the mole? Was I the bad guy and I didn't know it? Visegar did have the ability to plant a personality and knowledge in a person's head. Did they do that to me? Was this a *the call is coming from inside the house* kind of deal where the house is my brain?

If my brain was a house, it would be a massively expensive house - with lots of open space - that was in a shitty neighbourhood. Every other building was run down and busted like the leg, the chest and the liver. This was a really bad neighbourhood. Wait, in this metaphor was my ass the crack house?

"It ain't you, hoss," Drew said. "I ain't ever seen someone that wants to protect a girl he barely even knew."

"Either way, at least we're safe here. There's no way they could find us here." I nervously bit my lip. Jeff raised an eyebrow. "Ben?"

"She.....kinda works for Croxallé," I admitted.

"And Croxallé is owned by Visegar?" Jeff asked. I

nodded. Jeff fucking lost it. "What the actual hell, Ben? Are you a fucking moron? What are you doing bringing her here?"

"She's different," I snapped. God, I hope she was different. "Where else am I going to go? Sally's fucking dying or some shit and we can't go to a regular doctor."

"But she's one of them," Jeff yelled.

"But she's a doctor first. She's not going to let a fifteen year old girl die," I defended. "We make sure Sally's alive then we worry about her being safe."

"You three need to shut the fuck up," a new voice snapped. I looked up to see a very pissed off Christine standing in the doorway. "A) I have neighbours. B) It's not even 5 am yet and C) Sally is fucking asleep."

The three of us quickly let out a unison *yes ma'am* and zipped our lips. We may be dumb cowboys but we ain't that dumb to go arguing with a pissed off woman. Doctor Christine Hammett was roughly my age with skin that I could only describe as mocha coloured. She had bouncy brown hair, with blonde highlights, and brown eyes. She wore fuzzy pink PJ pants with a rose coloured tank top and she had a stethoscope hanging around her neck. She sat in a chair across from us and took in a deep breath.

"The girl is going to be okay," Christine began. "She was not having a seizure but she was undergoing some serious convulsions. I gave her a sedative and some meds for the pain."

"You keep that stuff at your house?" Jeff suspiciously asked.

"Croxallé doctors are ready to help at a moment's notice to do house calls or whatnot," Christine revealed. It was an official way of saying any of them could be called upon to quietly remove a bullet or whatnot for any of Visegar's black ops.

"What's wrong with her?" I asked, getting right to the point. I wasn't a cop. I didn't have to care about cop shit.

"Her body was having a metaphysical adaptive incident." I nodded. I didn't have a clue what she was talking about but I still nodded. Christine let out a small chuckle.

"Her body absorbed a lot of electricity. It's trying to adapt but it's struggling. It's going to be rough for her for the next couple hours but she'll pull through."

"Thanks, I owe you." Christine looked at the bedroom door and back to me.

"She's Sally Condon, isn't she?" I sheepishly nodded. Christine fucking lost it. "What the actual hell, Ben? Are you a fucking moron? What are you doing bringing her here?"

I glanced at Jeff. He gave me a cocky *I told you so* smirk.

"Every Visegar Ops is on the hunt for her," she snapped. "They told us if anybody knows anything and doesn't say something that they will come and literally burn my house down and since they switched the definition of literally to match figuratively, I don't even know if they're being clever or threatening. Why, Ben, why bring her here?"

"When you gave me your number you told me if it was serious that you'd help me. Not Croxallé; you. This was serious." Christine frowned. "She's fifteen. She's scared, she's tired and she's lost everyone. What the fuck was I going to do?"

Christine let out a sigh and nodded. I relaxed. "I'll hold off calling them until after Sally wakes up but after that you're on your own."

"Thanks," We smiled at each other. I looked around at her living room. "So what the deal with you and pink?"

"Fuck you, pink is cool."

"I need an answer, hoss," Drew said as the three of us waited. "I understand how the law works, it ain't my first rodeo, but we be kin now. So I need an honest answer. Who killed my Alexia?"

Jeff and I looked at each other. This was the elephant

we had been avoiding. I shrugged and passed the buck to the Marshal. It wasn't my secret to reveal. Jeff sighed and conveyed the truth to Drew. To his credit, Drew didn't overreact. He simply sat there, silent. Even when he found out that Ismael had been in the very same room as him and he didn't take the shot, he kept calm.

"Ismael Salazar," Drew said. He repeated the name over and over. I expected some Arnie rage fit and then he'd smash everything but Drew wasn't like that. Instead he did the one thing I did not expect. He started crying. It wasn't a slow start, it was like when the dark clouds above you suddenly rip open and dump a literal fuck ton of rain upon you.

"For nearly a year I have had the mystery of her death hanging over me," he sobbed. "I ain't even know who killed her. She was just another unsolved murder and I failed her. It was the burr in my saddle and the thorn in my side. It just ate at me, day in and day out. My fiancée was dead and I ain't done nothing to make it right but now I know. Now I have a name.

"She was the love of my life, that one. She was DEA and I was a Ranger, it was gonna be a right hassle but she didn't care and neither did I. Nothing of our union was going to be easy, not in Texas, but I still put on my Sunday best, my whitest hat and showed up at her door mounted on a horse. We rode out for hours before I stopped and dropped to one knee. The day she said yes was the happiest this cow-polk ever had."

"I....I'm sorry," Jeff said. "But I need Ismael alive. I can't let you end him."

"I know that. Rangers ride with honour, boy. I ain't about to end that streak on my own." He paused as he stoically wiped the tears from his eyes. "Alexis wanted nothing more than for the cartels to fall. She ain't the type of girl who wanted revenge and I ain't gonna taint her memory by killin' when an arrest can do more good."

"How did you meet?" I asked. I knew what it was like to lose the woman you love. I knew how talking about the good made the bad fade from memory. I also knew how drinking helped ease the pain but somehow I doubted Christine wanted us breaking into her liquor cabinet after we'd just broken into her house.

"I arrested her," Drew said with a laugh. "She was buying drugs and I arrested her. Turns out I busted up an undercover op. She exploded at me in anger. She was some federal dog and expected me to whimper away. I ain't the whimpering kind. I yelled back, we got to fighting and somehow we ended up in bed together. It kinda went from there."

Drew let out a sigh. His body was tired, his mind was tired and he was now emotionally drained, but somehow he looked relieved.

I crashed on the pink couch - sorry the *pink lemonade* couch - while Sally slept. Or at least I tried to sleep. I drifted in and out but didn't stay asleep for long. It was hard to sleep when I kept thinking about Sally in pain. I kept thinking about her life. I didn't ask to be a protector, I didn't want a kid in my life yet, but here she was. She was eager for my help, she was literally begging for it. I was happy to help but what happened later? What happened when all this came to an end? Was I going to be forced to say goodbye to Sally and watch her vanish in the Witsec system? Was I okay with that?

"Beeeenn." Sally's voice called out from Christine's spare bedroom. I limped over and entered the room, ignoring the pain that shot through my leg. I froze. Five seconds ago I thought the definition of *too pink* was Christine's living room. I was wrong. The definition of *too pink* was clearly the spare bedroom. The bed sheets were watermelon pink, the walls were bubblegum pink and the walls were decorated with unicorns. I was speechless.

"Ben," Sally groaned. I snapped out of my silent judgement and looked to the bed. Sally was sprawled out on the bed, clearly asleep but twitching and tossing. I limped over to her and sat on the side of the bed. I reached over and gently brushed the hair from her face. "Ben."

"I'm here, kiddo," I whispered. Sally suddenly sat up like she was WWE's Kane. I stumbled back. She turned her head towards me and stared with empty eyes. I was wrong. This wasn't Kane. This was Regan MacNeil, the girl from the *Exorcist*. I fought the fear and decided not to draw my M9.

"Ben," she said. The voice was clearly Sally's but it sounded different. "I need your help, Ben. I need you to protect me."

"I am, Sally," I admitted. "I'm here for you."

"I miss you, Ben."

"I didn't go anywhere," I said.

"I love you, Bright Eyes." Sally then fell back to the bed, still asleep.

Zoey.

I stammered for a second and tried to speak but nothing came out. I just stared at Sally. The teenage girl slept soundly now, no longer twitching or tossing. What the fuck just happened? Had that been Zoey, how?

The answer hit me: the second personality. Doc Balzary talked about the personality in her brain that protected her and prevented Visegar from withdrawing the remaining intel. Was that personality Zoey's? This circled back to my theory of a fourth faction, someone that didn't want Project: Whydah to see the light of day. But how did they have access to Zoey and Sally?

Van Cleef, the evil cowboy from my Zoey vision. It had taken me longer to piece together the name than I am comfortable with admitting. He was naming himself after actor Lee Van Cleef. The actor had been in dozens of movies but only one was important to the situation. Van Cleef was referring the single greatest western ever: The Good, the Bad and the Ugly.

Zoey's *true* cowboy - me - was Clint Eastwood, the Man with No Name. I was the Good.

Zoey's *other* cowboy was saying he was Lee Van Cleef, Angel Eyes. He was the Bad.

This left the all important question. Who was the Ugly?

I left the spare bedroom and returned to the living room. I glanced at the clock. It was 6:30 am. I plopped down on the couch and ran my hands through my hair. Arcel and Winnick had already left. Christine walked into the living room and plopped down beside me.

"You look like shit," she said.

"Thanks, Doc," I laughed. I let out a long yawn. "What do you know about psychic implantation?"

Christine's eyes narrowed as she looked at me. A look of concern and worry crossed her lips. "What do you mean?"

"I've come across it during my investigation and some of it doesn't make sense to me." I laughed. None of it made sense to me. "I've learned that people can have personalities put ontop of them."

"It's more than that," Christine explained. "They can put one person's skills, their knowledge and their personality onto another."

"And what, you walk around knowing you have a second person's mind in yours?" I asked. Christine shook her head.

"In some cases, yes; you can know there is someone else there but in most cases its nothing like that." She paused as she tried to come up with an example. "Let's say I'm Judy McFakename. I'm a high school dropout who works at a Wendy's. Visegar can go and take all the memories of Doctor Christine Hammett and put it into Judy. Now Judy isn't just walking around with a second personality, Judy thinks that she is Doctor Christine Hammett. Judy now knows everything Christine did in medical school. She remembers those long school nights, she remembers crushing on a professor and she remembers the feeling of relief when it all ended. Judy has every memory that Christine does. When Judy's lonely at night, she even closes her eyes and fondly thinks back to a wild night Christine spent in Mexico during spring break. Judy doesn't think like Christine, Judy is Christine and worse still, Christine doesn't know she's really Judy."

Silence.

"So what happened in Mexico?" I asked, suddenly distracted. Christine gave me a teasing smirk.

"What exposure do you have with psychic implantation?"

"Sally might have part of a personality in her brain," I said and shook my head. "They put intel into her mind and when they tried to get it back out, they found a partial personality protecting both her and the information."

Christine let out a low whistle. She glanced back at the bedroom.

"What is going to happen with her body adapting to the electricity?" I asked.

"Without my lab it is impossible to tell," Christine said. "But it looks like she reached her limit of energy absorption and blew past it. Her body is trying to hold more, to get stronger, but it's struggling. With physiologies like hers, it's difficult to predict what will happen. I've seen one guy who took electricity and turned it into speed. I saw a fire guy who ate too much flame and burned up from the inside. Sally isn't showing any negative symptoms but I still don't know what will happen."

"Do you always answer the door with a taser?" I asked. My mind was dead tired and was jumping all over the place. Christine, thankfully, just laughed.

"Only when someone slams on my door at 3 am," she smirked. "I live alone. I have to look out for myself."

My chuckle was cut short as another jolt of pain shot up my leg. Christine glanced at my wince with a look of concern. I shook her off. "If I put strain on my leg too much it fights back."

I put my leg through a lot this evening without my cane. It was definitely arguing with that decision. Christine walked away and returned a few moments later with a pair of pills and a glass of water.

"This is low grade stuff. It'll help you get through the morning but you need to lay off the leg, Ben."

"Thanks, Doc," I said as I downed the pills. "My Lazy-boy chair is calling me and I want nothing more than to sit down and relax. I'm really tired of this *True Lies* shit."

When I awoke next, I found myself back on the couch. My M9 was on a coffee table across the room from me. I had placed it there, safely out of reach, instead of trying to sleep with it on my side. In the distance I heard the sound of talking and eating. I climbed to my feet and limped to the kitchen. My leg winced with each step. I needed my cane. I had pushed my leg to its limits. It needed rest.

Christine and Sally sat at a kitchen table. Each were eating cereal from a bowl and surprise, surprise, the bowls were coloured pink. Between them lay Christine's taser. Why she hadn't put it away, I didn't know but I wasn't going to further question the woman who saved our bacon last night. Instead, I smiled at Sally. I was happy to see her up and about.

"Hey, kiddo," I said as I took a seat. "How you feeling?"

Sally just shrugged. I nodded. Sally grinned. I smirked. We didn't use words but we had just spoken volumes. It was a new form of wordless speaking.

Shrug: I'm okay. I feel better. I was really scared both in the van and on during the night. I wouldn't have made it through either event if it weren't for you. Thank you, Ben. You mean a lot to me.

Nod: I know, Kid. I was glad to do it. I'm here if you ever need me. In the few days since we met you have grown to be very special to me. I'm glad you're okay.

Grin: Did you know you can save hundreds of dollars

by switching to Geico?

Smirk: What, hundreds of dollars? You must be jesting. Wait, are we talking real dollars or Canadian dollars because I am not falling for that scam again.

Our own personal language wasn't perfect yet.

A knock at the front door pulled Christine away from the table. She returned a few moments later with Jeff and Drew. The cowboy trio was reunited once more.

"I feel very weird with three cowboys in my house at once," Christine said. She bit back an impish grin. "It kinda reminds me of Mexico."

I wanted to ask more but my phone buzzed. I glanced down and saw a text from Hotwire. Christine lent me a cord to charge my phone. It wasn't fully charged but it was enough for now. I glanced up at Jeff as he plopped beside Sally and started asking her a few questions. Drew leaned by the wall, standing all stoic and cowboy-esq. I was envious of that stance. I could never pull it off. I'm too fidgety. I glance back at my phone.

Hotwire: Just finished going through the doctor's iPad. Not much there. Just a couple follow up with a new patient called Michael Fletch.
Hotwire: Actually he's had several appointments recently including an emergency one about a week ago.
Me: Crap. Another dead end; thanks tho.
Hotwire: Still going through his cloud. Will update later.
Me: Ten Four good buddy.
Hotwire: So a downtown shootout and massive power outage occurred last night. What are the odds you were involved?
Me: I would have definitely put money down that I was.
Hotwire: Damn dude, what did you get into?
Me: It was nothing I couldn't handle. Winnick, Arcel

and I just fought Visegar.

Me: Spoiler: We won!

Hotwire: WTF Ben?!?!? You can't just go running into trouble.

Me: I didn't. I hobbled into trouble.

Hotwire: .....

Hotwire: At least you brought backup this time.

Me: Hell yeah and holy hell. Watching Drew shoot is amazing. That Texas Ranger is almost as big of a bad ass as an Army Ranger.

Hotwire: Yeah that girl can shoot.

Me: HAHAHAHA Autocorrect hates you!

Hotwire: What are you talking about?

Me: You called Drew a girl, again!

Me: Mr. Big Tech guy is beaten by autocorrect, again!

Hotwire: ......

Hotwire: WTF are you talking about?

Me: You called Drew a girl

Hotwire: She is a girl.

Me: No, Drew Winnick.

Hotwire: Drew Winnick is a girl.

Me: Texas Ranger Drew Winnick is not a girl.

Hotwire: Texas Ranger Drew Winnick is totally a girl.

Me: ......

Me: WTF are you talking about?

My phone beeped as Hotwire send a PDF file. I opened it up and stared at the file. It was the career record of Texas Ranger Drew Winnick and the face staring back at me was not the one I expected. I wasn't looking at the older, tired eyed Drew that I was used to seeing. I was looking at the face of a woman. She was younger, skilled and kind of looked like Emily Blunt in Sicario. What the actual fuck was going on? If this cowboy wasn't Drew Winnick, then who the fuck was he? I covertly snapped a pic of Faux-Winnick and fired it off.

Me: This is who I have been dealing with. WTF?
Hotwire: I don't know man but that ain't Winnick. I've checked and double-checked. Winnick is kind of a big deal in Texas. She's the first LGBT+ Texas Ranger and she's a crack shot to boot. She's big news there.

I looked up and stared at Winnick. If he wasn't a Ranger, then who was he?

Chapter 17
Punch Him in the Schnoz

Psychic implantation: the words ran over and over in my head. This wasn't Winnick, this was somebody else. This was what Christine was talking about. This man was walking around thinking he was she. But why would anybody put a girl Ranger into a boy Ranger? All it would take would be someone to look at her file and then she'd be exposed. If someone like me would go and look then......then..... Crap. I didn't bother to look at her file. I got Hotwire to summarize it for me.

My foes may know me way to well.

I had to be sure though. I had to find a way to confirm that he wasn't actually faux-she. I glanced at the phone and scanned for information. Sally looked at me with a concerned look. I showed her my phone. Her eyes went wide but she went silent.

"Drew." He looked at me. "How old were you when you won your first shooting contest?"

"I was fourteen. I won a long gun shoot," he said without hesitation.

"What did your Dad say when you won?"

"He was proud. He gushed and bragged for days." Drew narrowed his eyes. He gave me a suspicious glance. "What's this about, hoss?"

"Who was your first kiss?" Sally asked.

"Her name was Jenny Essiambre," Drew answered. "My Pa ain't too proud of me when he saw that. I assumed it was because he never did like the Essiambre family. What the hell are y'all asking for?"

"This is important," I said. "There is something going on but I need you to answer these questions for me."

"What's your favorite gun?"

"It's my Pa's classic Colt Peacemaker."

"Who's your favourite cowboy?"

"Sam Elliot." It wasn't Clint but I couldn't hate that answer. I love me some *Tombstone* and I love me some *The Ranch*.

"Favourite movie?" I asked, running out of ideas. Facts were proving useless.

"*City Slickers*." Drew shrugged. "I like city folk acting stupid."

I paused. I had just seen Drew cry over his dead fiancée. There was no faking that. He actually thought he was Drew. I needed something bigger to trip him up. I needed something deeper, something unforgettable that would rock his world.

"How old were you when you had your first period?" Sally asked.

"I was twelve," Drew responded quickly. He paused, suddenly confused. "Wait, I'm a guy but....I....what?"

His mind snapped and he fell to the ground. I leapt up from my seat and tried to bolt towards him but Drew quickly drew his pistol. He aimed it at me, keeping me frozen in place.

"Shit, he's cracking," Christine said. I glanced at her in confusion. "The personality in his mind just broke. His brain is trying to piece stuff together. His failsafe instructions will be kicking in right about now."

"Nobody moves," Drew said as he climbed to his feet. His demeanor had shifted and his stance had changed. I eyed Jeff. The Marshal nodded. We could rush him. "Don't even think about it, hoss. I could plug both of you before y'all took your first step."

I had seen Faux-Drew shoot. I knew he could do it. He dug a phone from his pocket and dialed. He spoke softly into the receiver for a few moments before hanging up. I watched as Drew stood there. The gun shook slightly in his hand. It suddenly made sense. It wasn't a trauma thing; it was a muscle memory thing. You could be taught the proper ways to shoot but good shooting came from hundreds of hours of practise and with that came muscle memory. Faux-Drew had the skills of Real-Drew but he didn't have her muscle memory.

"Drew, You---" I started. He glared at me and I shut up. My mind raced. Somebody here needed to do some quick thinking and make with the smarts. Sadly, all I had was me. Why would somebody send another cowboy into my presence? What was the point? Who was Drew, really?

We stood in silence for several minutes before Christine's door opened. Leo Anderson walked in. He locked eyes with me and shook his head. "I told you to stay out, Ben."

"What are you going to do, shoot me?" I taunted. "You can't shoot me and you know it. Once a Ranger, always a Ranger."

To be honest I had no clue if he would shoot me or not. I was bluffing my ass off. This was my *push all my chips in against John Malkovich* moment; anything to stay alive.

Leo looked nearly identical to his younger days with his military cut dark hair and piercing green eyes but a look of pain sat on his face. It was a look that reminded me of Jason. The man always seemed to carry pain on his face except when he was dating Annie.

"I don't have to shoot you to hurt you," Leo snarled. He glanced at Drew. "Good work. We'll get you sorted out."

My brain raced. I was confused as hell. Faux-Drew was working for Visegar but why would they send a cowboy? Why would they send somebody at all? Why not just hide in the shadows? I mean a cowboy was just going to catch my attention. If I saw a cowboy I was going to focus on it especially if they were a Texas Ranger. I love *Walker, Texas Ranger*. So

I actually met a RL Ranger I'd be so focused on his job that I would..... I would.....I would ignore everything else.

God, damn it!

I hate the fact that my enemies are using my love of TV against me. I swear if the next thing Visegar does is to hire Sylvester Stallone to kill me, I won't be overly surprised. I'll be star struck and probably dead, but not surprised.

As if by magic, the hamster that powers my brain started moving. It was hard work because that hamster is hella fat and normally doesn't have to do much but when he did start running in the hamster wheel, that's when the brain really starts kicking in. With a determined squeak, my brain shifted into gear and I started to piece shit together.

Visegar was watching Sally back in Chicago. They were using Doc Balzary to track her and withdraw the info. Then the cartel shows up and Sally pulls a Swayze. She bolts to my town. They need someone, and quick, to find her and she comes looking for me. Doc Balzary knows she's been dreaming about a cowboy and they figure that cowboy is me. So then send a Texas Ranger with a tragic past knowing I would be so enthralled with them and eager to help that I wouldn't be suspicious. This Ranger follows me, befriends me and then rats me out to Visegar. This was how Visegar knew to look for Sally at the bus depot. This was how Visegar knew to look for Sally at the cartel meet-and-greet.

Shit.

I was never going to trust a Texas Ranger again and if I ever met Chuck Norris, I was going punch him in the schnoz. That could only go well for me.

They chose Drew Winnick because her tragic past would motivate the host and make it so nobody questioned his/her motive. So where did Visegar get a Ranger and on short notice? They couldn't have had much notice that Sally was coming to me. Michael Fletch; it was Doc Balzary's emergency sessions. They implanted him and sent him out.

With an exhausted squeak, the hamster collapsed. His little chubby chest heaved as the little guy gasped for air. He was really not used to doing this much work. He looked at me and gave me a tiny thumbs up. It was like the end of *Terminator 2* just far more adorable. I loved that hamster.

Now I'm picturing a fat hamster in a leather jacket with a pair of sunglasses on his face. He looks at the feline cop and in a deadpan voice says "I'll be squeak."

Oh man. I'd watch the hell out of an all adorable animal version of *Terminator*.

I glanced at Leo and Drew. Leo's gun was still holstered but Drew's was out and ready. I needed to break him down. I needed to get Sally out of here. Leo was busy scolding Christine.

"The company won't like when they find out you were housing a fugitive," Leo berated. "You will be punished for this."

"You need to let us go, Drew," I pleaded, trying to talk over Leo.

"Shut up, Ben," Leo snapped.

"I know you're a good person. Michael Fletch is a good person." Drew's hand shook again as his mind battled. "You don't want to hurt us, Michael Fletch."

"Don't say that name," Drew said.

"Michael Fletch. Your name is Michael Fletch."

"Shut up, shut up, shut up!" Drew stepped towards me and pushed me against the table. He pressed the gun to my chin. "Shut up!"

This was exactly what I wanted. I had broken past the imbedded skill and forced the host to react. A trained Ranger would never get that close with a pistol, especially if they weren't trained on what to do in that situation. Drew was trained but Michael was not. Michael didn't have the skills or the muscle memory. Hs body didn't know what to do. Mine did. I twisted my body and knocked the pistol aside. I grabbed a bowl off of the table and slammed it across Drew's face. I grabbed the pistol and pointed it upwards. It fired off twice, putting two rounds into the ceiling.

Leo bolted toward me but Christine was on him first.

She grabbed the taser from the table and fired it at him. The electrodes dove into Leo's side. The solider screamed as the electricity dropped him to the ground.

"Tell the company that I quit," Christine snapped.

Drew kicked at my bum leg and I dropped like a fucking stone. Between the direct strike and the weakened state, the blow made me weaker than David when Annie starts yelling. Drew tossed me to the ground. He pivoted just in time to see Jeff charging at him. The Ranger fired and easily buried a round into Jeff. The Marshal spun as he crashed into the ground and Sally just screamed. Fear resonated in her body as she summoned an arc of electricity. The arc grew and Sally fired it forward. A bolt of lightning shot from her fingers and into Drew. The blast pitched the Faux-Ranger across the room and slammed him against the wall.

I scrambled to my feet and moved towards Jeff. Christine stopped me with a wave of her hand. She slid next to him. "Take Sally and run."

"Jeff," Sally sobbed. Arcs of electricity leapt from every inch of her skin, across her form and dove back into her body.

"It's a shoulder wound," Christine said. "He'll be okay. I'll look after him." She looked over at Drew and Leo and sighed. "I'll look after them as well. Now just go."

I looked at Sally and reached for her. She tried to pull her arm away, to protect me from harm, but I didn't let her. I grabbed her shoulder and pulled her close, ignoring the repetitive sting.

"He's okay," I whispered. "He's still alive."

I repeated it over and over until the arc diminished and eventually vanished. She looked up at me, relief taking hold. I smiled at her. It was a moment.

"Fucking run!" Christine yelled.

Oh right.

The Chevelle pulled into my driveway. As I exited the car I saw the door open and Puzo stepping outside, her pistol clearly visible. This wasn't good. I limped towards the house and Puzo quickly ushered us both in.

"What's wrong?" I asked.

"We're keeping this place secure," Puzo snapped. She signaled to the two FBI agents parked across the street before closing the door. "We had a visitor last night."

"What do you mean visitor?" I asked.

"The cartel showed up at your door," Puzo said quickly. "They met your sister."

"Is she okay?" I asked frantically. I turned around and called out loudly. "Annie? Annie?"

"Stop fucking yelling," Annie said. She emerged from the living room, my shotgun in her hand.

"Mom just said a bad word," Robby called out.

"Mom has a freaking shotgun," David replied. "She can say whatever the hell she wants."

"Annie, are you okay? Is everybody okay?" I frantically asked. Annie nodded.

"All is well, boy. All is well."

"Don't you fucking Dad on me," I snapped. "What the hell happened?"

"Some people showed up," Annie sternly said. "I handled it. That's all that matters."

I looked at Puzo but she wasn't saying anything. I sighed and pulled off my glove. Before Annie could stop me I pressed my bare palm on the door. A shiver and a twitch and I fell into the past.

The past was two hours ago. David walked towards the door to answer a knock. He opened it up to see a black 1970 Dodge Charge R/T in the driveway and several men in thick leather jackets at his door. The gaggle was led by a well dressed man with a charming smirk. I recognized him immediately as Ismael. Across the street I saw two Latino men holding guns to the FBI guards.

"I'm looking for Ben and Sally," he said with a grin.

"They're not here," David said.

"Why do I find that hard to believe?" he asked. "I feel the need to inspect for myself."

"You're not stepping one foot in here," David sternly said.

"I don't think you could stop me," Ismael said. He started to push David aside but paused as he heard the unmistakeable sound of a shotgun racking a round. David moved aside as Annie stepped outside. She held my Remington 870 shotgun in her hands and pointed it directly at Ismael.

"Put that away before someone gets hurt, chica," Ismael laughed. "You ain't gonna fire that."

Annie pivoted to the side and pulled the trigger. The shotgun roared to life as the Charger's passenger window shattered.

"Perra loca!" Ismael cried out. "That was my fucking car! Do you know how hard it is to find a Charger these days?"

"You are not stepping one foot into this house. You're not getting close to my son or my daughter and you're sure as hell are not getting close to Sally. You'd do best to walk away now, while you still have the chance."

"Listen here, puta," Ismael snapped. Annie cut him off by racking a second shell. Ismael gulped.

"Last chance: turn around, get back into your Dominic Torretto fetish-mobile and drive away," Annie snapped. "You are not setting one foot in this fucking house as long as I still live."

I have been asked why I fear my sister. This, right here, is the reason why.

Reality returned. I locked eyes with Annie. There was a Thompson moment where we just spoke without speaking. Annie just shrugged. I nodded. Annie grinned. I smirked. We didn't use words but we had just spoken volumes. It was a new form of wordless speaking.

Shrug: I'm okay. I did what was needed. I was worried for a while but I can hold my own. I will always be able to hold my own but it's good to know my baby brother is worried about me.

Nod: I know, sis. I'm glad you're okay. Shit. Has anybody told you that you are hella scary with a rifle? Damn, girl.

Grin: Did you know you can hundreds of dollars by switching to Geico?

Smirk: What, hundreds of dollars? You must be jesting. Wait, are we talking real dollars or Canadian dollars because I am not falling for that scam again.

Our own personal language wasn't perfect yet.

I frowned. How the hell did the cartel know where I lived? I heard a sad squeak as the hamster started to work again. It wasn't a long run but it was enough to find an answer. The Chevelle; they saw me drive it away and probably got the plates. They had men on the inside of the Marshals. Doing a search on a plate would be nothing at all.

"Where the fuck were you?" Puzo said. "I was worried."

I pulled Puzo into my office. I put my gun on the desk and fell into my couch. I sighed and rubbed my head. I was tired, I was fucking wired but I was dead tired. "Jeff was in trouble. We had to go save him."

"You could have called me for help," Puzo said.

"My phone was dead," I revealed. "Last night was fucked up beyond belief. You won't approve of any decision I made last night but we're all here."

I told her about psychic implantation and I told her about Drew. Puzo shook her head and swore. She didn't know what to say. That's when I decided to drop the bomb.

"I spoke to Zoey."

"What?" Puzo asked, shocked. "How? Where?"

"She's in Sally," I admitted. "Or a part of her is. There was a moment last night, when Sally was passed out, that Zoey emerged from inside of her. She sat up, called me Bright Eyes and told me she loved me."

Puzo sat beside me. She was silent. She didn't know what to say and neither did I. So I did what I normally do when I'm speechless. I ramble incessantly.

"Was this what she meant when she said she was still alive? Was this what she meant when she told me to save her?" I shook my head. Anger and frustration bellowed up inside of me. Confusion added to the mix. "I don't know what to do. I don't know how to save her."

"I know, Ben," Puzo gently said. "But you have to focus. You can't think about Zoey at the moment. You have to think about Sally. I need your head in the game."

"How? How do I focus when all I can think about is Zoey?" I cried out. "She's out there, trapped and with another cowboy. I'm supposed to be her cowboy."

"I'm so tired of hearing her name. Can't we go one day without you saying Zoey's name?" Puzo stood up and shook her head. "We keep having this fight over and over and I'm tired of it. I want you to find Zoey. I will help you as much as I can but you are stuck in the past. You can't move forward until you find her. So what does that mean about me?"

"This isn't about you," I snapped. "This is about her. This is about how fate keeps ripping her from me. This is how every time we tried to be together something would tear us apart. I thought I was over her and she showed up again, begging for my help. I need to find her; I need to be with her. I am supposed to be with her."

Silence.

"I thought you were supposed to be with me," Puzo said softly. A crack of sorrow seeped through her voice.

What did I just say? Oh fuck. Please tell me I didn't say what I think I just said. I glanced at Puzo and expected her cold, stern look. Instead I got an vulnerable look with a hint of pain.

Oh fuck.

"I---"

"Don't," she snapped. "Just fucking don't." She turned away from me and walked to the desk and leaned on it.

"I'm not doing this, not now. I have to focus on the situation at hand. I don't have time for our shit, not when a girl's life is on the line and not when your head is elsewhere. You need some sleep."

"Rachael--"

"Get some sleep, Ben." Puzo walked out of the office and left me alone.

I leaned back in the couch and just let out a single loud fuck. I just fucked up and it was big. I had to fix this; I had to make it better but how? I looked to the hamster for an idea but he just gave me an adorable shoulder shrug. He didn't know either. What use was my Arnie hamster if he couldn't come up with an idea? Why was I even using an Arnie hamster? I needed a Chuck Norris hamster with a little cowboy hat. I needed a Stallone hamster with tiny boxing gloves and American flag shorts. I needed a Vin Diesel hamster with polished eyes and goggles. I needed...I needed.... I sighed. I needed sleep.

A knock on my office door snapped me to attention. I sat up as Sally walked into the room. She sat down beside me. I looked at her and she looked back. We didn't speak, we just shrugged.

"You look like shit," she said.

"How very kind of you," I laughed. "Care to compliment my hair next?"

"Wearing a cowboy hat all day will eventually make you go bald." Ouch. That girl is mean. Doesn't she know that words can hurt? "How you doing?"

"I've been better," I yawned. "What's everybody saying out there?"

"They're worried about bad men storming the house," Sally said.

"Visegar won't come here. I don't think they're allowed to." Sally gave me a confused look but I just shrugged. "I'm kind of protected. I don't understand it but they won't come into my house for some reason. We just have to worry about the cartel. Annie scared them off but it won't be for long. They'll be back with more men. We need defenses." I suddenly stood up. "I need a moat. I need men with guns to stand on the inside of the moat. I need a catapult to fire the men with guns across the moat so they can bullet-tackle anybody who comes close to the moat. Then, we'll strap dozens of bombs to dozens of bees and then strap those bees to a cow. Then we put the cow into the catapult and fire it across the moat."

"Why?"

"Because the cow will hit the bad guys, then the bees will fly off and sting anybody who didn't get steak on them and then they'll explode taking out anybody who avoided getting stung. I'll call it the Buzzy Bouncing Bovine Bomb or Vitamin B4 for short."

Sally just stared at me. She had the widest eyed expression before erupting in laughter.

"Thanks for making me laugh, Ben. I needed that," she giggled. I stared at her with a serious look. I was totally serious. In my sleep deprived state, the Buzzy Bouncing Bovine Bomb sounded like a viable option. Oh well, I decided to run with it. I flashed a fake smile. "Yeah...a joke....that's the ticket. I'll go with that. She'll never expect that I was serious."

"Was that your inside voice?" Sally asked, "Because you're speaking out loud."

Crap baskets.

"Also a joke?" I suggested with a fake grin.

"You need sleep," Sally said.

"I really did need sleep. There was no way the kid knew how tired and exhausting the last couple of days had been for me."

"Inside voice, Ben," Sally reminded me.

Crap baskets.

"You need sleep." Sally took my hand and pulled me to the couch. She laid me down and put my head on a pillow. "We'll need you later so sleep now, cowboy."

"Yes, Mom," I said in a sarcastic voice. Sally smirked

at me. "Do I get a bedtime story?"

"Do you want one?" she asked. I gave an overly exaggerated nod. In truth I was touched by the fact that kid wanted to look after me. I decided to hide that emotion by making the entire situation awkward and weird. "Fine, I'll tell you a story."

Sally sat on the floor, leaning against the couch. She smiled and began her story.

"Once upon a time there was an immortal king. He ruled his kingdom for a thousand years and he watched his people grow. With his two sons, he guided his people and watched them grow strong and when great darkness emerged, the king and his sons would slay the monsters and protect the people.

"Whenever one of his sons would ask if they had made the people strong enough, he would smile and reply 'Our people need to grow stronger still. They need to be strong enough so they too can live for a thousand years. They need to grow strong enough so that they no longer need our protection. That is the greatest wish that a king could have.'

"One day the king grew tired and wished for a long sleep. This sleep would last five hundred years. He told his sons to rule as he would and bequeathed them his kingdom. Then the king went to sleep. The two princes tried to work together and rule as one but they argued over how to make their people strong.

"One prince thought that if he stopped fighting off the great monsters then the people would have to fight. Many would die and cities would fall but those that survived would be strong and the cities that were rebuilt would be grander than before.

"The other prince thought he must work on his people. He must coddle them and train them so when the time was right they could fight on their own. He would bestow magical gifts during their sleep so they could wake up stronger and wiser.

"Neither prince could agree on a method so they

split the great kingdom. Each side was ruled by one prince in whatever way they saw fit as long as neither strayed from the king's original wish for the people to grow strong enough so that they no longer need protection from the immortals.

"When the king woke up he looked out over his sons' work and stared in horror. His once great kingdom was gone and replaced with two that were constantly at war with each other. His people were strong but he was appalled by the horrors each underwent to get there. His sons had long since corrupted his dream, each consumed by greed, power and hate for the other. Worse still, his people had forgotten him. Unable to reunite the kingdom he loved, he was left with only one option: to watch from afar.

"The king built a city in the sky, high above the clouds where only the gods could reach. From there he watched his sons and tried to protect the people of his once great kingdom. His sons had become too strong to simply smite so he made a new vow. He was no longer eager to strengthen his people, they would have to do that on their own, instead he would have to protect his people from the greatest evil ever known: his sons."

Chapter 18
No War for Anyone

"Benny!" Annie pounded on my office door before storming. I bolted up with a scream. I was really tired of waking up this way. I glanced at a clock. It was well into the afternoon.

"Benny I ---" Her words trailed off as she stared at my murder board. "What the fuck is this?"

"It's a case," I muttered as I rubbed my eyes. "What the hell is wrong? You burning down my house now?"

"Sally is gone," she said urgently. I bolted up to my feet. My leg objected to the sudden movement. I winced and pushed through the pain, Thompson style.

"What happened?"

"She was sleeping in Robby's room," Annie said. "I went to check on her but she's gone."

"Did anybody get into the house?" Annie shook her head. I frowned. I pulled my phone out from my pocket. It was dead. I limped to my bedroom and plugged it in. There is nothing worse in this world than when you are in a hurry and waiting for your dead iphone to turn on. When I die and get sent to hell, 'cause all Thompsons go to hell - it's a family curse -, my punishment will be having all of my exes berate me at once and the only way to escape is to use my iphone but its dead and I have to wait for it to turn on.

David walked in and glanced at Annie. I looked at

both and noticed a weird look between them. I also noticed a letter in David's hand. I raised an eyebrow. "What's up with the letter, Kevin Costner?"

David blinked in confusion. Annie rolled her eyes. "How many years has it been and you still don't speak Ben?"

"I speak Ben perfectly, thank you very much. I just missed that reference," David defended. He looked down at the letter and suddenly let out a chuckle. That's how I knew he got my *The Postman* joke.

"The letter's not important right now," Annie said. "We have to find Sally."

My phone buzzed. It was back in the land of the living. I grabbed it and instantly saw an imessage from Sally. I tapped it and saw a video file. The movie was taken from her phone in selfie pose.

"This is my goodbye video. I wasn't going to wake you but I had to say goodbye. The cartel is coming for me. They need me dead. They will hurt anyone to get that. I can't let them hurt you or your family. I can't be responsible for another death."

Tears formed in Sally's eyes. Despite her best efforts, the tears rolled down her cheek.

"I haven't told you the whole truth. I didn't tell you who was really responsible for my Dad's death." She sobbed as she spoke, the tears falling stronger than before. "Dad is dead because of me. It's my fault he's dead.

"When Dad noticed the drug trade he didn't know what to do. He talked it over with me. He didn't want to get involved. I told him that he had to do what was right. When he fought me on it I used Mom's name to change his mind. I told him Mom always did what was right and he needed to as well. That's when Dad went to Ms. Pike. Dad got involved because of me. He died because of me. I'm not going to allow that to happen to you. The king had to accept that his son's actions were his responsibility. I have to accept that the cartel is mine. It is selfish of me to allow anybody else get hurt because of my actions.

"I have been dreaming about a cowboy lately. I didn't know what it meant. In my dreams I was saved by this cowboy. I'm from Texas. Cowboys are a dime a dozen so I didn't care. Now I know I was dreaming of you. You are the man of my dreams, Ben. Thank you and goodbye."

That's where the video ended. Annie gasped and David dropped to the bed. Neither of us knew what to say.

"That poor girl," Annie said. David just nodded.

I swiped through my phone and texted Hotwire.

Me: 911 - 911 - 911
Me: I need an urgent phone trace.

I fired him Sally's number.

Hotwire: On it.

"I'm going after her," I said suddenly. "I'm not letting her die today."

This was my moment. This was the moment where the reluctant hero stepped up and entered into the fight. This was where the dramatic music played and the audience swooned and fawned. This was movie-life.

"No fucking way!" Annie snapped.

My big sister telling me what to do was not movie-life.

"Annie," David said. "What are you talking about?"

"You're going to war with the cartel. What the fuck am I supposed to do, be happy about this?"

"No but.....what options do we have?"

"We?" Annie's worried look turned to a glare.

"He's not going in alone," David said sternly. He motioned to the letter. "There really isn't anybody else he can call." What the fuck was that letter?

"Dude," I began. David cut me off.

"No. She needs help and it's about time we do this together." David put on a fake smirk. "I'm tired of being left out."

"Left out? Did you forget us taking on a damn army at your house?" I reminded him.

"I will always be there for you, dude," David said. "Thick or thin."

"Rangers for a moment," I started.

"Brothers for life," he concluded.

"Rangers lead the way," We both said.

"Bro."

"Bro." We chest bumped.

"No...why....why?" Annie desperately stuttered. "I want her to be safe but...why can't we just hide in the bedroom until this all goes away?"

"Because it's not the bedroom walls that save us," I said. "We have to save each other."

"Why does this always keep happening to us?" Annie asked.

"Because we're shit disturbers." I turned around and saw Robby standing in the doorway of my bedroom.

"Watch your language," Annie snapped. Robby gulped and tried to ignore his mother. Gutsy move kid.

"When we last saw Grandma, before she died, she told me that Thompsons are shit disturbers. We poke where we shouldn't and do what others won't because we want to help people. Shit disturbers do good but we always end up to our eyes because of it."

Our mother had a way with words.

"And Belledins ain't that different. Grandma said she was happy you found a shit disturber of your own to marry."

"I actually kind of thought your mom hated me," David whispered.

"You want to save her 'cause she's basically family, which I'll admit is worrisome for me," Robby continued. "When I was in trouble what did we do? Uncle Ben hunted me down and when shit came to our doorstep, Dad and Ben dove into the deep end. Even today, when shit came to our door, Mom faced it head on. We don't turn our back on family and we don't ignore people who need help."

"Because we're shit disturbers," I finished. I looked at Annie. She sighed.

"Go be shit disturbers," she said. "Just make sure you come back."

Hotwire texted me with an address; he was keeping a trace on her phone. "I'm calling Puzo. We need all the help we can get," I said. David let out a hesitant wince as he clutched the letter. "What the hell is up with that letter?"

"It's not important at the moment."

"Okay, David. I trust you. If you say it's not important then I will leave it alone for now and -- yoink!" I yanked the letter from his hand and opened it up. It was a hand written letter from Puzo.

Ben;

I don't have the strength to do this to your face be-cause I don't know if I can go through it but this isn't working between us. I love you, Ben, and I don't doubt that you love me but I am not the only person you love.

I want the best for you and the best for Zoey. I want her to be free and safe but until you save her, until you get over her, there is no room for me. You love Zoey and that's okay; that I can deal with. But you love her more than you love me. That I cannot deal with. Because of that, I'm ending things with you. We're breaking up.

The only way we can have a future is if you choose me over her and the only way that will happen is if you get over your feelings for her. I can't wait for you to do that. I waited for you once, Ben. I cannot do it again. I will not do it again.

If you ever get over her, look me up. I may be single, I may not. Who knows what the future holds but maybe we can try again. Maybe we can't. Deep down I hope this isn't the end of you and me, I hope this only ends

up being a pause, but until both of us are in better head spaces, this has to stop.
I wish for only the best for you, Ben. You deserve good in your life.
I love you and I always will. I just can't be with you.
Goodbye
Rachael.

I just got Dear John'd. Fuck. Fuck. Fuck. Sadness and sorrow billowed up inside of me as my hurt grew. I had just lost Puzo. The universe didn't take her from me, I lost her.

No. I didn't have time to deal with this. I had to do what Thompsons did best and take those emotions and shove them so fucking far down that they never saw the light of day, ever again. I walked to my office and pulled open the desk drawer. I dropped the letter inside and watched as it fell beside a small black engagement ring box.

I would deal with all of my emotions later.

I needed to save Sally, I just needed a plan. Arnie Hamster let out a determined squeak as he climbed into the hamster wheel. With an adorable resolute look, he started running. It was time to use my brain.

We were doomed.

I needed backup. I needed a wheelman, I needed troops and I needed a way to equalize the playing field. I need that movie moment where the good guy outsmarts not one group but two. I needed that epic movie-life moment.

"Squeak!" I glanced at my Arnie Hamster. He leapt out of his wheel and rapped on the metaphorical glass that separated us. He was eager and excited. My hamster had an idea. "Squeaky, squeaky squeak-squeak."

"Squeak me!" I swore. Hamster had a plan. It was a good plan. It was freaking great plan. I had to make some phone calls.

A roar of an engine and a knock signaled the first step of my plan. Annie answered the door, shotgun at the ready. A punk chick with a studded leather jacket, an arctic blue Mohawk and more piercings then I could count quickly raised her hands into the air.

"I'm think I'm at the wrong house," the punk said quickly. A devious grin crossed her lips as she eyed Annie up and down. "Then again, I might be exactly where the fun is."

"What type of name is Harm?" Annie asked, her shotgun not wavering.

"It's mine, what's it too y'ah?" the punk snapped back. "Enough with the foreplay, let's you and I get down and dirty or let me get to work. Either way, lower the boomstick."

Annie lowered the weapon and let Harm inside. The car thief walked in and froze. She looked around and saw my entire family ready for war. Everybody was doing their part. David and I were readying for battle, Annie was guarding the door and Robby was googling our destination's location and rattling of important intel about the area. Even Alice, with her giggling and laughter, was doing her part by keeping the tension low.

"I did not expect family fun time," Harm said. I did a rounds of introductions. Harm nervously waved.

"Seriously," Annie said as she entered the living room. "What type of name is Harm?"

"Back in school I used to hang with this girl called Melody. We were damn close. They called us Melody and Harmony. Then one day some guy smack around Melody so I smack him back. They started shortening it to Harm."

Annie gave the nod of approval.

When I put Arnie Hamster's plan into action, I made three phone calls. The first was to Harm. I needed a wheelman and she was the best I knew of. She was shocked at my call but jumped at the chance to clear her debt. I told her there was no debt. She insisted there was.

Harm glanced at me. "Seriously, Ben, who are you?"

"What do you mean?"

"You saved my life and we ain't even met, now you going to fight the cartel to save some girl that ain't even blood? People don't do that."

"People should," I said.

"People should do a lot that they don't," she responded. She nervously fished a smoke from her pocket and tossed it into her mouth.

"I'm offering you a guilt-free out if you want it," I said. "I know this is a lot to ask of you---"

"Zip it. If I ain't wanted to be here, then I ain't going to show up," she snarled. She flicked open a lighter and lit the smoke. "I ain't killin' tho."

"We got that part covered," I replied.

"No smoking indoors," Annie snapped.

"But they let you in?" Harm flirted.

A second knock at the door signaled my next ally. Annie opened the door, shotgun in hand.

"Damn girl," a familiar voice cried out. "You remind me of an ex."

Jack Walker was here.

My second call was to Jack. I needed backup and since Arcel was out and I didn't have the nerve or strength to call Puzo, I called someone I knew I could trust and who could hold his own. That list started and ended with Jack.

That left the third call.

Annie let Jack in. He walked in the living room and gave me the bro hug. He gave an identical one to David next. He eyed Harm and flashed a smile. "Hey. You look fine. Wanna tussle?"

"Wrong tree, dog," Harm smirked. "I'm more Annie's style."

David's eyes went wide and a devilish smirk crossed his lips. Annie took one look at her husband and let out a single, solid *no*. I just shook my head. I didn't need our wheelman trying to sleep with my sister. Jack looked at me.

"This you just making ends meet?" he asked.

"Trust me, I want to be out," I said. "I just ain't very

good at it."

Jack just nodded. It wasn't a judgmental nod. It was like the upwards nod that every guy gave to a guy they knew only this time there was a sparkle in his, like he was excited to see someone he hadn't seen in a while.

"I got the gear," Jack said as he tossed his bag onto the ground. David pulled open the bag and withdrew several tact-vests. Robby stared with a look of hesitant wonder. The kid was still off around guns and gun accessories but this was too cool for him to shy away from. "Who has the party favours?"

That was my cue. It was time to get my surprise under the back porch. After my adventures with Joseph Price and Tyrone Straub I needed to have some equipment ready for the big event, for something just like this. But I couldn't just have dangerous weapons out and about. I needed somewhere to hide them. That's where my burn box came in.

My burn box was a metal deck box three feet long and two feet high. It locked from the inside and had no key-hold on the outside. All it had was a keypad. How it worked was simple. I had to punch in a keycode to unlock the box. If I punched in the wrong code it destroyed its contents. This is where things got complicated. The code was randomized every time and the only way to see the code was read it off of a small screen -- located on the inside of the box. So how did someone open it? The only way to safely open it was to touch the box, use your psychic powers to see the code on the screen and then punch in that exact number. It was literally a box that only I could open.

I touched the box and felt a shiver and twitch. My vision brought me inside the box. From there I read a code off the screen: 386738. Reality snapped back and I quickly punched in the coed. I heard a positive beep and the latch un-locking. I pulled it open and glanced inside. Waiting for me, crisp and clean and surrounded by ammo, were three FN P90s and three FN Five-Seven pistols. They were clean weapons with numbers belong to organizations across the globe. One was registered to the Jagdkommando special ground of the Austrian Army, the second to France GIPN counter-terrorism group and the third to the Halifax Regional Police in Canada.

Are you shocked that Canada needs guns? Yeah, me as well.

We exited the house and walked to Harm's acquired car. It was a maroon four-door Nissan Maxima. Jack just laughed. "That's your get-away car?"

"It blends into the crowd instead of standing out," Harm began. "It also gets 300 horsepower from the 3.5-liter V6, has a continuously variable transmission and comes with front-wheel drive. Mock if you want, but this pep will do the job nicely."

"Nice. What does it go for?" David asked, slipping into Dad mode. Harm just shrugged.

"How the hell should I know?" she said. "I stole the damn thing."

We all climbed in. Jack took the front and instantly pulled out his phone. He connected it to the car via Bluetooth. David and I climbed in the back. Instantly, David shoved me away from him. I shoved him back.

"Jack! Ben's on my side! He's touching me!"

I leaned in close to David and held my finger right by his left eye. David started to squint and glare at me I smirked. "Not touching you. Not touching you. Not touching you."

"I don't want to hear another word from either of you," Jack said in a fake snarl. "Neither of you will like what happens if I hear another peep from the back."

David and I looked at each other and smirked. At the same time we both said a single word. "Peep!"

"That's it," Jack snarled. "We're turning around. No war for anyone now."

The three of us laughed as Harm started at us like we

were idiots. She wasn't wrong. This was old Ranger goof-balling. We laughed like this before going out on patrol.

"What the hell is wrong with you guys?"

"We keep it light until things get dark," I said in my best Stallone. "Then we go pitch black."

Harm just shook her head. She started the car and pulled out of the driveway. With a roar the car sped down the street. Jack reached for the silent radio. He turned up the volume and looked back at David and me in the back, a wicked grin on his face. My eyes went wide.

"You don't?" I asked in disbelief.

"I do."

"Kick it," David ordered.

It wasn't often that David, Jack and me went on missions together but when we did there was one song we'd play. The song was old school even in our soldiering days but for some reason it rang true. We loved the song. I hadn't listened to it in years but I instantly knew the words.

"Don't call it a comeback," LL Cool J began, "I been here for years."

Chapter 19
Thanks, William Dafoe

Sally shivered in the darkness. It wasn't because she was cold; nobody could be cold in this heat. She shivered because she was afraid. She was taking a big risk. If things went according to plan then she'd forever be a prisoner. If they did not then she'd be dead. Either way, my family and I would be safe. She was fine with either option.

She hid beside a parked car on the third floor of an all-night parking garage. It was dark with scattering of lights that that decorated the roof. It was the type of place that drug deals and deep throats happened. For those that are wondering there are two different types of deep throats. One is a sexual move that involved swallow a lot of -- sausage -- and the second was a whistle-blower that hid in the shadows and helped bring down Nixon. I was pretty sure both types had happened in this very parking garage. She looked up as three vehicles approached and stepped out of the shadows as the cars came to a halt before her. Ismael exited the charger.

"I did not expect you to text me, chica," he began. "It is brave of you to meet me face-to-face."

"I have come to offer you a deal," Sally began. "If you say yes then you benefit greatly."

"And if I say no?"

"You can shoot me." Ismael paused to think for a second before nodding. "The ways I see it you need me quiet.

There are two ways to do that. One is killing me. I'd rather not die. The second is I swear my allegiance to the cartel and work for you for the rest of my days. If I'm a member of the cartel then I can't rat you out."

"That sounds like a lot of work. Why would I want to recruit you when I could just kill you?"

"I can offer you something nobody else here can."

"Colour me intrigued." Sally eyed one of the other cartel goons. She raised her hands and formed a small ball of lightning. She fired it into the goon and sent him flying backwards. The dozen remaining men quickly drew their weapons and aimed at her. Ismael waved them down. "Mierda! That is spectacular."

"This could be yours," Sally offered.

"Why would you offer us this? Why risk death to join us?"

"Too many have died because of me. I don't want Ben or his family to die as well." Sally tried to keep a stoic face. "Here's the deal: I join you and forever be a powerhouse for the Imperecedero and in return you leave Ben and his family alone."

"Is this another trap, chica?" Ismael asked. "I am not the fool twice. I have a dozen men before you and another dozen hidden."

"Ben doesn't know I'm here," she said. "I've said my goodbyes."

Ismael silently stared her down. Eventually a smirk appeared. He stepped forward and put his arm around her and pulled the girl close. "You will be a great asset for me, child. You will be the cause of my ascension. With you I will surpass my father." He looked at his men. "Tell the second team to hold position." He eyed Sally. "Order the *third* team to sweep the area. I don't trust this girl yet."

Suddenly a silent bullet dove into a goon and dropped him to the ground. Two seconds later a second goon fell. Ismael drew his pistol and pressed it to Sally's head. He pulled her back as he used his Charger for cover. Logic said he should have shot the girl but greed had taken hold.

"Qué chingados!" Ismael cried out. "Return fire!"

The cartel men fired into the darkness. Two second later a canister skipped across the floor. It exploded in a loud flash of light and sound. Some cartel men were blinded and stunned, others dove for cover. As the flash faded, a gaggle of men stormed the floor. Billy Idol, Jerface, Two-Pump, Faux-Drew and Rasputin marched on the cartel men with guns a blazing. They were being led by Leo Anderson.

This brought me to my third phone call.

"Ben?" Leo picked up the phone with a surprised tone. "You have some nerve calling me. I should beat you within an inch of your life for what you did to me. I swear, protected or not, the next time I see you I will fucking---"

"I'm sorry," I said truthfully. "I need your help."

"What?"

"I'm in over my head," I said. "I need your help. I've come to make a deal."

Silence filled the air. Leo didn't know what to say. I took his silence as permission to keep going.

"I can't protect her anymore," I admitted. "The girl, I can't protect her. I can do my best to keep her from you and the company but I can't fight the cartel. I'm one guy and now they're threatening my family. I need help."

"What do you want from me?"

"She's gone to offer herself to the cartel," I said. "She's going to sacrifice her life so me and my family stay safe. I can't deal with her dying. What I'm offering is this: save her and you can keep her. Just promise me Visegar won't kill her. I would rather see her in your hands than dead."

"You're fucking with me, Ben. Do you think I'm an idiot? I kno---"

"You know what I've lost. You know who I've lost.

You know what it did to me. Do you really think I can handle losing someone else?" I snapped. "We're brothers and if that means anything to you then you'll know I cannot let her die. I need you do to this one thing for me. I need you to save her life."

Silence.

"Text me the address."

I am a horrible liar. The funny thing about lying though is you can do it while still telling the truth. Everything I said to Leo was true. I couldn't fight the cartel and I couldn't deal with having someone else die because of me. The lying part came with what I didn't tell him. I did plan to let him have Sally, what I didn't tell him was for how long. Spoiler: it wasn't going to be for very long.

I needed an army to fight the cartel. Now I had one.

Leo's team was outnumbered but they were better armed, better equipped and better trained. This time Leo's team wasn't using little MP5Ks. They were fighting with full-on balls to the walls assault rifles. Each - except Billy Idol - held an M4 in their hands and none of them were afraid to use it. Leo moved down the center of the line with Faux-Drew behind him. Jerkface and Billy Idol took the left flank as Rasputin and Two-Pump took the right. In the distance was Chicken-Head with a silenced rifle playing over-watch.

Half of the cartel started returning fire with pistols as the other half retreated to the trunks for bigger guns. This was a shit storm of gunfight. This was hell in bullet form. There was only one man who could properly describe what happened.

"There was a firefight!"

Thanks, William Dafoe.

Bullets flew back and forth. Leo's team dropped cartel goons with precision and expertise and when shit got deep, Billy Idol summoned the flame. Balls of fire lit up the darkened garage as they collided with their attackers. Men screamed in pain as their skin burned at the mere contact with the balls of fire.

"Hijo de puta!" Ismael looked at Sally. "There are more of you?"

"There is a whole world of us," she replied. He held the teen tighter to his body while returning fire. He motioned to the Charger and Sally pulled open the door. Shoving her inside, he told her to keep her head down. Ismael walked to his trunk and popped it open. He lifted the hidden compartment and withdrew a WAT-FB MSBS-5.56. The weapon was a modular assault rifle made in Poland and was used by the Polish, Swedish and Portuguese armies. The weapon was a new model that had quickly proven itself on the field. It was an expensive gun but Ismael was a rich boy who only wanted the best. Ismael loaded a grenade into the modular launcher and smirked. He walked out from behind the Charger and fired several rounds before launching the grenade into the distance. A ball of fire took out a car and the sniper fire stopped. Ismael had just taken Chicken-Head out of the fight. Shit was cray-cray but it was about to get worse 'cause now it was my turn to get involved and nothing makes a situation more calm and relaxed as a Thompson entering the room.

"Momma said knock you out!" Music blared through our car speakers as the Nissan Maxima sped up the garage ramp. For a split second everybody froze, gunfire ceased and everybody tried to figure out where the music was coming from. It was like the legendary Christmas Truce except there was no soccer and everybody was more confused than anything. The Nissan leapt up the ramp and Harm quickly shifted. The car turned and Harm drifted through the corner all while the legendary rift from Europe blared. Jack and David fired out of their respective windows and I fired from mine. Our P90 gunfire ripped through an unlucky few but mostly it caused everybody to dive for cover.

Our presence had thrown a kink into the mix. Before

we showed up it was 1v1. Now it was a fucking free-for-all. Did Leo team up with me? Did the cartel team up with me? Did Leo and the cartel decide to put their differences aside to boot stomp me into the curb?

David didn't wait for the car to stop before he popped open the door and rolled out. He was back on his feet in less than a second and opened fire. Back in my prime I was a damn good soldier but David was smooth. I could never pull off a move like that. I'd end up tripping over my own feet and then I'd get run over by the very car I was trying to climb out of. David was like a cat. He was smooth and always landed on his feet. David bolted to the right towards the nearest car. He slid across the hood and slammed his foot into the face of one goon before filling the second with bullets.

The jerk was a total show off.

Jack dashed to the left. With one hand he slapped aside a cartel weapon and with the other he fired. He grabbed a second goon, spun him around and used his leg to pin him to the ground as he opened fire on a third. This was Jack's specialty; the dude could CQC like a god. He was my own personal John Wick.

The jerk was a total show off.

Now it was Ben's time to shine. I bolted out of the car and instantly tripped. I slammed into the ground with a thud. I groaned. Worse still, I think everybody saw that happen. I looked and saw a cartel goon rush towards me to get a clear shot. Good. He was here to kill me. At least I'd die quickly before this embarrassment kicked in.

The Maxima slammed into reverse and slammed into the approaching goon. He flew backwards. He hadn't even hit the ground before Harm shifted the car into drive and sped forward. She took a corner and drift-slammed a second goon out the way. Harm was Memphis Raine. She could steal, she could drive and she could make a car dance.

The jerk was a total show off.

I was super glad all three were on Team Ben!

I bolted towards Sally. I dove behind cover as Ismael opened fire at me. I popped up and let my P90 fire back. Sneaking around a car, I popped out and fired when I had the chance. I needed to save Sally and I needed to put an end to Ismael. I'm often filled with an urge to protect and save, it's one of the reasons I enlisted, but for Sally it was different. The instinct was stronger. The instinct was deeper.

"Sally!" I called out. I was done hiding. I was ready for a fight.

"She's with me now, el vaquero."

"The hell she is!"

"Go away, Ben," Sall cried out. I could hear the fear and the tears in her voice. "Please leave me alone. I can't stay with you. It's wrong and it's dangerous."

"Squeak?" Arnie Hamster said. I glanced at him. I had the same idea he did but it was really stupid. Arnie Hamster nodded at me. "Squeak!"

I stepped out with my weapon raised only to see Ismael pointing his at me. "This is one hell of a Mexican Stand-off."

"In my country we just call it a standoff, el vaquero."

"There is nothing that is wrong in wanting you to stay here with me," I said. Ismael gave me a weird look but I wasn't talking to him. I was talking to Sally. I was speaking her language. "I know you've got somewhere to go but won't you make yourself at home and stay with me?"

Sally popped her head out of the car and stared at me. Tears were full-on pouring down her cheeks.

"And don't you ever leave." I pressed on. "Lay down, Sally and rest here in my arms. Don't you think you want someone to talk to? Lay down, Sally, no need to leave so soon; I've been trying all night long just to talk to you."

"What the fuck?" Ismael said. I ignored him.

"Are you sure?" Sally asked between tears.

"I long to see the morning light coloring your face so dreamily," I continued. "So don't you go and say goodbye. You can lay your worries down and stay with me."

A bolt of electricity slammed into Ismael's back. The

boss' son few across the garage and slammed down into the hood of another car. Sally ran toward me and into my arms. I pulled her down into cover and hugged her tightly. She cried into my shoulder and I fought back droplets of meat.

Man tears.

"Don't you ever leave."

"Don't skip ahead in the lyrics of that song and we got ourselves a deal," she sobbed.

"I was trying to make a point," I laughed. "Eric Clapton can sue me later." I leaned down and kissed her on the forehead. She smiled and hugged me closer as bullets flew all around us.

Chapter 20
Don't You Ever *John Wick* Me

With their boss down, Team Ismael began to scatter. This just left Team Leo versus Team Ben. The lines were firmly drawn. I peered up from behind my cover. I saw Leo standing there beside Billy Idol. Rasputin and Jerkface stood nearby. Faux-Drew and Two-Pump were nowhere to be seen.

"It's over, Ben," Leo said. "Give it up."

I wanted to fire on Leo but I couldn't. He was still a brother. I looked at Sally.

"Stay down and run," I said. "I'll deal with this."

"Like fuck," she snapped. "I'm done being the damsel in distress. If I'm here, I'm here for the fight."

"Just stay down," I snapped. I tossed my P90 on the ground and stepped out from cover with my hands raised.

"I told you to stay out of this, Ben," Leo said as he approached me. "I told you to stay out of the game. Is this your way of saying you're back in?"

Oh my god. This was it. This was my *John Wick* moment. It was stupid and dumb but how often do you get a *John Wick* moment?

"You know, people keep asking me if I'm back in the game and I haven't really had an answer but now, Yeah, I'm thinking I'm back in." Damn that felt good. Damn that felt like movie-life. Leo walked up to me and without saying a word slammed his boot into my bum leg. It hurt like hell.

"Okay, I'm out, I'm out. I'll stay out."

"Don't you ever *John Wick* me," Leo spat. He raised his gun to butt strike me with it but a bolt of electricity slammed into him. It wasn't strong enough to pitch him into the air but it staggered him a second. A second bolt flew towards him but Billy Idol stepped in front and deflected it with a blast of fire. I'm not sure how the science works for that but who the fuck cares, it was a super-hero fight.

Billy Idol threw a big blast of fire and everybody scattered. I limped away and dove behind another car. Sally popped up. Her eyes held the canary glow of lightning as she summoned blast after blast. Each one she fired at Billy Idol. The blaster wasn't one to simply stand there. He dodged what he could, deflected the rest and summoned flames to fire back.

In the distance I spotted Rasputin. He raised his weapon to fire but suddenly felt a hand grab the back of his vest. Jack pulled the man back and threw him to the floor. Rasputin hit the ground hard but quickly recovered.

"Jack Walker," Rasputin said with his Russian accent. "I've heard many good things about you."

"I don't even know who the fuck you are," Jack said. "Nobody says good things about me."

Jack raised an eyebrow as Rasputin dropped his M4 and instead drew a pistol and a combat knife. A sparkle in Jack's eyes suddenly appeared and he did the same. "I wish to test you."

The two men stepped into each other. Their blades and hands moved quickly as one limb tried to deflect an attack while the other struck back. Back and forth the two men went. Knife and pistol; gunshot and slash: the attacks were endless.

Lt. Jerkface had a mess of his own to deal with as he suddenly faced the cat-like fury that was David. Jerkface would move like a soldier, firm and rigid. Each move was directly out of the infantry's book of military training. David had read the same book but he moved differently. Jerkface would fire and move, making sure he had solid footing and squared shoulders. David was a more on the fly type of guy. He knew he was smooth and could improvise a risk or two. David would shoot on the run, he'd dive over cover and he'd roll with the punches, slips and falls. It was like watching two people cook. Jerkface was the type who would follow the instructions to the letter. David was the guy who could improvise. He'd throw in a dash of seasoning, taste it and try something else. To him cooking and soldiering was an art.

Ismael climbed off of the car hood and tried to limp away. He needed to escape. The boss' son got only five steps away before a shot rang out. It bounced off of the ground mere inches in front of his foot. Isamel turned to see Faux-Drew approaching with his coyote brown P226 drawn on him.

"My mind is a mess. I know I am Michael Fletch but I still feel like Drew Winnick." His voice had changed and the drawl had vanished. The Faux-Ranger took another step forward. "I am filled with Winnick's mind. I am filled with her memories and her feelings and of them none are more powerful than the urge to kill you."

"What did I do to this Winnick?" Ismael said.

"You killed the woman she loved. You killed Alexis Pike." Ismael's eyes went wide. He tried to bolt away but Faux-Drew fired twice, putting a bullet into each kneecap of the escaping man. Ismael fell to the ground, screaming and wailing in pain. "I feel the sorrow Drew felt the day she found out her love had died."

"Tu novia es una puta fea!" Ismael spat.

Anger filled Michael. He raised his pistol and leveled it at Ismael's head. Every inch of his body wanted to revenge, every inch save one. Suddenly the drawl returned. "It don't mean much but I long to say the words. Ismael, you're under arrest."

I scampered around a car, desperately looking for my P90. Sally and Billy Idol were still firing at one another. I needed to give her a hand but as I looked up I saw a form in the shadows with its weapon raised at Sally. I didn't think; I just dove. I tackled the man to the ground and we both tumbled along. I rolled to my feet and look up. I was staring at Two-Pump.

"You!"

"The cowboy," he snarled. "I'm getting very tired of cowboys."

"You tried to shoot Sally," I said, the rage growing in me. "Not once, but twice."

"Yeah I'm badass that way," he laughed. His chuckle drifted off as he suddenly saw the pure hatred in my eyes.

"You threatened to paralyze her," I roared. Two-Pump needed to pay for that. He needed an ass whooping unlike any other. He needed to get a beat down and I had to channel the greatest beat-down expert in all of existence.

Stelios

I lunged at Two-Pump and grabbed him by the shirt. I fired punch after punch into his face. After the third I pulled him into a spin.

Stelios Kantos

I pulled him towards a car and released, the power of the spin sending him headfirst into some car's side window. The glass shattered but I wasn't done. I pulled him free and slammed his face down twice against the hood.

Stelios.

I threw him against the ground. Using the car as leverage, I slammed my foot into his face. I kicked over and over, rage pillowing through me. I screamed as my foot struck.

"Never. Hit. A. Child."

With one final kick, and a satisfying crunch, I slammed Two-Pump against the car and knocked him out cold.

Stelios Kantos.

I looked up at Jack and Rasputin and I gasped. Jack was cut and bruised and blood dripped down from his face. He panted heavily as he tried to keep up. Rasputin was also cut but he seemed fine. Shit. I hated Rasputin. He could bone the Russian Queen and get away with it. He could survive poisoning and even gunshots. That never happened to me. I've been shot and blown up and I'm barely standing and no queen wants to sleep with me.

Jack looked injured but he looked determined. The more Rasputin cut him, the more he seemed to adapt. His strikes became faster and more precise. Jack lunged forward. He slashed with his blade before thrusting with his pistol. Rasputin sidestepped and struck with his foot. He caught Jack by the knee and watched as Jack's leg buckled. Seeing an opening to finally end the fight, Rasputin stepped in.

This was what Jack wanted. He twisted his body, put all of his weight on his good leg and then pushed off. Jack grabbed a shocked Rasputin, slapped aside his knife-hand and stabbed his blade into Rasputin's side. The Russian screamed. Jack pressed his pistol against the Russian's gut and fired twice. Rasputin fell.

David ducked behind cover as Leo and Jerkface opened fire. The two had paired up and had David pinned. Round after round slammed against the car, preventing him from moving. David looked at his options. He needed to move, his cover was not great, but he couldn't move left or right. That left only one direction. David raised his P90 and wildly blind-fired. Leo and Jerkface dropped under cover.

"Ben!" David called out as he dropped his empty P90. I glanced over and saw David taking a running leap off of the hood he was using as cover. He leapt into the air and came down into a rolling dive. I don't know how he did it but David rolled up behind Jerkface and Leo, uninjured by his stupid-ass stunt.

Then I realized why he called me. Leo and Jerkface quickly turned around. David only had a pistol. He could drop one foe, not both. I quickly drew my Five-Seven and leveled it at Leo. This was supposed to be a difficult choice. How do you pick one brother over another? Leo was my brother but David was my brother-in-law and he was my best friend. There was no contest. Like a coordinated duo, I fired twice into Leo's chest as David fired twice into Jerkface's. Both men dropped. Both men had vests but they were still down.

I spun as I heard a frustrated roar. I spotted Sally standing atop a car hood, the canary glow weakening in her eyes as she fired another big blast of electricity. Billy Idol looked hurt but worse still, his composure had finally cracked.

"I have tried my best to control any emotional outburst as to diminish the risk of someone receiving a devastating injury." Billy Idol let out a blood curdling scream. There was no controlling his emotions. Flames suddenly appeared everywhere. Cars caught on fire, the skin on his arms began to welt and bubble and the balls of flames in his hands began to exponentially grow. "Now I'm about ready to fucking hurt someone!"

"Oh shit," David said. "He just went Super Saiyan Blue." I glanced at him and gave him a weird confused look. David shrugged. "Robby and I watch it together. Shut up. It's kinda cool."

Billy Idol's hair was no longer blonde. It was fiery red. A massive shockwave of flame ripped through the parking garage and tossed everybody on their asses. I swore. What the fuck? If a heat-wave wasn't bad enough now I had this fucker?

"I guess kill him with fire's out?" Jack said.

"Ben?" David asked.

"Why the fuck is everybody looking at me?" I yelled. "Shoot him!"

The three of us aimed our Five-Sevens at Billy Idol and opened fire. We each fired three shots. None of the bullets made it. Each melted before even reaching him. I don't know if the science behind that worked but who the fuck cared, this was a super-hero fight and I was losing.

"Keep him busy," Sally said.

"How?" I asked.

"Talk him down?" she suggested as she ran for the wall; yeah, because my voice was always known for soothing the enraged. Instead I fired again. My bullets didn't make it. Billy Idol formed two balls of flame. "Scramble!"

He flung one at me. He missed, barely, but the shock-wave pitched me into the air. I slammed against a stone pillars. It hurt, like a lot.

He flung the second at David but the cat did some fancy dodge that landed him safely behind a car. There are some days, when I'm trying to get my back to feel again, when I fucking hate my BFF.

Jack spotted my discarded P90 and bolted for it. He scooped it up and turned. He unleashed a torrent of FN 5.7×28mm rounds towards the fire bat. But none reached him. They did, however, get closer than before.

"Spread out," Jack called. "Wide attack."

All three of us fired again, each from a different angle. The bullets got closer and closer but still none hit. I suddenly understood what Jack was doing. Billy Idol could summon great heat and flame but only in a focused direction. If he spread out and taxed his limits, soon it would break. We just had to make sure we survived until then.

I glanced at Sally. She stopped at a fuse box and ripped it open. She looked at me and smiled before grabbing the wire and ripping them free. The live wires sparked and arced as Sally grabbed them. The lights started to dim as she started to absorb the electricity. She was super charging.

The three of us kept firing. Finally a round passed through his heat shield and tore through his leg. Billy Idol dropped to one knee, screamed and turned to the source of the bullet. Who fired the bullet? You get three guess but the first two don't count. Billy Idol looked at me. He summoned a burst of flame and readied to fire. That's when Sally stood in front of me.

"I chose the name Lucy for a reason," she said suddenly. She took all of her anxiety and fear and threw it back into her powers. Much like my super-visions, Sally was about to activate hers. "I've only done this once before. I hope it works."

Billy Idol fired his massive blast but it never reached me. It was instantly absorbed by Sally. I blinked. Sally wasn't harmed. Instead, her body was a glistening diamond. Every inch of her skin had been replaced by diamond. In this form she was no longer Sally. She was Lucy, Lucy Diamond. She was my diamond in the rough.

Billy Idol fired a second blast and a third. Each collided with her body but none left a mark. She was impervious to all physical harm in this form. She was indestructible. She raised her hands and with a scream, summoned the biggest bolt of electricity I'd seen since Robby dragged me to Thor: Ragnarok. She blasted Billy Idol in the chest and sent him flying backward. He flew through a concrete pillar and fell into several cars. By the time he touched down, his body was still. Billy Idol had passed out.

"Nobody was there to catch your fall!" Lucy screamed. "You dick!"

"We'll work on your banter," I offered.

Leo groaned as he tried to stand up. As he did, he saw me standing over him. I offered him a hand. He took it.

"Mr. Anderson," I said in my best Agent Smith. "This

is over. The girl's with me."

"It doesn't work that way," Leo said. "You know the company won't stop."

"Tell the company that whatever protection circles me, now circles her. If anything happens to her, I will rain hell down upon them."

"Ben--"

"Then take her and see what happens. I have fucked things up in the meta-world three times now and those were accidents," I interrupted. "Imagine what I can do if I decide to put my mind to it."

Leo just stared at me in silence. Eventually he just nodded. I turned around and walked to the Nissan. Leo called out for me. I glanced back at him.

"It's nice to see the old Ben," Leo said. He offered me his hand. I took it and we shook. "Next time, aim him somewhere else."

Chapter 21
Minnesota is Fictional

The next couple of days sucked. It was emotional, it was scary and worse still, I had to do all of it with a couple broken ribs. Being tossed against a pillar was not as fun as they make it look on TV, but whatever is?

The hardest part wasn't the injury or the berating we got from Annie when we returned home, broken and bruised. The hardest part was when we said goodbye. After the fight the five of us vanished from the garage. Harm made sure we didn't have a tail. The girl could drive. When the cops descended they found Ismael in possession of several illegal weapons. He was picked up for gun charges among others. He was off the street but his family wasn't. Sally was still in danger and my place was no longer safe. The Marshals had to take her and make her disappear yet again.

She stood in my hallway, looking nearly identical to the day she showed up. Jeff Arcel stood beside her with two additional Marshals. The cowboy wore an arm sling but he was still standing and was still smiling.

"I owe you big, Ben," he said.

"I just did what any other cowfolk would do," I laughed. I offered my hand to shake but paused and I remembered his right hand was in a sling. Instead I made and fist and bumped with his left. "By the way, where are you from? Is it Minnesota?"

"Don'cha know, Ben. Minnesota is fictional." I knew it!

I looked over my shoulder and saw Robby and Sally standing side by side. Both were silent. Robby glanced at his Dad and got a nod of encouragement.

"I...I....I'm sad you're leaving," Robby stuttered. "You're basically the coolest person I've ever met."

"And y'all the biggest dork I've ever met. You're basically the king of dorks," Sally replied with a stern face. Robby's face dropped. A mischievous grin crossed her lips. "But the king of dorks is still a king and that's pretty cool." Sally leaned in and gave Robby a kiss on his cheek. His jaw dropped and his eyes went wide. Sally walked to the door and towards me. "Be seein' ya, King."

Robby's cheeks turn a deep crimson red. David laughed and Annie slapped his shoulder. She also wanted to laugh but knowing her, she'd at least wait until her son was out of the room. David was proud of the boy, their talks had paid off, but Robby's reaction was still funny as hell.

Sally stopped by me. The two of us silently looked at each other. I looked past her and locked eyes with my sister. Annie nodded. She ushered David and Robby out of the hallway. Sally glanced at Arcel and he did the same with his Marshal flunkies. Now it was just her and I.

"You, looked at me as you walked in the room. Like the red sea, you split me open," Sally said. "Somehow I knew these wings were stolen. All you did was save my life."

"Tried to run but I couldn't move. Well I paid for these concrete shoes," I replied. "But like a singer that sings the blues, you saw hope in the hopeless."

We both smiled.

"If you ever need me, Sally, you know where I am," I said. "No matter what, I'm only a drive away."

"What if they put me overseas?"

"I didn't say it was be a good drive," I chuckled. She smiled back.

"I love you, Ben."

"I love you, Sally."

We hugged. Then she opened my door, walked out and left. She got into the car and Arcel drove off. I watched them drive down the street. I watched them until they were out of view and I kept watching for a few moments longer. Steaks and pork chops dropped down from my eyes.

Man tears.

That was the last time I ever saw Sally Condon.

A couple days later David and Annie moved out. They got the all clear to return to their house. That left me alone. I limped around my apartment. There was no Annie, no David, no Robby, no Alice, no Puzo and no Sally. There was nobody but me and my thoughts. There was a time, many years ago, when this was what I craved. Now, I loathed it. I was amazed at how far I had come.

I plopped down in my chair and grabbed my phone. I had an important call to make. It rang twice before a female voice picked up.

"Howdy, this here's Drew Winnick," the woman on the phone said. "How can I be of some assistance?"

With Jeff's help I had gotten the phone number for the real Drew Winnick. I had to call her. I had to tell her something important.

"My name is Ben Thompson," I began. "I'm a PI from up north."

"I don't normally get calls from your end of the woods. What can I do you for?" Her drawl was identical to Faux-Drew, just with a feminine touch.

"Alexia Pike was killed by Ismael Salazar," I said suddenly. I heard a gasp on the other end. "He's the son of the Imperecedero Cartel's boss."

"Who....what....." her voice trailed off.

"I know this question's been eating you up inside. I

know it's haunted you, I know you thought yourself a failure but you aren't. You're a great cop and Alexia would be proud of you." I head a sob come from the phone. "I can't say more. I don't know any more but I can tell you who can. Call US Marshal Jeff Arcel and tell him Ben sent you. He'll help clear things up."

There was silence for a moment. Drew didn't speak and I didn't speak. I just waited. Eventually she replied. "Thank you, Ben. I don't know who you are but thank you."

A couple days later Harm showed up at my door. I invited her in and we had a drink. She wanted to drink something new so I made her my signature drink. She took a sip and nodded.

"What do you call it?" She asked. I smiled. I finally had a name.

"It's called a Lucy Diamond."

Lucy Diamond:
- 1/2 Citron vodka - adds character of lemon and lime with a note of lemon peel
- 1/2 Coke - Can or glass bottle. No plastic. Tastes better that way
- Ice - I like ice in drinks. I feel cool swirling around booze in ice.

"I need to thank you," Harm said.

"You don't have to keep thanking me," I defended. "I would have saved anybody's life."

"Nah, I'm over that," Harm said with a chuckle. "I wanna thank you for setting me up with Iris."

"Did she get you a good deal with the cops?"

"Even better, she got me a job," Harm said. "Rutin Haley paid me to figure out how Edwin pulled off the heist.

After that contract he offered me a job. I'm now a security consultant for his dealerships. I start next week."

"Well shit, congrats." We tapped glasses and had another sip. I put on a jesting face. "So is the part where you throw yourself at me in thanks because I'm single and ready to mingle."

Too soon, Ben; too soon.

"Wrong tree, dog," Harm said. A mischievous grin crossed her lips. "Now if your sister wants to be thanked."

"Stop trying to sleep with my sister!"

It had nearly two weeks after Sally left when Iris showed up at my door. It wasn't unusual to see her, she did throw a lot of work my way, but this was different. This time she had a massive file that strained the seams of the brown folder. I eyed her suspiciously.

"I have an offer for you," she began. "But it's not something to take lightly."

That's when she started to explain. For the next two weeks I saw Iris almost daily. We dealt with paperwork and the legal ramifications of her proposal. I listened carefully then politely asked her to repeat it using small words. I reminded her that I was not a smart man. Once she even explained it to me using puppets.

I had a lot to change in my life and my appartment. David helped me with renovations, Annie helped with the decorating and Robbie helped me with shopping. On the last day Iris sat before me with another file. It was double the size of the last one. Damn, I hated paperwork.

"What we're about to do cannot be reversed," Iris explained. "Under normal circumstances there would be a trial period and testing but this is so far from normal that it's scary. If you sign this last form, if you agree to this contract, then it is for life. Do you understand?" I nodded. She pushed the file towards me. "Are you still interested?"

I didn't answer her. I quickly grabbed my pen and signed the final form. Iris smiled at me and nodded. "Then we're done. I'll see you tomorrow."

A knock on my door caught my attention. I eagerly limped to the door and pulled it open. Jeff Arcel stood in my doorway. His arm was no longer in the sling but its movements were still rigid and stiff. We shook hands.

"I'm supposed to ask if you're 100% sure." Jeff said. I quickly nodded. "Then I'd like to introduce you someone."

Jeff stepped aside and I saw a teenage girl standing behind him. She was a head and a half shorter then I was. She wore tattered jeans, a screen-printed tee and had a black choker with a metal heart around her neck. She wore a man's black leather jacket. It was too big for her and she was basically swimming in it. Her eyes were like a pair of vibrant emeralds. Her chest-length hair was well kept, vibrant and several layers were dyed a shamrock green. She was clean, well fed and on her face was the largest smile I'd seen in weeks. It had been a month, almost to the day, since she left me but here she was, standing in my doorway once again.

"This is Lucille Sally Thompson," Jeff began. "But she prefers to go by Lucy. As of today, you are her guardian."

Lucy looked at me and smiled. I smiled back. I looked back up at Jeff. "I heard this was your idea. Thank you."

"After we cleaned house, we needed a place to put her. I didn't want her back in foster care and we needed someone that could deal with her special abilities. There was really only one choice." He looked at Lucy. "You sure about this, munchkin?"

"Country roads, take me home," Lucy drawled. She glanced at me and smiled. "To the place I belong."

"I'll take that as a yes," Jeff said with a relieved

smile. He looked at us both. "The cover story is Lucille is your cousin's daughter. Your cousin passed away suddenly and you were the only remaining family. You agreed to take her in."

"Gotcha."

We shook once more. Lucy gave Jeff a final hug before the Marshal departed. Now it was just her and I.

"Lucille?" I asked with a chuckle.

"I was named after Lucille Mulhall. She was a famous cowgirl and wild west performer," Lucy explained. "Naming people after cowboys is kind of a tradition in our family."

"You have a bunch of traditions to learn," I laughed. I escorted her to what was once Robby's room. Aside from mine, he used to have the biggest bedroom. He happily sacrificed it and took a smaller one for Lucy. I opened the door and showed her the inside.

The room had dark wine coloured walls, a large bed and a chalkboard-headboard above the bed. There were speakers in each corner and a subwoofer on the floor, all hooked up to a Bluetooth system for her phone. There was a small record player in the corner and several records beside it. A large Halestorm poster hung on the far wall. Hanging on the side wall, carefully placed in display frames, were a vinyl copy of Eric Clapton's Slowhand and Halestorm's Vicious.

She smiled and tossed her bag onto the bed. She walked into the living room and looked around. She noticed that I'd rearranged the living room. Gone was the second couch and beside my Laz-y-boy was just a large empty space. "You're missing a couch."

"I got rid of it. I needed the space." She shrugged. I turned her around and looked at her with a serious look. "I'm new to being a father. I don't know what I'm doing so I will make mistakes. But I need you to know two things.

"First: despite what our cover is, I'm not trying to replace your father. Nobody can. I'm just trying to be here for you. I'm trying to be what you need."

"And the second?"

"You are not - repeat not - responsible for your Dad's death. Your Dad knew what was right and he knew what he had to do. You did not force him into working with the cops. He did that because he wanted to show you that a good person does good things."

Tears formed in her eyes as Lucy nodded. She instinctively wrapped her arms around her body as she nervously tried to formulate the next words. "You do want me here, right? I'm not just here 'cause you feel sorry for me?"

"There is nothing that is wrong in wanting you to stay here with me. I know you've got somewhere to go," I said. "But won't you make yourself at home and stay with me?" Lucy wrapped her arms around me and held me tightly. I kissed her forehead. "And don't you ever leave."

Steaks and pork chops fell to the ground.

Man Tears.

"So what do you wanna do?" I asked as we separated. I glanced down at my phone. I had an app open that was tracking an approaching delivery truck. It was almost here. "Wanna order food and watch a movie?"

"Why don't you show me this Stallone guy," she said as she plopped down in my Laz-y-boy. "I wanna see shit explode."

"Then its time I show you The Expendables," I gleefully said. I tapped her on the top of her head. "You're in my spot."

"Really, that's how we're going to start this?" She mocked. "You ain't gonna let me sit in your chair?"

A loud knock at the door startled her. I flashed a devilish smirk and limped to the door. I opened it and let the delivery men enter. I escorted them to the living room and pointed to the empty space beside my chair. The two men lowered a large piece of furniture wrapped in plastic onto the spot. I thanked the men, tipped them and sent them on their way. Lucy looked at me with suspicious eyes.

"What the hell, Ben?"

"Open it up."

She flicked open her pink knife and tore at the plastic. As she pulled the last piece off she stared in wonder at what I had bought. Sitting beside my brown Laz-y-boy was a pink Laz-y-boy.

"Pink?"

"Fuck you. Pink is cool," I replied. Lucy laughed as she plopped down in it. She wiggled her butt and shimmied her back as she tried to get comfortable. Eventually she flashed me an approving smile. "I want you here, kiddo. I want you to be a part of my life. I will get anything you need to show you that."

"Anything?"

"Within reason," I said.

"Cool."

I put in the movie and sat down in my chair. We both watched the opening credit as Stallone and crew approached the pirate ship. I smiled at Lucy. This could work. After what I went through to get her I didn't think there was anything I couldn't handle.

"Because I need tampons," she said quickly. "My period's about to start."

......

......

......

Well – crap.

Epilogue

Rania Nimr yawned as she walked into the kitchen. She glanced at the clock. It was 9:30 am. She grumbled to herself and reached for the pot of coffee. It was a couple hours old but it was still warm. The first person awake brewed coffee and it was always the same person. Rania cocked her ear and listened. She could hear the sound of the treadmill, thumping below, as their *guest* put it to the test. Rania scoffed. It was way too early for physical fitness. Even after all her years in the military, she still loathed an early morning.

Rania poured a cup and topped it with two sugars. She like the way sugar fought the bitter taste of coffee. It made it just sweet enough to feel like drinking warm candy. Rania liked candy. She leaned back on the counter as she sipped her coffee with her left hand, her right resting on the revolver holster on her belt. Rania was a righty. She shot with her right hand, she threw with her right hand, she boxed with her right hand and when she made love - or just enjoyed some carnal fun - her right hand was the hand with the magic fingers. Yet when it came to sipping coffee, she always did it with her left. Maybe it was because years of service in dangerous areas had taught her to keep her weapon hand free or perhaps she was trying to counter the weight of her large revolver. Either way she was a southpaw drinker and she was fine with that.

Rania walked to the living room window and peered

outside. This house was a suburban townhouse and had a front lawn to match. It looked like a normal house, each of the houses on the block did, but it wasn't and neither was this neighbourhood. The further out it went, the quicker it became evident that this community was nothing more than a fancy prison. On the inside it was meant to replicate a suburban neighbourhood with its look and none of its guests were free.

This was Malpaso Prison.

Rania walked away from the window and returned to her room. She wasn't a guest in Malpaso. She was a guard. VIP guests had live-in guards. Rania was a highly trained soldier. She used to be in the Egyptian Army before being recruited into Unit 777. Then Visegar showed up. They offered her better money and Rania leapt at the chance. She was loyal to her country but there was a very low ceiling for a female soldier, especially one of her persuasion. Visegar didn't care about gender or orientation. They wanted skill.

Rania pressed her palm on the digital reader. The door unlocked and Rania walked in, placing her coffee down on the nightstand. She removed the weapon from her waist and placed it on her bed. She was required to be armed at anytime she wasn't in the bedroom. Rania stripped out her clothes and walked to the on-suite bathroom. She showered and cleaned, readying herself for the day. She looked at herself in the mirror. Her amber hair was falling past her shoulders. She frowned. It was getting time to get it cut, she loathed having long hair, but her guest liked it long. Rania bit her lips. Perhaps she could let it grow just a *little* more before chopping it off. She quickly pulled it into a bun. Rania pulled on a tight pair of jeans, a sports bra and a basil green tee. She grabbed her revolver and returned it to her waist.

Her revolver was her pride and joy. It was a Taurus 'Raging Judge Magnum' revolver with 6.5 inch barrel, a blued plasma-finish and a gingerbread-finished handle. It had a seven-round cylinder that chambered .45 colt ammunition. Rania loved a good revolver. She had always used pistols in the service and on missions but even then, on instinct, she'd twist her elbow to absorb the recoil. That was a revolver technique. Her Taurus was expensive but damn if it wasn't worth it.

Rania grabbed her shades and placed them over her cinnamon eyes. She grabbed her coffee and exited the room. She walked into the basement. It was time to check in on her guest. Rania sipped her coffee as she descended the stairs. She entered the basement gym and paused at the door. She watched as the guest - Prisoner 1401 - ran on the treadmill. She was a fit woman and it showed on every inch of her skin. There was not an inch of flabby skin across that body and Rania knew that for a fact. She had spent hours studying it from afar.

When she was given the job of prison guard, she scoffed at it initially. Then they told her about Malposa and the people they'd be holding there. Rania again said no. Then they showed her how much she'd make. Rania still said yes. She was reluctant to go, even after the money, but one look at Prisoner 1401 with her wild red hair and hypnotic eyes made her weak in the knees. After that she had no choice but to say yes.

Prisoner 1401 was wearing a pair of tight shorts and a sports bra as she ran on the treadmill. Rania could see nearly every inch of Prisoner 1401's body. She could see every scar and blemish. Even the faded stretch marks that came from her recent pregnancy were visible. Rania still found 1401 gorgeous, stretch marks and all. Rania smiled as she watched, knowing full well that 1401 was dressed in this fashion to grab her attention. There were some benefits to this posting.

"We all have sunglasses, Ms. Nimr," 1401 said. "No need to show off yours indoors. Please remove them."

"Good morning, Prisoner 1401," Rania said as she removed her shades. She hung them from the front of her shirt. "How many hours has this been today?"

"I have been up since 5 am. I've pretty much been on the treadmill nonstop," 1401 said. "And what will it take for you to call me by my real name?"

Four hours of running. Rania whistled in admiration. This wasn't light jogging, this was full on running. 1401's endurance never failed to impress. It was like she had the ability to never tire. Even now, after four hours, she didn't look drained or tired. In fact she looked like she'd barely sweat at all.

"Your real name *is* Prisoner 1401," Rania reminded her. 1401 stepped off the treadmill. She walked over to Rania and gave the guard a pleading look.

"Please, Rania," she said, trying her best to appeal to the woman's kindness. "It's been so long since I've heard my name said out loud. I've almost forgotten what it sounds like."

Rania sipped her coffee to hide her wavering spirit. She wanted to do anything Prisoner 1401 asked of her. She was enthralled with her. No, it was more than that. Rania dared not to say it aloud but she was in love with 1401. She longed for her. The worst thing a guard could do was to fall in love with a prisoner but Rania had done just that. A cry from the baby monitor ripped through the tension. Prisoner 1401 sighed. Rania smirked.

"He beckons," she said. "Now be a good girl, Zoey Harris, and go check on your son."

Zoey flashed a smile of thanks and Rania just melted. As Zoey took the stairs two at a time, the guard followed behind at a slower pace. Rania scolded herself. Why did she do that? It was her job to break the prisoner's will, not secretly build it back up.

Rania reached the upstairs bedroom. Zoey held a small child in her arms, soothing the nine month old child with small bounces as she hummed. Zoey was a beautiful sight but she was also a trained spy. She was a dangerous woman but Rania had always been attracted to the dangerous ones. The dangerous ones were more fun.

"Hey there, cutie," Zoey said. "You slept through the night. Mommy's so proud of you." The kid giggled. "You're a big boy, Clint, and Mommy is very proud of you."

Rania walked to the window and sat on the ledge. She

sipped the last bit of her coffee, finally feeling awake. She looked out over the fake suburbia. Every female guest was here for the same reason. The company wanted powerful meta-children and they would get it by selective breeding. Zoey - Prisoner 1401 - was one of those breeders and there were dozens more like her, right outside. This was their prison.

This was the town of Malpaso."

THE END

Benedict Thompson will return
in
The Future Sold Out

AUTHOR NOTES

Here's a little something that you need to know, it's how I went from nothing to an author with flow. Now I may not be a poet - not even close - but I am an author and in the five years since doing this racket I have learned two very important facts.

1) No author works alone.

2) Debt collectors for bars aren't afraid to get violent.

With Ben's return to the world, I have many people to thank but none more so than the fans. There was a time I thought I was done with Ben. There was a time where I did not think I would return to him. It was the demand of the fans that made me return. People would ask when Ben 3 was coming out. They would poke me and ask for the next book. When that happens there is only one choice: you listen and you write. So write I did.

Friends: Cliff, Lenny, Sam, DeYoung, Chelsea, Kayla and Megan. Thank you for being the support that you were.

The Legion: MM, BH, CL, KF, KC, SP, CW, MA, AH, MM and more. You are among those who helped in countless way and motivated me. I feel like you've each given me your energy and I've used it to make my book into a *very similar to but legally different enough* Spirit Bomb.

Family: You are my biggest supporters! Thank you!

Mom: I wouldn't be here without you encouraging my writing and reading from a very small age. Thank you and I love you!

Val: There is more of you in this book than any before it. You put in endless hours to make this a reality. I can't begin to properly thank you. I love you.

Zid: I do as thy commands.

All Hail!

My name is Benedict Thompson and I am a superhero. With a single Touch, I can read an item's past. I can tell who used that pen before you, I can describe how that shoe was made and I can describe everything that has been done on that motel room bed.

The problem with having superpowers is that people want you to actually use them.

I just want to watch TV but here I am dealing with a movie-quoting assassin, murderous celebrities, kidnapped children and secret government conspiracies.

My family's in danger, my life is in ruins and worst of all, my TV is being ignored.

I miss my TV.

NOT EVERY
SUPERPOWER
IS A BLESSING

THE BENEDICT FORECASTS

Author **Larry Gent** transports you into a world spies, espionage and superpowers. Each book is an action-packed thriller that'll keep you on the edge of your seat.

Winner of the silver medal in the *Best in Halifax* award, the Benedict Forecasts deleve deeper into the ever growing Lycotta mystery

WHO IS MAC?

The mysteries of the Visegar Company, Polaris Industries and the Lycotta gene grow deeper with the introduction of the deadly young raven called Mac.

>The Prague Riots
>The Port Alexander Explosion
>The Clockwork Killer

She shows up at each and brings death with her. Who is Mac and what is her connection to all three?

The TOP SECRET Mac Files
Book 1: She Who Trains Under Death
ON SALE NOW

The Lycotta-Verse expands with a look behind the Visegar curtain and a glimpse into the evil that dwells beneath.

TO ARMS, SOLDIER

LIGHTYEARS TO GO
BEFORE I SLEEP
ON SALE NOW

Allana Guiver was the Legendary Soldier that all of history knew. She won the great war but lost everything she knew and loved doing so.

400 years later, Major Guiver wakes up from cryo-sleep to find a world she doesn't reconize.

Earth is gone, humanity floats through space on a massive ship searching for a new home and a new alien threat wants to rid the universe of every human.

Humanity needs their Legendary Soldier but how do you ask a woman who gave up everything to give up more?

YOU'RE NOT DONE YET

WHAT'S WORSE THEN BEING STUCK IN A VIDEO GAME AND NOT BEING ABLE TO LOG OUT?

My name is Rake and I'm stuck in a MMO. It wouldn't be so bad if I was in my max level main but I'm not. I'm stuck as my level 1 Rogue. I'm stuck in my bank alt.

Now I'm running for my life, I'm fighting to stay alive and I'm trying to figure out how the hell to get out of here.

Where's a GM when you need one?

HELP!

BEING STUCK IN YOUR BANK ALT!

Vörissa's Catalyst

—ONLINE—

Patch 1.01: New Game+
Patch 1.02: Escort Mission
Patch 1.03: Corpse Run
Patch 1.04: In Another Castle
Patch 1.05: Silent Protagonist

In this new series by Award Winning author Larry Gent, we dive in the action and mystery of the *Stuck Online* genre.

Follow Rake and company as they fight in a harsh digital world. If they're smart, they'll keep their lives. If they're lucky, they'll keep their sanity and if they're both, they just may find a way to log out.

STORIES WORTH STAYING UP LATE FOR

 @midnightreadingpublishing

 @MR_Publish

Photo by Lisa Liteplo

ABOUT THE AUTHOR

Larry Gent is a is a bottomless well of know-legde on historical wars in worlds that are, sadly, fictional.

Larry is an enthusiastic gamer whose dreams as a child was to be either a detective or a TARDIS Repair Man (it's like a VCR repair man except you just see the ending of the movie first). He got into writing to give back to the worlds he's enjoyed so much from.

A Perth, Ontario native, he lives in both Ottawa and Halifax where he works as a freelance writer and full-time dreamer. He lives with his wife Valérie and his owner Zid the cat.

Website:	Larrygent.com
Twitter:	@42webs
Instagram:	@xan_in_the_hat